INTO THE SILENT SEA

Claire Stibbe

BOOKPRENEUR

United States of America

Published by Bookpreneur in 2018

An imprint of NLP Publishing
3906 Pat D'Arco Highway
Rio Rancho, New Mexico 87124

Printed in the
United States of America

ISBN-13: 978-0-9982027-4-7
eBook: 978-0-9982027-5-4

Cover Artwork by ekdesigns.co.uk

Editing by Jeff Gardiner, Sandra Mangan, Booklab,
Famelton Publishing, Twisted Ink Publishing
An Tig Beag Press & The 13th Sign.

www.cmtstibbe.com

Also by Claire Stibbe

The Detective Temeke Series

THE 9th HOUR
NIGHT EYES
PAST RITES
DEAD COLD
EASY PREY
SILENT ADMIRER

Never miss a new release!

Sign up for the author's email list and never miss a new release - plus get a free book and other special offers. Your email will never be shared and you can unsubscribe at any time.
Sign up: http://eepurl.com/bqCQhv

"The thorns which I have reap'd are of the tree
I planted,—they have torn me—and I bleed:
I should have known what fruit would spring from such a
seed."
Lord Byron

PROLOGUE

Berkeley Road, Southampton, New York
Present Day

I dream of you. I dream of killing you.

Sometimes I see your face in the window. Sometimes I catch a glimpse of you on the beach. I map every tiny nuance in my head and I copy everything you do. I must memorize those lines, I must recite them perfectly.

I must be you.

And so I watch you gaze out at the ocean, fingers teasing a crease in your bottom lip. I wonder why there are pearls of sweat on your forehead when your heart is so cold.

I wonder what you're thinking.

Now you stand between luminescent spots of light that roam among the algae. It's like you are somewhere deep in the woods looking up at the stars at night.

I shudder at the weights that have anchored you into the bottom of the world, the stench of seaweed and rotting things. I cannot imagine those precious few moments of panic but they are delicious to me.

Pale skin drawn over cheekbones and moonlit limbs. You hang there, jeans shredded at the knee and deep gouges in the flesh at your calves. Bubbles dart through an open mouth and then a final sigh goodbye.

You are in my dreams. I can still reach out and touch you.

My conscience won't allow me to separate myself from you completely.

Not yet.

1

There had always been something about the dark that made me want to cry and I looked for that pinprick of light. My lips quaked out his name but nobody answered. It hurt to speak and I tasted blood.

The air shifted around me. Then a strange silence, an unusual quality of silence. Ryan had not slept in our bed last night and he hadn't called. My mind buzzed with the usual excuses. He was working late or his car had broken down on a lonely road, where a frayed power line had been ripped from its housing in a freak thunderstorm and he was lying in a ditch with two severed limbs.

I remembered sitting on the couch listening to an audio book. A hazy memory of staggered screams, animal sounds I never knew a human could make. My screams.

I lay on my side, looking at a slender bar of moonlight that trickled in beneath a stubbornly tilted blind. Shards of ice ebbed under the pleated skirt of the couch, coffee table on its side. I choked on my tears and tried to speak.

"Ryan."

My fingernails were like tiny claws, tracing an arc over the carpet and I could smell the ferrous stench of congealing alcohol and wool. There was a gnawing in my stomach like a spasm of food poisoning and I tried to take small sips of air. It was my churning place; a tiny hole below my ribcage that sent out warning signals when ugly things were said.

A memory drifted past, snapping a piece of the puzzle back in place. An image of his eyes, disconnected and empty. I lifted myself up on my elbow then rolled to a squat. With some effort, I detached myself from the pain, swallowing blood as I swallowed my pride.

Rewinding the day, I saw an image of Ryan, hand curled into a fist, pummeling at my stomach until I couldn't catch any more breaths. I can't place the words he used, fragments that make no sense and I scrambled for orientation.

"Sign it, damn you! Are you listening?"

I nodded over tears, tasting salt as they seeped into the corners of my mouth. He thrust a pen into my hand, lips curling around each word. Then the sound of his fingernails clicking on the table like a rat scurrying across a hardwood floor. I let the pen hover over the signature line, giving myself a taste of control. What I shouldn't have done is crumpled the papers and thrown them across the room.

That's when it happened.

There had been something strange about his eyes, a window into a life that was suddenly unfamiliar, a zigzag of crossed lines we couldn't hope to reconcile. Thrown off by my calm demeanor, he hesitated before swinging a fist. I lifted my arm and braced for impact. The force ruptured my lip, and somehow the playback of this event seemed to slow, globules of blood hanging in the air.

I'm sure I flew over the coffee table but everything faded after that, springing briefly back into focus before the light winked out altogether.

It wasn't the first time Ryan had hit me but I swore it would be the last.

Scattered images streaked past, blaring with grim shrieks: a brutally efficient male with eager green eyes and a whip for a tongue. Every little glance he snapped occupied the damaged spaces of my mind. I felt like a dog jerking on the end of a chain to get away and I didn't care if the collar dug deep enough to bleed.

I dragged a shallow breath through my teeth and felt a bolt of adrenaline. I wanted to strip my mind of the memories: how we met, our wedding and our fifteen-year marriage. They were no more than scant, emotionless details. I had cared for Ryan deeply but now, for some throbbing, aching reason, I couldn't fathom why.

I wiped away a film of tears and decided I deserved no sympathy. If a man was close enough to hit me, then I hadn't jumped far enough. If I hadn't fought back, then I never had a plan. What Ryan didn't know was how much of a plan I did have. I knew where she lived, what she looked like, where she shopped and more intimately, when she took her swim in the ocean.

I looked around the room. Coffee table angled beside the armchair, ice bucket spewing slush. I scooped up a handful, dabbed it against my lip.

A discarded newspaper straddled the arm of the couch like a sleeping lion. There was an ad I had circled in the classifieds. *Hamptons Home Help.* A number I had called from Ryan's phone many times and hung up. A number he had programed in his contacts.

Hers.

It hadn't taken me long to track her down once he'd called out her name in his sleep. I worked for the police department, for crying out loud.

But fear began to press in, squeezing and throttling as it circled the house. I crushed my eyes closed. *I will fight it. I won't let it in.* Then came the shivers—throttling, creeping things that started low and bubbled up through my gut.

My heart began to pound.

He's gone. Won't be back until midnight.

The voice in my head sounded pinched as if I didn't believe my own words. It gave me a little time.

I will fight it. I won't let it in.

I knew I could.

2

Monday, 25th July, 2016

I must have fallen asleep on the couch because I awoke at 5 a.m. to a flabby vibration against my arm. My mouth was open. I had been snoring.

Morning light puddled the carpet and the coffee table was upright now. The smell of fresh air wafted through an open window and the blinds were open.

Ryan was in the kitchen. Would today be any different? I promised myself no more beatings, no more psychological warfare, no more whining like a rusty bolt every time he hit me.

I stared through the window at the street, looking for anything on display. The house opposite seemed to gawk at me, dormer windows like two raised eyebrows over a paneled front door. Lieutenant Joe was pulling weeds along the driveway and shoveling half-digested kibble into his rose bed. A work colleague.

Two houses down, old Mr. Kipfer rocked a beer gut and sifted through a handful of envelopes at his mailbox, while his wife stood in a nightdress at the front door. Berkeley Road was buzzing.

"Clo!"

Panic flared and I tried to rub away a thin layer of sweat on the back of my neck. Grazing one hand along the wall, I swayed down the corridor knowing I needed more than mental strength to reach the kitchen.

He tossed his jacket over a bar stool. I heard it slither to the floor. He wore a clean-cut shirt and cufflinks and looked every inch the executive.

"Clo. Look at me. I expect last night was a blur. Do you remember what we agreed?"

His fingers traced his lips as he waited for a response. But I had learned that any response was the wrong response and there was no point screwing up a second time.

"I've been doing some thinking," he said. "You've been drinking a lot. Might be an idea to see Doctor Howarth."

I wasn't an alcoholic. I had GAD: Generalized Anxiety Disorder, where stomach upsets and restlessness were only some of my symptoms. Worrywarts didn't need doctors. They needed a safe environment to live in, they needed—no—*wanted* a commitment. Faithfulness for instance. Was that honestly so hard?

Ryan had been very clear in his unrealistic prenuptial agreement about me turning a blind eye to the occasional one-night stand. A fundamental desire to procreate with as many women as he wanted. To spread his seed, which in his tiny and somewhat distorted mind must have been worth spreading. To me it was like horse shit on a rose bed.

He chose me because I was uncomplicated. Made no demands. Ordinary enough for other men not to stare at in the street. He reminded me of Scotty in *Vertigo*. Always trying to remake me into something I wasn't. From my clothes to the color of my hair and the way I spoke.

"No point living in a permanent daze, Clo. Can't be healthy. Do you know who you spoke to in the last twenty-four hours? Or where you've been? It's dangerous."

He was right. The past eight hours had receded into a bank of fog and I stood there trying to piece it all together. He pleated the newspaper and dropped it into his briefcase, then tapped a wedge of papers on the countertop.

"You need to sign these. There's no point dragging it out, Clo. It's been over for years now. It's not good"—I cringed—"for either of us."

My lip gave a little jolt. A vibration if you will, as if connected to a circuit that had been thrown. Somewhere deep in my subconscious my voice protested, screaming the words *Someone help me*.

"Is that how long you've been screwing her?" The words were out of my mouth before I could stop them.

He took a step forward. Then hesitated. His mind was ticking. I could tell by the twitch in his eyebrow, the sudden flinch he thought I hadn't seen.

"You're paranoid, Clo, acting out. It's that destructive scenario thing."

"What scenario thing?"

"You're doing it now." He pointed at my head. "Your brain ticks over at a hundred miles an hour thinking things that aren't happening. There's nobody else."

Of course there was someone else. I had seen the letters and the photographs, scores of them tucked away in his briefcase. A pair of panties trickling under the flap of his jacket pocket, small and lacy and not the granny-panties I wore.

"You'll get the house, Clo. It's a good deal."

When did divorces start feeling like buying a new car? In any case, there was no deal when you were slapped with a hefty mortgage.

"Your salary…" I pointed out, "hasn't been going into our bank account."

"No, Clo. It's been going into *my* account." His voice trailed off. He knew he sounded callous. "Your salary is enough."

My basic salary as a forensic photographer for the Nassau County Medical Examiner wasn't enough. Not unless I supplemented it with overtime and I'd been doing a lot of that recently.

He tapped his lip as if he could feel the pain in mine. "I shouldn't have done that. Probably best to cover it up."

"Why?"

"Oh, I see."

He didn't.

"I see exactly where this is going." Green eyes regarded me coolly over a slack mouth. "You think it's some kind of trophy you can show to the police, your buddy Joe, for instance?"

Now you mention it.

"He's not interested, Clo. Joe knows better than to interfere."

"Good God, Ryan. Listen to you!"

"Clo, Clo, it's not about me—"

"It's always been about you. What you want. What you don't want. Our marriage… you checked out years ago. Think that's responsible?"

My words drifted to a halt. I couldn't risk telling him all the things I knew. About the woman he'd been seeing. The woman I'd been stalking. Complicated things I still needed to research. He'd only snap and snarl, tell me how unhinged I was. It sucked. It really did.

"Clo, don't get all worked up and I don't want you saying any of this to Lucy Kimball."

When was I ever likely to talk to Ryan's boss's wife? All cocktails and prissy women and work colleagues.

Squads of them.

Talking, no. Emailing, maybe.

"Clo? Promise me you won't talk to her? Keep my work colleagues out of this. Our separation, our divorce—it's none of their business."

My gaze bore through a photograph of our wedding in a thick black frame and then, without turning my head, I flicked my eyes back at him. "For now."

A brittle silence. He was nervous.

"Clo, look I'm sorry. I really am."

"Sorry for what?"

"For running out on you like this. I didn't mean... I didn't mean to hurt you."

"Oh, you think I enjoy being treated like shit?" I thrust my head forward as I said it and angled my body toward him.

Ryan's expression thawed and he took three steps toward me, hands capping my shoulders. I flinched. He let his arms drop to his sides and gazed past me.

"You can use the car," he said. "I'll get a ride with Shayna."

"She outside?"

"Yes."

"Does she know?"

"Of course she doesn't know, Clo. What do you take me for? I'll rent a car just for a few days until we can sort this out."

My jaw clenched and flashes of yesterday flitted through my mind. I felt as if I were nosediving through my own head, arms over my belly to still the tremors. I knew what he was doing, tapping into my subconscious where he had found a broken synapse, a place of weakness. He knew because he'd been there so many times before.

"Here," he said, holding out the pen. "Let's make a clean break. Legally and emotionally. You're going to need it too."

He assured me if I didn't sign there was nothing to stop him petitioning on his own. I didn't believe for one minute I would ever receive a court summons. Nor would I turn into a shriveled and dispirited woman if I didn't sign.

I walked over to the countertop, pen twitching in my hand. I could see he had gifted almost everything to me. Yellow flags indicated where my signature needed to go. The pen didn't hover this time. It scratched. It rushed. Finally, a gash of ink at the bottom of the page.

"I'll be back tonight to get my things. Oh, and I'll be renting an apartment for the time being," he said, tucking the papers in his briefcase and jamming the house keys in his pocket. "It's better this way."

I could feel a stream of air against my cheeks as he pushed past me and then I heard the growl of Shayna's car as it sped along the road.

Silence. Impossibly big and everything I dreaded, until a new sensation crowded my mind.

Rage.

3

A delicious thought drummed through my mind. One that could only be relieved with a gun.

Makeup couldn't hide the swelling on my lip and there was no use rolling with a lie. Everyone would suspect I had been back-slammed into the floor. I called my supervisor and asked for time off to deal with personal issues. He was more than happy to grant me leave. I could act a part when I needed to.

A knock at the door.

It took a few seconds to think my way through it. I could see the street from the window and there was no sign of a delivery service. For a long time, the only sound I heard was a shallow breath from the air vent and I shrugged it off and went back to the voices in my head.

The bottom half of Ryan's face kept twirling into my line of vision. A smile, where only one side of his mouth tipped upward as if yanked by a thread. When we fought, he tactfully refrained from admitting he was the one who needed help. He had a genius for hurling toxic arrows and then acting with calm indifference. It was the side of him

I hated.

Unspooling a reel of memories, I realized we had been living on this street ever since we got married. Ryan had been promoted to a Relationship Banker at Chase after several years in sales. He was an expert at interpersonal skills they said. Had the Midas touch. Not sure what happened to the Midas part, but the touching got him fired. It wasn't referred to as a firing. More like a gentle nudge overboard with a life raft. But somehow he managed to get hired again. Kimball Aerospace. Finance Manager. Quite a career jump.

The knock at the front door sounded again, fainter this time. Half-hearted, as if the person had already given up. Light shimmered on the bathroom wall and then retreated. I saw the back of him walking across the street. Lieutenant Joe, T-shirt and washed-out jeans shredded at the knee.

Had he seen Ryan hit me? Couldn't have. The blinds had been closed last night.

Another thought compounded the first. A breath of fresh air and a breath of fresh stalking. I was already nine stalks deep—if I was counting, which I wasn't—and a few more wouldn't hurt.

Looking at the clock, an idea flared in my head. Five feet ten and two liquorish black eyes. She would be walking alone on the beach this afternoon because let's face it, a tan needed a top-up. I couldn't casually make a move, I hadn't devised a plan for that yet. It was probably five more stalks into the future. But I had devised a plan for the *how*.

A heavily weighted scuba belt, snug in the duffel in the back of my car. A prescription I needed to call in for sedatives and a couple of flathead screwdrivers in the glove box. Nobody could say I wasn't prepared.

I took a shower and climbed out onto cracked linoleum. Wiped the condensation from the mirror with a fist and glanced at red hair sagging over my shoulders like creeping thistle. I wouldn't miss the puddle in the recessed soap dish, creamy shards sticking up like icebergs. I wouldn't miss the yawning toilet with all its stains and cracks or a bathroom that needed repainting. I wouldn't miss any of it.

I tugged on four layers of sweatpants under my clothes and instead of weighing one-twenty, I could easily pass for one-sixty. With a wide pair of overalls, a T-shirt and lace-up pumps, I could honestly say even my mother wouldn't have recognized me.

My head began to ache, then settled into a numb buzz. I tilted the blinds closed in the living room. Lieutenant Joe was looking up at the peeling paint on his gutter, hair bristled as if he had pulled off a T-shirt and forgot to gel out the static. His presence swallowed my mind and I could almost hear the lingering rasp of a cigarette.

I opened the hollow china duck which nested on the ornament shelf, incubating the check from my mom's lawyers. Unknown to Ryan, probate had cleared weeks ago. The money was already mine and mom's old Buick sad idly in Mrs. Nita's garage a few streets away.

Renting a car wasn't cheap. It also left a paper trail. So I decided to use my gold 2001 Toyota Camry with its dents and dings. Not exactly a rad ride and would probably go unnoticed in most areas except where I was going today.

I pulled out of the driveway and exchanged a smile with Lieutenant Joe. He seemed satisfied to study me with a dark stare, mouth set in a tepid smile.

He waved. I waved.

When I turned the corner of the street, I slowed down and tucked my hair up in a baseball cap. Changed my sunglasses and applied a smear of 'career-girl' lipstick. Light colors, I had been told, were better for thin lips. What would I know? I never wore the stuff at work.

I couldn't help thinking I had been stripped of my

identity and reshaped. That all my uncertainties had been shut down and I was stronger than I had ever been. But it wasn't true. Every time I thought of Ryan in the early days—the steady grunt as he slept, the faint pulse, his mouth on mine—I gripped that wadded up tissue even tighter and cried all over again.

I can still smell him. I will always smell him.

No one knows it's over. Not even my sister in Queens and my mom, an Irish transplant, was too far gone with Parkinson's to remember my name before she died. My father left us when I was five. There's no one else.

Honestly, it was a relief because family members complicate things and there's never any escape. I relished my peace. Jealously guarded it, actually. That's the way I am.

I took Southern State Parkway to NY-27. The coastal towns of eastern Long Island were crammed with fund managers and sunbathers who drove vintage collectors. My Camry wasn't among the beach cruisers and German convertibles that traveled to the island's east end. But idling in the parking lot of a large store, it slotted in nicely with a few of its own kind.

I checked my face in my rearview mirror. Not pallid and blotchy but silky with foundation. Then I slammed on my brakes. My heart almost stopped.

Some drug-addled ignoramus walked across the road without looking. He barely glanced up, raised his hand as a signal to say he was sorry and continued on, earphones blocking out the sounds of traffic.

I hated driving. Never knowing the right way, one hand on the wheel and one hand tapping out addresses on Google Maps. Cars going too slow. Alumni stickers in the rear windows: Riverdale, Trinity, Dalton. Private schools I had never been to.

A quick stop for an espresso roast and then the bank. I suddenly felt as if I had low blood sugar and started to pant through an open mouth. Was Ryan already two steps ahead?

The teller greeted me with a warm smile, gave me the privacy I needed to take my passport and a necklace my mother had given me out of the safety deposit box. I was ablaze with stories of how we were moving and wanted to take our money out of the joint account and put all our savings into a credit union. Banks and their charges. Surely she agreed?

She nodded, eyes traveling to my lip. "There are no funds in the joint account, ma'am. Your husband closed it yesterday."

"Closed it?" A swarm of flies deep inside my head. A tilting lobby. "Well, then I don't need to worry."

I felt myself being sucked toward the door as if dragged by a giant syringe. I sat in my car. Turning on the ignition felt alien to me as I inched out of the parking lot before swerving into the main road. Drivers flipped me off and tailgaters tried to ram me from behind.

As it happened, I arrived at a bank on South Main Street an hour and a half later, deposited the passport and the necklace in the new safety deposit box under my maiden name, Turner. I had never legally changed my name to Shepherd and my driver's license and bank cards were still unchanged.

A new life. That's all there was to it.

4

I noticed another old Camry almost identical to mine. Same color. A few less dings.

It was parked rear end in on the south side of the bank. Food wrappers littered the sidewalk and a flotsam of used condoms were banked up against the corner of the building. The car appeared to be abandoned. I had about thirty minutes to waste and I eased into a space on the other side of the street.

Lifting plates in broad daylight meant two things. You had to be quick and you had to know your cameras. The nearest Viacom housing in the area was tilted in the opposite direction, servicing what appeared to be the front doors of the bank. Other cameras did not provide a view of the car.

I groped in the glovebox for the screwdriver and slipped it in my pocket. Limping toward the vehicle—posture is everything—I crouched behind the back bumper. There was only one other person in the parking lot; a woman leaning in through the passenger door to buckle up a baby. She hadn't seen me, hadn't heard the clatter of a plate as it fell on the pavement. I waited a few seconds before sliding them both under the hem of my sweatshirt and limping back to my car.

I could have killed for a Xanax, anything to stop my fingers from tapping against the steering wheel. *Tap, tap, tap.* The precursor to short breaths and then the whirligig before the blackout.

Breathe.

Anxiety deserved sweet coffee and helped my brain to navigate through the wreckage of what was left of my life. Normally a shock like a divorce would have taken me down for several days but it was going to be different now. Charged with a stronger bolt of confidence, I gripped the wheel like I had in my driving test.

There was no use worrying. Worrying cost years. It was time I could never get back. Xanax was addictive, or so they told me, and deadly when taken with alcohol. I had done that a few times.

But the thing was—and I had to think this through carefully—Ryan said I needed medication. Why? I can't sodding remember, unless it was the time I had a terrible case of Tourette's, a maddening tic when meeting the HR manager at his work. I can't imagine what had excited me so much about finding out I had been taken off the family medical insurance. But I do recall a stapler flying through an open window and latterly being walked out by a security guard.

I had been manipulated by Ryan for fifteen shagless years. Who could blame me?

I had to carry on as if everything was normal, turning my mind to the better things in life. A cedar-clad mansion with white chimneys and a privet hedge, for instance. One that stood on the beach front with views of the ocean, one that epitomized the elitist order. I couldn't imagine what the house was like inside. Nothing like the rectangular footprint of a shoebox we lived in.

I headed for the Southampton Tennis Club. Found a shady parking spot and exchanged the license plates for the ones I had just taken. Covering the windshield with a sunshade, I must have slept for four hours, waking up to crushed lips against the driver's window and a smear of make-up on the glass.

I eyed my lip in the rearview mirror the way a victim's impact advocate would appraise a case. A fracture in the stucco that cried out for a daub of cement. I scooped a mixture of sweat and foundation from my forehead with a finger and applied it to the swelling. It was good enough.

It occurred to me as I reversed out of my space and idled at the entrance of the tennis club, that I didn't remember how I got there. Streets and turnings were all a blur as if the car were in autopilot. What if years of trauma had sawed away at the nerve cells of my brain? As if one half had been dangling on the end of a frayed piece of rope and then… snap! It struck two ledges before disappearing into a gully. It wouldn't just be a reason for memory loss. It would mean death.

I shook myself out of it. Ryan couldn't say it was all my fault. He had accused me of flirting with the neighbors and trying to ruin his career. That was a lie. The only neighbor I ever waved at was Lieutenant Joe as he scooped up a pile of dog leavings. Good solid bones. A man who looked as if he had been raised in the ragtag streets of Brooklyn rather than the orderly rows of Hempstead.

Joe was into all kinds of things and entertained a psychic to help with his cases. A man called Owen Sykes —big afro, big smile—who owned a pub in Holtsville called The Outsider. I had been there once after photographing a particularly ugly crime scene in the area...

A car roared past, almost clipping my hood as I pulled out of the driveway. A slate gray Porsche with dark tinted windows. The sound of the engine guttered and died as it turned right at Foster Crossing. I couldn't see the driver but the fly line profile of the car was distinct. Vanity license plate with a black frame.

PRFXN. *Perfection.*

I had seen it many times down Gin Lane. This time I followed at about fifty feet. Watching brake lights blinking on and off as the car slowed before a white mansion with crimson shutters. An arm flopped out of the open window and two fingers flicked upwards at a red Thunderbird steaming the other way. A neighborly greeting? Or a warning to slow down. I couldn't decide.

The speed limit was twenty-five. The Thunderbird was going ten over. Maybe.

The Porsche accelerated again and then came to a stop outside the house with the white chimneys and balled privet hedges. I passed him as he loitered outside the front gate, window down and texting. His face was in shadow but I recognized the thatch of grayish-black hair and luxurious moustache. David Kimball.

I kept my eye on the rearview mirror as I cruised toward the intersection of Wyandanch lane. Without a village parking permit, I couldn't leave my car at the end of the road, where it tapered to sand before hemorrhaging onto the beach. Because Kimball, Ryan's inscrutable boss, was watching.

Instead, I circled Old Town Pond and drove under a canopy of trees before doubling back to Gin Lane. I figured Kimball would be gone by then and unable to report my car.

I figured wrong.

He reversed out into the road and began following me, slowly at first and then giving off a growl of acceleration. I could see livid headlights in my rearview mirror, filling the window like two large teardrops.

My vision began to buckle, and all I could see was a

thin smudge of green spinning like a thread of DNA. I had to slow down. Had to look as if I belonged.

Breathe, Clo, remember?

A plan evolved in my mind. I had Googled the area enough times to know that if I shot down any of the side roads, most were cul-de-sacs with no egress. But by hugging the perimeter of the lake, I knew there would be a side road leading inland where I could circle back the way I had come.

An impatient revving, nose almost kissing my bumper. I tapped the brake twice to warn him of the white wall that marked the bend to Old Town Road.

He was insistent. Car swerving around me—a haze of gray—as if there were an invisible outside lane. It was an illegal maneuver that almost cost me the contents of my bladder. I flinched, foot pumping the brake and hands locking around the wheel. He had just enough space to overtake between me and the frosted glass lamp he narrowly missed.

I slammed on my brakes and slanted a glance at the Porsche as it made a wide loop around my right side, taking the bend like a pro. I made out a face through the driver's window, eyes forward, not a dot of sweat.

I told myself to focus. To take deep, slow breaths. Dizziness was a common side effect of the Xanax, not to mention a pinch of nausea. I couldn't risk taking it and driving.

So I let my thoughts drift in the stifling heat and I let the car idle with the glare of the road ahead.

5

I slumped forward, limp as a rag. My skin was burning and shuddering from the vibration of the engine.

I tried to tell myself I was okay. But I wasn't. Fear lingered along with a sense of panic. Had Kimball taken a note of my fake license plate? Questions kept tiptoeing through my brain and I asked myself why he had followed me.

It had been a few months since I'd had a full-blown panic attack. An episode, my doctor called them. He promised me if I stuck to his rigorous schedule I could dispense with taking the medication. In return, I promised to pay better attention to my choices, to my friends, to those damaging situations in which I had found myself. Since then I had been waiting for the menacing images to hit because with all my good intentions, I was now breaking those promises.

Seagulls screeched across a cloudless sky and a tiny strand of wind curled through the open window. A butterfly drowsed nearby. I could smell the ocean.

I drove slowly along the road, hearing the shift of

bulrushes and the faint ripple of water. A rank of maple trees and white gables rushed past before I turned into Old Town Crossing.

Easing around the corner, I heard the snarl of an engine about forty feet up. Narrow tail lights flickered under a straight brow and the rear end of the Porsche scrutinized me like a predator.

Acid churned in my stomach and it hurt to swallow. I couldn't see the man through the sloping rear window and I had no idea if he had seen me. The engine purred and revved, taunting as if gearing up for a race.

Which way? Left or right?

Left. It was the road that led to the beach. I yanked on the steering wheel, shoulder slamming against the driver's window as I leaned into the corner. The car strained at the sudden surge and then burrowed into a mouth of trees, where the road appeared like a gray tongue, unfurling into the distance. I kept my eyes peeled on the rearview mirror and back at the windshield and when my car emerged from the shaded canopy, there was still no sign of him.

Above me stretched a deep blue sky, sun blazing against gates and wide lawns. I squinted at the brilliance of Gin Lane as it swung into view and I could almost taste salt water.

I slung a quick glance toward the closed gate where Kimball had briefly parked before following me to the end of the road. My chest heaved and my heart popped. All clear.

Ahead was the private parking lane to the beach and I slipped in between a red Honda and a Jeep Wrangler, and turned off the ignition. Pressing my head against the back of the seat, I was bleary with exhaustion, eyes seeping tears.

A sense of isolation gripped at my ribcage. A why-didn't-I-live-in-this-gorgeous-stretch-of-paradise longing that always came with not belonging. I hiccupped a sob.

My stomach cramped, a scratching, clawing contraction. It was there to bring me pain and to teach me a lesson.

A strong breeze blew a discharge of sand across the windshield, bunching up against the wipers before dwindling into tiny dots. I needed to get busy. Dig a hole. Bury the tools. Follow my target. Sounded a little too much like a 1930s counter-espionage thriller. The one about a notebook that eventually took a man across the Scottish moors. I had forgotten the name.

I dragged the duffel bag from the trunk and shouldered it down the path. Took a sharp right turn, hugging the embankment in front of the house. There was a spot in the sand hills I had noticed on an earlier visit; a patch of marram grass circling an eye of sand. From the air, it would have looked like a donut.

The strap of the duffel kept sliding down my shoulder and I jostled it back into place. There was a distant mingle of surfers riding on the deep face of a wave and a display of Chelsea-boy flesh, tanned and toned and bobbing in the swell.

I yanked a bottle of water from the duffel and snapped off the cap, drinking enough to temper the buzz in my head. Hearing laughter, I watched the beach through a screen of grass. Six female swimmers cut through the waves, slits of tanned cleavage and well-oiled arms. Too far away to see me as I scooped out a hole in the sand.

Within ten sweaty minutes the duffel was buried.

6

I saw Marion Kurchel as she jogged along the viewing deck at the back of the house. Then down the steps to the footpath that straggled away into a wide belt of sand. She did the same thing every afternoon.

She didn't know she was going to die. Not then. She didn't know about the scuba belt. Five pockets of ten-pound weights, almost equivalent to being pinned down by a five-year-old.

I knew killing someone wouldn't be easy. It would be a workout. In my case, this *someone* would need to be sedated. I could already see her taking tiny sips of air, hands clawing and eyes pleading. Mouthing the word *why* over and over again.

I was about forty feet behind her, swinging a bottle of water. She walked on tiptoe; a narrow silhouette dressed in white jeans cuffed above the ankle, clean and crisp as if they had been pressed that morning. An understated black and white top with a tie front. Could have been a high-end swimsuit. It was hot enough to wear one.

A carefree and self-assured woman, who paired her

innate femininity with grace and willpower. A woman who dared to be herself. It took guts.

I had ingrained every inch of her tight little body into my memory. How she talked. How she did her hair. And when I got close enough, I could see the fine arch of her brows and the contours of her cheeks. I wanted to copy every nuance until I became her. The low-rise jeans, revealing the swelling of her hips and a waistband that barely grazed the hollow of her belly.

I filled her footprints with mine and wondered why I wasn't genetically predisposed to well-defined calves and ankles. My calves had merged with my foot. There was no in-between with cankles.

I noticed a ring on her left hand. I couldn't see which finger, but the diamond was like a pulsing flame every time the sun bounced off its many facets. It must have been at least two-and-a-half carats.

A young man appeared through a gap in the dunes—blond and limber—and fanning his face with a letter. He folded it and slipped it in her back pocket. His arms seeped over her shoulders, hers fluttered around his waist. They stood there for a while until he pushed her back, head angled and lips opening and slamming. He pointed toward her house, then shrugged, palms up toward the sky. She dusted a finger beneath one eye. Shook her head.

They strolled together. His hand sometimes flat against the small of her back then creeping higher to the nape of her neck. I noticed how attentive he was, head turned down and finger pointing to a piece of driftwood she might have stepped on. There was a moment where they stopped and he gave her a flash of white teeth before jogging inland between the dunes.

These were some of the many sights I saw.

The air was salty and over the brow of a white dune I could hear the cries of seabirds against an enormous sky. I seemed to have burst into another world. A remote, halcyon world, where the hull of a fishing boat slapped against the ripples of a turning tide and torn shrimping nets hung from the stern.

I sat in my usual spot below the house, knees drawn up to my chin. She waded ankle deep in the surf, drinking in the emptiness of land and sky without turning to look behind her. What Marion lacked in intuition, she certainly made up for in looks. Here I was thinking every woman had a warning light that flickered inside when something wasn't right.

I don't know how many times I had Googled her. No LinkedIn. No Twitter. Just a meager profile on Facebook with one post linking to Montauk Models, an escort agency. Her profile was tastefully done. Black bikini in several poses—face blurred to protect her identity. Perhaps Marion Kurchel wasn't her real name and she was running from someone. It made her all the more mysterious.

I was still lightheaded. No use feeling a prickle of guilt when a killing was on the cards. Drowning hardly counted as murder. Not if lacing a drink with a powerful sedative was anything to go by. If you can make it look like suicide, then so much the better.

I was about twenty feet from her, arms around my shins, trying to make myself as small and tight as I could. It would be so easy to slide up behind her, tap her on the shoulder and say *boo*. But in those few moments, she turned, eyes barely grazing mine before scrambling up the bank toward the house, hands clinging onto tufts of grass.

She was fast. I would have to make note of that.

Since I found out about Marion and my husband, I had spent nearly every spare minute of last month on this beach. My assignment? To monitor my target. Time seemed to pass quicker here and it was possible to become infected with ambitions of owning your own mansion.

I had also become a member of the Southampton Yacht

Club, where I had been taking sailing lessons for the past six weeks. Their website had an email signup for all updates, which included incoming and outgoing tides and up-to-date weather information.

So I had this idea. Kill Marion and get the house. It was a terrible idea in the irredeemable, I-would-be-committing-murder kind of way. But nothing was impossible. At least not the way I saw it. The best part of this scenario is how much it would hurt Ryan.

Using a sedative was spot on. In the moment. Provided everything fell into place, a body would be undetectable to the naked eye if weighted down and pushed over the side of a small dinghy. I had one in mind.

If the drowning method wasn't practical, I bet Marion's house was equipped with a high-powered meat grinder. You could seal human remains in about ten different coffee cans and send them to an undisclosed address in *Meh. Hee. Ko.* I was feeling a little stoked.

If Marion deigned to talk to me out there on the beach, I would tell her I had just moved into a house nearby, one she wouldn't have heard of and with a man she wouldn't have known. An obstetrician who drove a gray Lincoln Navigator. Perhaps she had seen it?

She must have seen me trying to look sleepy and disinterested when she rushed past. Yet not a word passed between us. Why should it? She didn't know me.

She didn't care that my breathing was often ragged, brought on by anxiety and flashes of fear. That my medication left me feeling worse than before I took it. It didn't make it any less humiliating. Any less real.

Women like her rarely suffered chills on a hot day or the tug of depression that threatened to take away the ability to feel. I've always likened it to the worse type of stage fright. It's there just under the skin like a ganglion, growing bigger and bigger. Uglier and uglier.

I started to seethe. This was the problem when I had

too much time to think. I wanted to shut out the deep footprints Marion had made in Ryan's world. The memories, the smells, the sounds.

In a way, I had two worlds. A world of sadness in a pokey little house in Hempstead. No friends and a neighbor who smoked until 1 a.m., where the glow of a cigarette flickered on and off like a blinking eye in the darkness. And another world here on the beach, where boats swung at anchor and gulls swooped overhead. Sometimes if I stayed long into the evening, I could see the reflection of the sunset in the window of her house. Like today.

I wanted tell her about my husband, how he had left me and shacked up with some hornet's nest of a whore in the village. What would she say? Would her eyes be a shine of tears like mine?

It mortified me to consider that she wouldn't understand. Wouldn't acknowledge a dumping because it had probably never happened to her. I was glad and sorry.

If she met me she would have disapproved of me. My brusqueness, my lack of class, but that's because she wouldn't know real talent if it bit her in the ass. I was dead to her.

A part of me was excited. Because when Marion was gasping for breath to the bottom of the ocean, I would finally start living.

7

I sat staring at the fading sun, its belly almost brushing the horizon.

There was not a hint of crime here, not so you would notice. No 'hood kids hanging out in gangs, watching an arrest as if it were another day. No stench of death in a back alley. The worst stench you would get here would be someone's bag of dirty diapers that didn't quite make it into the dumpster. This was paradise.

Unreal.

My phone rattled out a cheerful rhythm. It was probably Ryan saying he would be home late to pick up his things. I studied the screen. Didn't recognize the number.

"Yes," I snapped, giving the ocean a dirty look.

"You're drawn to everything bad. Like a fly to sticky paper."

I froze. It wasn't Ryan. It was Lieutenant Joe. "What?"

"You know what. You shouldn't be out there doing what you're doing."

"What am I doing?"

"Snooping."

I looked around. "Are you following me?"

"Would it bother you if I was?"

"Well kinda, because I am in a lady's bathroom." I stifled a giggle.

"Public or private?"

"The bathroom? Private."

"Now you know that's a lie. And you know what happens to bad girls."

"No, tell me."

"A frisking. A few tricky questions and a nice long ride. Sound tempting?"

It kinda did. "Maybe another time. Wait… you get this number from work?"

"Yeah. There was a rumor you were taking time off. I just wanted to know how much time."

"That's none of your business, Joe. So if you don't mind—"

"You be careful out there."

He hung up before I did.

I didn't know whether to be riled or flattered that he'd called. Neighborly concern mixed with police loyalty. I hoped he would back off.

My thoughts drifted back to Ryan. He was still at work. But today was Monday, the day he worked late. He wouldn't be home until midnight because the bastard would be sniffing around this very house. Only this time I would be waiting for him.

A dragonfly buzzed past my ear and I batted it with a hand. There was a young man collecting shells; slender and sunburnt. I recognized him as the man Marion had met earlier.

An incoming wave washed up the beach and then receded and he crouched, picking things out of the sand and placing them in a straw hat. He looked lonely and I wandered over to talk to him.

"Hey," I said, studying a throat and chest all creamy with sunblock.

"Hey."

I crouched beside him. "Find anything?"

"Yep. A few shells."

"Good ones?"

"Maybe. They're for my mom. She makes things for Hildreth's."

I knew the home goods store on Main Street and had always loved the beach-themed mirrors and wreaths.

"Wow, I bet she's really talented." A trite answer.

"Yeah. She's cool." He stood, hands on hips, chin jutting inland. "I've seen you around here before. Last week, I think."

I nodded. "I like walking."

I thought he was probably around seventeen or eighteen. Nice voice. Educated, like everyone else.

"Jax," he said, holding out a hand.

"Great name." I could see confusion in the squint. "Do you live around here?"

He pointed at a house further down the beach.

"So you know the people who live in this house?" I pointed behind us at Marion's.

"Yeah. Old man. Has a Porsche."

"Nice car."

He gave me a cheeky grin and then winced.

"What?" I asked, staring at my reflection in his sunglasses.

"He's a dirty old man."

"No kidding."

"Yep. Shacked up with a girl about twenty-seven or so. It's really gross."

I laughed. Marion was older. "Sometimes mature men like younger women. Nothing wrong with that."

"It's not that. I don't have anything against age. But... well, you see things. Through the window."

"Oh, you mean, they don't draw their blinds?"

"Curtains. Exactly."

I made a face.

"She's nice though," he said. "Swims here in the evenings. Do you know her?"

"Marion?"

"Yeah, Marion. She's nice," he repeated. He picked up his hat and stuffed it under one arm. "Well, it was good meeting you. I better go before I get sunburnt."

Too late. "You too."

He took off with his shells. I had made a friend.

I turned and gazed at the house with the white chimneys. A house with a quiet, mellow façade and lit with a peachy glow. I lay belly-down in the long grass, studying the furnished deck; four club chairs, a loveseat and a table. It wasn't long before the living room behind was illuminated by a bright chandelier, and standing neatly within the frame of the open French doors was Marion.

She was the perfect ideal of a woman, someone who had realized her value and potential long before the rest of us. A woman who wasn't confined to the limitations society had placed on her. Having climbed the social ladder effortlessly, I could see the power she possessed over men.

I crawled forward several feet until the image sharpened. Excitement seemed to live-wire through my body and I thought of every occasion I had seen her and not seen her dressed like this. It was a curiously corseted silhouette; a square-necked dress with an overskirt of beaded lace. Purple, I thought, but I couldn't be sure. Short sleeves exposed her shoulders and a high waist reminded me of the Titanic era. There was a pear-shaped amethyst around her neck and two more danced from twisted pendants, each dripping down the gorge of her cleavage.

She cradled a phone between her cheek and shoulder. Kept rolling her eyes as if the caller was droning on about something she couldn't care less about. She seemed hypnotized by the darkening ocean and a plunging sun.

I sensed a flicker of pleasure as the wind soughed through the marram grasses and I thought I could hear music. She was still talking on the phone, pacing along the lit deck now, dress sucking at her tiny waist.

A blood-red horizon reflected in the windows and the sky around it had turned to dusk. Water lapped against a buoy and then the sudden squawk of a hovering seagull, piercing as if torn from a woman's throat. I wanted to curse at the bird for giving me a fright, beak tilted to one side, eyes roaming over the land.

Marion gave the bird a cursory glance and went back to her yacking. Twisting a tendril of hair around one finger and eyes tracing the balustrade. She couldn't hear the rattle of rigging against a mast, nor did she notice the revolving beam of a navigation light. It was all so familiar to her.

I caught a sudden flicker of movement behind the French doors, white curtains flickering as if a draft had suddenly entered the room.

Marion spun toward the sound and lowered her phone. She was expecting someone and that someone waved her in with a key dangling from his hand. Peppery hair and a walrus moustache. Ice cold smile.

David Kimball, President and CEO of Kimball Aerospace.

He took the phone from her and laid it on the coffee table. It seemed like a fatherly gesture until he sat on the couch and patted the cushion next to him.

I studied both of them, confused. He was neither father nor friend. He was something in between. He flashed a brief smile at the phone. Marion's caller had not been disconnected.

With his knee a little closer to hers, I sensed she was trying to ice him out. Only he wasn't buying it and I felt like pummeling the window and telling him what an asshole he was.

He turned his head to one side and pushed up his chin with one hand. I could almost hear the crack. Then he clawed a hand through a flip of hair above a widow's peak. I'm sure it was done to see if she would lunge for the phone, but she didn't.

Marion talked to him, patted his arm, dark eyes pointing toward the stairs. He held up a hand and pointed to the couch. Her eyes were silent and pleading.

I took a deep breath, hands slick around my phone. I made sure my flash was disabled and snapped a few pictures. Not sure why. But whatever he was about to do, I had a strange feeling I wasn't going to like it.

He took off his jacket. His tie. His belt. Pinned her against the couch and raised a knee between her thighs. I couldn't bear to watch.

Bile rose in my throat, thick and oily, and I tried to tell myself to relax. I had no intention of leaving vomit in the sand for the police to find. If this was what Jax was talking about, what he referred to as *a dirty old man*, I could see why he winced. Kimball was hurting Marion. No doubt about it. If I had seen it then so had Jax.

The grooves in Marion's forehead were scored deep and her eyes were tightly closed. I could hear her groans through the open door. The whole scene was not a G rating. More like an NC-17.

One thing crossed my mind. Did they know walkers on the beach had a front seat viewing at dusk? Did Marion and her old man know how many shots I had already snapped through those big screen windows?

I could have kept going as long as they did. Stock-taking I called it. Taking stock of my surroundings.

He broke from her abruptly and dressed. Wrapped his

tie around one hand before stuffing it in his pocket, eyes watching intently as she pulled the hem of her dress over her knees.

His fingers traced the line of his throat as he spoke, eyes burning into hers. He picked up her phone, hand deflecting the shake of her head. Whoever was on the other end would have heard everything.

They both stood, her rushing to dim the lights and him getting in her face with an I-don't-like-your-attitude. My stomach was pounding. Should I call the cops? The idea seemed ridiculous in light of the fact that I wanted Marion dead. All I could think of was a Roman emperor giving the *police verso* in gladiatorial combat, while the mob in my head shouted encouragement from the arena.

I crawled closer to the house, belly brushing against sand and grass until I reached a stone urn engraved with the words *Sparky. We will never forget*. An animal grave marker. I lay low in its shadow.

Floodlights flashed on, aimed up against the back façade; a tinge of blue that now gave the house a cold, dank feel. It was harder to see through the windows since Marion had dimmed the lights but I could hear a voice shredding the air with a torrent of S's, similar to a rape whistle. Both mouths were a grill of teeth, snarling like two lions in a viral wildlife video. The action was so fast, I almost lost the part where he backhanded her and she fell against the coffee table.

I gawked in disbelief. A gigantic set segueing from erotica to thriller in less than three seconds. He shrugged on his jacket and set off—not toward the front door as I had expected—but toward the deck and down the steps to the beach. His face glowered like a skull as he tripped along the sand, ear turned to the rumble of waves.

Marion sat on the couch, slashing the screen of her phone, face plasma-bright in the glare.

I wanted to crawl under the steps where I would be safe

and hidden in shadows. But that was stupid. I was already thirty feet inside the boundary and surrounded by thick clumps of grass. No one would see my yam-colored hair tucked into a cap. It was almost dark.

The muscles in my back were wound so tightly I struggled to sit. It was the waiting that bothered me. With the man on one side and the house on the other, I was hemmed into my hiding place. I would have to wait for hours.

The roar of a distant car startled me and I swung my eyes inland. The fields had turned blue in the glow of headlights and a plume of exhaust haunted the driveway. A car horn sounded, then silence fell like a blanket. Someone desperate to defend Marion. Someone, I sensed, who had been listening on the other end of the phone.

Kimball suddenly veered inland as if he was about to loop back into the house.

Perhaps I didn't have to wait after all.

8

The water bottle lay against the base of the stone urn, where a breeze tried to dislodge it, rolling first one way and then the other until I tapped it with a finger.

It was getting cold. I could have eaten a whole plate of shrimp and cocktail sauce instead of chewing the remains of a piece of gum.

Marion was in the living room, sluicing a glass of wine. I was surprised she wasn't in the shower, scrubbing off every last remnant of her last caller with a slug of shampoo.

As far as I could tell, she displayed all the hallmarks of panic; demeanor bright and glowing one minute and deathly pale the next. This was, after all, only an impression as she slung a few nervous looks toward the front door.

She walked further into the room and out of sight. It must have been about ten minutes before she reappeared again. Her fears must have drained away with the wine as her hand reached around her back for the zipper, dress sloughing to the floor. One hand pressed against the

French doors as she climbed out of a pool of sequins.

Then she did the oddest thing. She turned out the living room lights and walked outside. I heard the latch as the French doors swung closed behind her and there she was wearing tiny boxer shorts and an even tinier bra. She shivered.

I dropped my head in case she saw me and pressed a couple of fingers against my temple, kneading away an approaching headache and hoping my brain wasn't about to evaporate from all the adrenaline. I doubted she would come out and press charges in her underwear and she couldn't have seen my head, dark like a combat helmet inching upward from a trench.

Time seemed to stand still, lurching forward only when Marion did, huffing air through an open mouth and likely tasting the cold tang of sea air on her tongue as she sprinted toward the beach.

There were few light poles near the house and the only other source of illumination came from a buoy, the revolving beam that made an arc across the beach every thirty seconds.

I felt like a celebrity stalker as I watched her pause, knee deep in spume. Instead of unsnapped her bra and slipping out of the lacy boxers, she rushed into the sea sending a spray of foam in her wake. No flopping into the surf like a walrus. This was an elegant streak of flesh, peeling through the waves with long alternating strokes.

The one remaining factor I hadn't counted on was how fit Marion was. Even when she waded back into the shallows and squeezed her hair, I could see tone and definition in her thighs and glutes, each muscle group flexing as it should.

Grabbing the water bottle, I crawled closer toward the edge of the dune and peered down at Marion through a swarm of grass. The thought of her suddenly becoming roadkill, either by me or someone else made my head pound. I began nursing the thought of wrapping my fingers around her neck. The same fingers which, until now, had been wrapped around the plastic water bottle.

Once I'd delivered the coup de grâce—the death-blow that will end my suffering, not hers—any sharp cry she made would carry all the way up the beach. It was a gamble.

My stomach whirled. No sign of Kimball but there was a patrol boat cruising close to the beach, port and starboard lamps lit. I could just make out two men inside the cabin—faces steely blue in the moonlight—and heads jutted forward against the window.

One of the men appeared on deck. He waved to Marion, who was standing in a pane of moonlight, one hand resting on her chest. I couldn't make out his face, merely a wild swath of hair that lifted suddenly in the wind. I could hear something about a choppy ocean and a stiff wind out of the west-southwest, between fifteen and twenty knots.

The light from the buoy swung around, focusing down the beach before rushing out to sea. Marion was briefly lost in shadow as she ran up the beach toward the house. My eyes swept back and forth, hoping for a glimpse of her. I was willing the beam from the buoy to hurry up as it swept around, sending a long gleaming tail over the water.

Then a splash. I stiffened. One of the coast guards had jumped into the shallows. The boat jerked a little and then with three loud grunts, swung out to sea. I looked up at the house and the French doors were closed, suggesting Marion must have gone inside.

The officer, however, was walking down the beach, khakis wet to the thigh. He turned inland toward Wyandanch Lane and I decided to follow him.

I cowered along the crest of the dunes all the way to a row of streetlights. As I turned the corner, I saw him peering into my parked car.

He reached into his pockets for something. A flashlight? A pen? Then he walked around the back of the car and peered at the license plate, lips working over the numbers as if he could commit them to memory.

The car didn't have a permit to be parked there. As far as I knew he was arranging for it to be towed.

I watched him saunter down the road, receding into the shadows. Assuming he had been dropped off at the end of his shift, I crept down the lane, hit the remote and slid into the front seat of my car. The engine coughed into life and I slammed my foot on the gas, turning sharp left on Gin Lane.

Before I could apply the brakes, there he was in the middle of the road. I slammed into his upturned hand, his body rolling over the hood and up the windshield. He was catapulted several feet before landing against a neatly trimmed privet hedge.

I didn't wait to check if he was okay. I just hoped he was.

9

My fingers drummed on the steering wheel as I looked ahead at a shiny string of windswept traffic. The window was open a crack and I could smell rain and blood. The fuel gauge flashed an angry red and after three blocks, I turned off a busy road and parked under the canopy of a gas station.

There was a small vapor cloud on my windshield and it was then I realized how close I was to the glass, gripping the steering wheel until my knuckles hurt. I could still hear the thud as the car almost sheered into the curb. I should have stopped for that man. Should have pulled over and helped him. But I wasn't supposed to be in the Hamptons. I didn't belong.

I closed my eyes for a few moments, feeling the vibration of a large truck behind me. An idling engine. I could have slept for hours if it hadn't been for a man stooping and posting his lips through the gap in my window.

"Hit a deer, ma'am?"

A deer? I followed the direction of his finger. Thin

streaks of blood streamed down the windshield, painfully visible under a dazzle of lights.

"Oh, no, it was a bird. Not sure what type."

"Must have been pretty big," he said. "There's some on the roof. Want some help?"

"No, I'm fine thanks."

I watched him in my rearview mirror, sauntering toward the cab of his truck. He pulled out and didn't look down as he drove past.

A bucket of water was hooked beside the pump and I sluiced it over the roof, droplets running down the windows in a trail of pink suds. I kept telling myself to go back, to do the right thing. How I had no right to take a life.

As I pulled away from the garage, I felt weightless, as if the car accelerated without any intervention from me. I barely registered flashes of red and white racing either away or toward me. I don't remember arriving home. The decision to park two streets away from my house had become a habit. The car was now tucked inside Mrs. Nita's moldy old garage, next to mom's old Buick, where it would remain buried and undiscovered. I could never drive it again.

Trees rattled in the wind and the street was deserted. I ducked under the canopy of a weeping willow, branches clawing my face and peeling off with an angry *whap*. Blasting through the alley to my back yard, I squeezed between two rotting panels in the lattice fence. The back door scraped against flaking linoleum and I was already panting out a rhythm before I reached the living room.

The fact remained. I'd screwed up. This was the kind of shit you learned when you first start out on a killing spree. The kind of shit you hoped washed down the drain at the carwash. I began to wonder if I was cursed, tainting everything I touched until there was nothing left.

My body was a film of sweat and stink and I was

shaking like a whippet. Cringing in the beam of a standard lamp, I peeled off my clothes in the living room, walked naked to the bathroom and wrapped myself in a toweling robe. I wanted a bath. But I wanted a drink first.

Six glugs of wine couldn't put a stop to my conscience and I pinballed between the couch and the living room window, rummaging through my mind about what to do next.

Oh God, I had killed a man.

A coastguard's disappearance would make headline news. I tried to count off the possibilities of a neighbor having heard or seen anything. They couldn't have. It was too dark out there. Too deserted.

I slumped on the couch, must have nodded off before my eyes pinged open, flicking to the digital clock on the mantle. 1:47 a.m.

Lights flashed past the front window at full beam. The runners on the garage door should have squealed like a skinned rabbit by now. My ears were wired for that sound, even in the deepest sleep. But it wasn't Ryan.

The motion sensors across the street heralded the return of the Lieutenant. He was late—an hour to be precise. Window open, his mouth was pressed into an 'o' and smoke leaked from between his lips

He flicked the cigarette away from his cruiser before creeping forward into the garage, brake lights blinking red and then going out altogether. I watched the jointed panels of the garage door as it rolled back down and I could see the glowing end of that cigarette as it lay in the driveway.

Why hadn't Ryan been to get his things? There were no texts to say he would be late. Late, my ass. He was probably hammering Marion to the bedhead.

It was his fault I had gone to the beach in the first place. His fault I had hit a man. Tears pricked at the corner of my eyes as if something deeply significant had happened. Something too profound to grasp. I couldn't get Marion's pictures out of my mind. Body shots, beach shots, standing with her back to the camera and hair blowing in a gust of wind. I didn't have to wonder who had taken the profile picture and I shouldn't have cared.

I knew where Ryan was, in the same way I knew the exact minute—the exact second—he touched her. I sensed it in an out-of-control fretting that wouldn't go away. Even my dreams were fractured by sudden awakenings and I always asked myself the same questions.

Why me? Why us?

If I thought about it for long enough, tears seeped from swollen eyes that had taken on the conical and scaly appearance of a chameleon. Life didn't make sense anymore.

I looked through the shuttered zone between my house and the outside world. The motion detectors had gone out and there were no lights on in his house. Tall lamps were staggered all the way to the main road, casting a circle of light at the base where I expected to see a stranger wearing a mac and hat. There was no one there.

Knock! Knock!

In a screwed-up way, it started to hit me. Change always hurts, especially the kind where killing one person hurts the other. Perhaps Marion needed to ride the opiate wave; eleven mashed up pills in a glass of wine. The colliding of poisons would take her down without a fight.

Knock! Knock!

Someone at my door? It was deeply disconcerting to hear someone knocking after a hit-and-run. More so, because I had a bell.

I staggered around to the hall and tried to identify the blur through the pane of stained glass in the door. A dark shadow, arms crossed. Hard to calculate height and weight. If Ryan had forgotten his key, then too sodding bad. The bastard could wait until the morning.

I covered my ears from subsequent knocks. I wasn't opening the door at nearly two in the morning.

The knock was louder this time, followed by the obligatory announcement I had come to dread.

"Police! Mrs. Shepherd? Are you in there?"

Of course I'm sodding in here. In a strange way the drinking would save me from being accused of a hit-and-run. I didn't drink and drive. No good citizen did. I'd been here all night.

Tying the belt of my robe even tighter, I opened the door a crack. Joe. *Lieutenant* Joe.

"Yes," I said.

"Can I come in? It'll only take a second."

He was alone and the word *second* took away the wound-up tension in my joints.

"I'm…"

"Undressed," he said, staring at the robe.

We stood in the hallway, me swaying a little and him with his arms crossed.

"I don't want to alarm you," he said. "We had a call this evening."

"Ryan? Is it Ryan? He hasn't returned my calls."

"From a Ms. Kurchel?"

"Ms who?" *Work it, work it.*

"Marion Kurchel. Owns a house in Southampton."

I hated to burst his bubble but Marion wasn't the homeowner. I had done enough research to know that. I was surprised he hadn't.

Joe grimaced and raised his chin. "There's no easy way to break this. Ms. Kurchel claimed your husband was at her house this evening, that he became belligerent and took a priceless painting off the wall. A William Bliss Baker? I believe she said it was of a woodland brook."

"Ryan's never stolen anything in his life. He's Baptist."

Now me, that was different. I was an accidental

criminal; a label I would have to come to terms with. Although I hadn't graduated yet to the *serial killer* category it wasn't out of the realms of possibility, considering how long my mental list was becoming. But the coastguard was one I hadn't seen coming.

Why had Marion accused Ryan of stealing? Last I knew she was skinny-dipping in the ocean with her house wide open for Ryan, much the same as her legs.

"She said Mr. Shepherd—your husband—didn't steal the painting. He smashed it. She also claimed he plowed into a pedestrian on the road. Would you like to sit down?" He peered down the corridor to the living room.

My face was already doing an excellent job of contorting, more from confusion than shock.

"I'll need to ask you a few questions," he said. "Can I get you anything?"

No, I didn't want anything.

"Were you out this evening?"

"No."

What time had Joe come back? Before me? After me? When?

It was *after*. He wouldn't have seen the car at Mrs. Nita's and he would naturally assume Ryan had been driving it. The fact that Ryan was possibly using a rental would have escaped him.

"Watching TV?" he asked.

He was trying to lock down my activities by the movies I had watched. No luck there, Joe. "Reading. I couldn't sleep."

"You don't mind if I take a look around?"

"Go ahead."

I followed him into the living room. He threw a cursory glance at the couch and the pile of dirty clothes, underwear splayed out on top.

I never used the word *panties*. Hated the word. Too 'booties' and 'blankies' for me and more appropriate for small children. But he was looking all right, eyes trying hard to gain control of themselves.

The cushion, under which my car keys were hiding, was angled slightly against the back of the couch. If he looked hard enough he would have seen a black fob and a blade of silver teeth.

Instead, his eyes settled on a large book on the coffee table with the title *B-29 Missions in World War 2*.

"Isn't that the Spearhead?" Joe said, pointing at the bomber on the cover.

"Yep. Lots of pictures of the combat crews. Want to borrow it?"

Joe gave me a wide-eyed nod. "Really?"

"Sure, take it. Ryan won't mind. Especially not now he's in jail."

"Who said anything about jail?"

"Well, that's why you're here, isn't it? I'm guessing he was arrested."

"No. He was gone by the time the police showed up. Not my jurisdiction so I can't give details. But I wanted you to know."

Great coms the cops had. I wish Joe could teach Ryan a few lessons.

"So, you haven't heard from him?" he asked, eyes dropping to my robe and back up again.

"No. That's the problem. He was supposed to be working late tonight. He's incapable of taking a break. Bit of a workaholic."

"Welcome to the club." Joe angled his head and smiled. "Did you guys have a fight?"

As a matter of fact... "No."

He looked at the floor and slowly nodded his head. "So everything was hunky dory when he left?"

I nodded. "What's the connection? With Ryan and this Kurchel woman?"

"Work related?"

Good answer. Marion is a working girl.

"Ever seen any unusual activity? In the street?" he asked, leaning in a little closer on the pretext of examining my hair but he was either smelling my breath or looking down my robe.

"Just poor old Mr. Hancock with his pants down."

"Yeah, dementia will do that," he said, creases getting deeper around his eyes. "I was thinking more like unfamiliar cars, that kind of thing."

"No. Have you?"

"Would you notice the occasional drive-by?"

I shrugged. "I doubt it. All cars look the same to me."

"You sound tense."

"I sound tense because my husband's been accused of murder. How am I supposed to sound?"

"Not murder. A hit-and-run."

"It's the same thing, isn't it?"

Joe's head banked toward the hall as if he had heard something. "Would have been a misdemeanor. But since he left the scene, it's a felony. Victim is in hospital. Dinged up pretty bad."

I noticed Joe referred to the driver as *he*. I also noticed how his uniform hugged a narrow waist, belt sagging from the weight of his hardware.

He narrowed his eyes and scrutinized my face. His voice was soft and sad when he spoke. "He hits you, doesn't he?"

I almost jumped, as if he'd shone a flashlight in my face. "No, no. I'm clumsy. Always have been."

"C'mon, Clo. We work together. I see you almost every day."

"Yeah, well, we don't live together, Joe."

His eyes dropped to the 'V' of flesh at the collar of my robe. "If I asked you to take this off you'd be covered in cuts and bruises. That would be my guess."

"If you asked me to take it off, I'd tell you to take a

hike."

He smiled.

I sensed a woody, spicy scent, which almost masked the last cigarette he had smoked, and the gum he had latterly chewed. It reminded me of summer.

He leaned in a little closer, breath brushing my ear. "I would also guess you're a little relieved he hasn't come home."

I backed up a little and said nothing.

"Well, Mrs. Shepherd, until you feel like talking."

He broke away and walked down the corridor, peering into every room and the empty garage until he was satisfied Ryan wasn't hiding under a piece of furniture.

"Oh, I nearly forgot." He returned to the living room and hooked the bomber book under one arm.

He paused in front of the window for a few seconds, head turned sideways as if he wanted me to think he was scanning the upper end of the street. I couldn't see the direction of his gaze but I guessed it pointed at his own house.

"I'll bring it back in a day or two," he said.

"There's no need to knock. Just leave it by the front door."

He crossed the street without looking back.

My luck was turning. I wasn't going to be strung up on the flagpole outside the courthouse or face-to-face with a screaming judge. If Lieutenant Joe couldn't conceive I had committed a crime, then no one would.

Home run.

10

I hadn't anticipated Joe's visit. In a way it scared me.

He wouldn't leave the bomber book on the doorstep. He'd keep knocking until I opened the door. It was an excuse to keep tabs on me like he had been doing for some time. I had seen him watch me when we worked the same crime scenes, but never thought much of it.

Better keep up the pretense and let him go full tilt into an investigation. Let him think I was the dumb housewife who didn't watch her back. Because I hadn't. I had left a piece of myself behind.

The water bottle.

It was a wake-up call. I was going to have to ramp up my game. If serial killers had categories like hurricanes I would be a Serial 1: Very dangerous and will produce some damage.

It was no use thinking I could get past Joe. Cops had antenna that went way beyond the norm. Take Ryan for instance. He wouldn't know if you crept up behind him with a sledgehammer, even if he was looking out of the window at night. A cop would feel a change in the wind, he would sense movement behind him. He would see your reflection long before you reached him.

That kind of antenna.

I wasn't going to crumble. I wasn't going to let the world tear me apart. But I couldn't relax and I needed the familiar confines of a hot bath. It wasn't to scrub off the guilt. It was to lie there and think about what to do next.

With bubbles up to my chin, I could feel a cool draft through the slit in the window. Watched the limbs of an old sycamore, leaves doing a belly dance in the breeze outside.

I regretted not having access to Ryan's bank accounts. It would have given some indication which car rental company he had used and where he was planning to live.

I had to admit that I needed a better plan. Still, the nagging feeling something wasn't right and the night seemed to be warning of dangers ahead. I could see a silver moon, waning in the west and mocking me with a fixed grin.

Snap!

I froze. Listened to my heart slamming in my throat.

A male voice. "Henry? Get your ass over here. Now!"

I exhaled. The dog, a bloodhound I think, was chuffing in the alleyway behind my house. I could imagine his ears dragging through a heap of old fish bones and baby's diapers. Taking the stench home with him as an offering to his owner.

My chest ached. For a terrible moment, I thought Lieutenant Joe could see me through the frosted window above the bath. A wave of nausea washed over me and I splashed water on my face.

Relax, Clo. Relax.

My phone lazed in the over-bath caddy. I wiped the bubbles from my hand and checked Ryan's location from the Find Friends app. He was either a no show or he had turned off his location settings. I typed in Marion's address from Google maps and stared at the satellite view on my phone. Zooming in on the vast grid of streets, each roof was so sharp it was as if I were hovering above the house itself.

I Googled 'Montauk Models' and found her profile. Swiped through the tabs and found she had added one called *Today*. It appeared to describe her feelings at the time. It also gave her artificial self an extra layer.

We should never take things for granted. The touch of another human being. The sweet smell of air. A hot shower on a cold night. Sleep. The simple things.

They can all be gone in seconds.

I ask you if parties and promotions are important. If wanting to be noticed is worth the effort. Perhaps it's all a fantasy. Perhaps you're sick of it.

Perhaps you want to wrench yourself from an unhappy marriage. Perhaps you want something new. Ha! Don't we think the strangest things at the oddest times?

Let me ask you this. What if the last two days have been the loneliest in your life? Where do you go? What do you do? Would you call me?

Or would you stay in your suffocating hell trying to work out why she left you, why he left you. Why you left them.

Tell me what your crystal ball tells you. Humor me.

Dread crept into my bones. There was something very abnormal about the piece. Certainly not relevant to the website. I had the impression she was talking to someone she knew.

I looked down at my body through a gap in the froth. At thirty-nine, I wasn't as slim as I once was. I had begun to bore Ryan and I caught the tell-tale yawns every time I reached for him in the night; the same short attention span; the same quick glance at his watch and the *uh-huh, uh-huh, uh-huh* as his eyes scanned the door for any means of escape. How often had he walked out of the room when I was mid-sentence?

Then I thought of Marion Kurchel, as graceful as a cheetah and just as powerful. She was attracted to men with investable assets of several million. But Marion, much like any credit strategy, wasn't without her risks.

When I first saw her standing inside her house, my mind was a riot of emotions. She would not have seen me behind the hedge, staring at a lawn that in the winter looked like a patch of brown corduroy and in the summer a baize of the purest green. She had no idea how much I had studied those dark eyes and the tilt of her head.

I remember following her to the open-air lounge at Oreya, a high-end Mediterranean restaurant, where only the privileged dined. There she sat on a bar stool and it was like someone had tossed out a sexual hand grenade. A near-naked thirty-two-year-old packaged in a lace sheath with no lining and no underwear, the type to incite edge-of-the-party whispers. I doubt she was content to inhabit the same room as other females. No, this dazzling concoction of charisma and style was somehow above all that. It was the men who had deified her.

It was hard knowing I could never be one of *them*. While we owned a small house on Berkeley Road worth a little over one hundred and fifty thousand, Marion Kurchel lived in the Hamptons, on Long Island's South Fork in an 18th century shingle house. Four-car garage, swimming pool, sweeping drive. A holiday house worth well over eight million.

My mind whirred back to Ryan. He had allowed himself to be seduced by her; a name I found in the contacts list on his cell phone under the pseudonym Buy-and-Hold. A woman who had suddenly ripped through the peace of my life. A number that, when I called, went through to a voice that claimed to be Marion Kurchel.

Three times a week, he would come home around one o'clock in the morning, hair slightly damp in the shallows of his neck, where it grew in thick dark tufts. I would caress it after he had fallen asleep, bringing my finger under my nose to smell the sharp scent of grapefruit zest. Not a flavor of shampoo we had in our house. That's how I knew he took his showers elsewhere.

But did he know he shared Marion with another man? A tall, gray-haired man who habitually squeezed himself into his death-trap of a Porsche Panamera to race off to her house every Monday, Wednesday and Friday between the hours of six and nine.

Ryan drove a rattle-trap of a sedan and turned up on the same nights between nine-thirty and eleven. I knew this because I had rented a car and followed Ryan on five separate occasions as he blew along Gin Lane without a care in the world. I couldn't help feeling a flash of irritation at his stupidity.

Ryan lived in his own world, loving himself and pretending he was perfect. A narcissist, if I could give it a name. Touching him was like touching a veneer of ice. He was smooth and emotionless, and like every man he was prone to breaking. If the moron thought he was God's gift to women, then let him.

Life comes down to two things, I thought. *Wallet and ego*.

Ryan didn't have much of the former. But he had plenty of the latter.

11

The sun had hardly cleared the horizon when I awoke, coiled on the couch and hugging my pillow. There were two waking thoughts. The first was:

I had hit a man.

Technically, Ryan had. I think that's where I got off feeling detached somehow. But my conscience was the kicker and even if it couldn't be traced back to me, the man at the garage would remember the woman who had hit a bird. I wanted to tell someone. Someone who could keep a secret, like a counselor perhaps.

Marion's neighbors had windows that pointed toward the ocean, not the road. At least, not that stretch of road. It was no use coming up with scenarios of witnesses walking dogs either. Or kids playing hoop in the driveway. It had been too dark for that.

I picked up my cell phone and headed for the bathroom, rear plummeting hard against the toilet seat. I Googled *hit-and-run* and found a Long Island news article. A neighbor had heard the crash and called the police. There was background on the coastguard, whose injuries were surprisingly minimal—cracked rib, cuts and bruises—and family members were asking for the person responsible to come forward. It was an active investigation with a hotline number to call Southampton Town Detectives.

I huffed out a loud breath. Thank God he was okay.

The second thought was that Marion had informed the police about Ryan's misconduct and latterly his road rage. Marion was chock-full o' shit, that's all I knew.

I missed him. The old Ryan. I missed how we had coffee together on the couch. When it snowed he would take my hands in his and blow warm breath through his thumbs. When we walked in the park he would tuck his hands in the scoop of my armpits and make me squeal from the cold. I miss how we were in our bed.

The pain spurted from me in a deluge, an outpouring of whys. The marriage had faded like an old photograph, curling at the corners and covered in dust.

I felt wooly from crying.

Two hair color boxes graced the sink and if the model on the front was to be trusted, I too would be exquisite. I twisted off my wedding ring, heard a definitive clink as it settled at the bottom of the soap dish.

I mixed the color and sectioned my hair, squeezing the foul-smelling cream to the ends, my hands encased in a pair of plastic gloves. Forty-five minutes. That's how long I waited, parked on the edge of the tub.

Thinking.

Backtracking.

Sliding down memory hill, recalling the first time Ryan had tried to get me to sign the divorce papers. Two weeks ago over a tight-lipped frown. That's how he always tackled awkward things.

Typed on the letterhead were the words *Petition for*

Dissolution of Marriage and under it *Ryan Anthony Shepherd*, petitioner. *Clodagh Bridget Shepherd*, respondent.

"We need to talk about money, about the bills," Ryan had said.

My eyes had meandered over walls and windows and hovered somewhere above his head. It was enough to hear him humiliate me, but it was another to drag my name through the mud to someone on the phone. Latterly I had lost interest in his threats. It should have mattered, but it didn't.

"I'm not being unreasonable, Clo. It's the only solution. I can't go on like this."

He couldn't go on like it because he was in love with *her*. How predictable of him. The spineless son of a bitch.

Didn't he think I'd check? Of course I checked. Like I checked everything: Facebook, Twitter, Instagram, until I found a few daring moments Ryan had posted on Snapchat.

Why blame me?

I plucked up enough courage to follow him along the same scenic routes he had brazenly videoed. Think of it as a game, I kept telling myself. A game where you outsmart your prey. Where you stick it where it hurts and you win, win, win.

When I thought of him, I saw a man in sport mode, as if his gear shift had somehow got stuck. Everything he did was planned with discipline and precision. Only he hadn't planned this.

He wanted to know what was in the package FedEx delivered three days ago. I assured him it was only a couple of books, dreading he might see *The Sportsman* logo on the side and realize it was a box of ammunition.

Call it neighborhood watch, but I began sitting at my window more than I used to. Jogging up the street after Ryan had left for work and memorizing faces, cars, addresses. Keeping myself to myself. Not a bad thing when your marriage is in tatters.

This was why Lieutenant Joe asked me about unusual cars in the neighborhood. He knew I had been keeping watch.

Snapping back to the bathroom, I checked the GPS on my phone. It was 5:45 a.m. and Ryan's location was still unavailable. I decided to shrug it off because today was the day I took control and became the person I had always wanted to be.

Through the blinds, I saw a vast horizon streaking out like a pale finger that separated the earth from an inky sky. That's what I loved about this time of day. A thick silence where a wrinkled floppy-eared dog in Lieutenant Joe's front yard, nosed through an upturned trash can and made off with a paper bag. He was the size of a small pony and when he took a leak it was wise to stand back.

The street was alive with sounds. The airbrakes of a truck, the distant rumble of traffic on the freeway, the squeal of many garage doors as residents began their early trips to work. But the one sound I loved the most was the rasping scream of a red-tailed hawk. There was one nesting nearby, though I had never seen it.

Tugging a fresh towel from the closet, I eased into the shower to rinse off the dye. Beads of water burned into my back and scalp, and muddy brown trails dribbled down my calves.

I half-wanted to call Ryan again. If he was at Marion's enjoying a full continental breakfast the call would only incite suspicion. If he had left me for good, I wouldn't have to suffer his whiny monologues, his pitiful attempt at empathy, his arched eyebrow and you've-gotta-be-kidding expressions.

I could never be myself around him, especially the times when he expected me to explain why our marriage was not the one he'd planned and why I sneaked around like an unwanted stranger. It was because Ryan stewed over the most insignificant things and lately, he was convinced I was hiding something.

Hiding something? Feh. What's to hide?

The only thing I could think of was the stalking and he couldn't have known about that. Ryan was a math wizard, a bottom-line kind of guy, but he sure didn't have the foresight to look in the bank account. I had been siphoning a few dollars each month.

I could always tell when he was lying, could feel a change in his mood even before he came home. Today I felt nothing. As I finished combing conditioner through my hair, I knew with absolute certainty. There would be no more squeaky hinges or the growl of the garage door. No car catching its breath before revving out into the street.

Ryan wasn't coming home. Ryan would never come home.

12

I was now a medium brown with beach waves, at least that's what it said on the box.

It was a nugget of an idea that kept flashing in my mind. An idea that I needed to be more Marion-esque. Except for my copper eyes, I could have been her.

Maybe.

How easy would it be to turn the clocks back to when I was 115 pounds? I had already rid myself of the red cap of hair I was born with and with regular exercise, Marion's flat stomach was mine.

It was her regal bearing that said, "I am beautiful. I am desirable. I am a professional." I wasn't sure I could pull that off.

I'd often thought of breaking into her house, knowing that every room was probably rigged with CCTV. My face would need to be distorted by a mask so no one could identify me and my hands covered with latex. I'd get away, of course. But that's after a brutal police chase across two state lines.

I snapped off the plastic gloves and stuffed the empties

into a grocery bag, toweled myself dry and stared long and hard in the mirror. There wasn't a blemish on my skin and a smooth décolletage was something to be envied. I shrugged on a long T-shirt before pausing in front of the closet.

There was a medium-sized suitcase of clothes and personal items on the top shelf, things I had been accumulating for some time. I pulled it down and rolled it to the kitchen.

The gun was slim and compact, belonged to my grandfather and had never been registered. It was concealed in a carrying case beneath a solid wood cabinet between the floor and the lower shelf. Today, it belonged in the trunk of my car.

Slipping the gun in the upper compartment of the case, I hesitated at the sound of a knock.

Then the stutter of the doorbell.

The urge to run across the back lawn was overwhelming and the fact that I was underdressed jolted my thoughts. A long T-shirt, no shoes, no underwear; not a pretty sight. Rolling the suitcase to the back door, I left it on the step in a light drizzle of rain. Tugged a clean towel from the laundry basket and wrapped it around my head.

There was a familiar outline through the stained glass in the front door—a quirk of the houses in the street. I waited for the sound again, only this time it was more urgent, like the trumpets in *Reveille*.

I flipped the lock and opened the door a fraction. "Yes?"

"It's me. Joe."

I opened the door a little wider and I could smell hand sanitizer and nicotine. His legs were planted wide and his arms were folded across a Kevlar vest.

"Are you okay?" he said.

"Yes, I think so."

"Heard from him yet?"

His forehead was creased with lines, eyes skating up and down my front and resting somewhere on my forehead.

"No, he hasn't called. Didn't come home. Do you think I should file a missing person's report?"

"It's only been… what, a few hours?"

I don't know. You're the one counting.

"He's an adult," he said. "Probably—"

"Left of his own accord? Yep."

"Listen, it's none of my business, but I understand things have been stressful, what with him being fired and all."

"Fired?" My stomach cramped. "What do you mean he was fired?"

"He didn't tell you?"

I sensed Joe was on edge, shifting gears. I bet he wished he had a cigarette speared between his lips.

"All I know is there's a big investigation going on," he said. "You should have received a letter. One of our detectives said Kimball Aerospace sent them out a week ago."

"Well, I haven't been to the mailbox in about that long. You probably noticed."

He paused. "I hope you didn't think—"

"Not at all. I don't mind you checking on me. It's very comforting actually."

He cleared his throat. "I know you've been through a lot lately. I'd like to help."

I shook my head in frustration. "Why?"

"I've asked myself that a few times over the past year. Word got out that he's seeing the Kurchel woman. I'm sorry… if that was news."

My jaw flopped open.

"Getting divorced?" he asked.

"That's a bit personal, isn't it?"

"Well, are you?"

I began to wonder if I was supposed to supply Joe with a progress report each week. "He already filed and I signed."

"Better that way. Being in love with an egotistical jerk is like loving banana bread pudding. Hours of misery on the treadmill. He's out there, Clo. Keeping tabs on you."

If Ryan was out there stalking me—the liar, the snake, the devil himself—then I'd shoot his ass the first opportunity I got.

Joe looked down at his pager. "So, if you do see him, you'll let me know."

"Yeah, Joe. I'll let you know."

"And if you need anything. I'm only a whisper away."

He looked me dead in the eye before I closed the door. My throat hardened. No point in getting worked up and all wrung out because Ryan had been fired.

Fired? Shit, Ryan. Why didn't you tell me?

Stuffing the box of hair dye in a grocery bag, I walked along the hallway, swinging it in an arc and into the trash. I tied my hair into a tight bun and let it dry that way. The mirror confirmed how much brown hair suited me. It made me look... exotic.

If Ryan saw me now, I mean, really *saw* me, what would be his reaction? I like to think open-mouthed amazement as I dressed in skinny jeans and a long, lean T-shirt.

Skinny jeans! When did I last wear skinny jeans?

It gave me the confidence I needed to slip back into the world unnoticed. I had been dead tired and too afraid to sleep, but the steady patter of rain against the roof seemed to revive me for a moment.

It was better to assume someone was following me than to blindly head out into the open without watching my back. Opening the back door, I wheeled my suitcase down the path to the gap in the fence. Lugging it between the wooden slats, my eyes swept the street for an unfamiliar car with a driver faking a nap behind a sun visor.

Nothing so far.

I kept my head down—an amateur runaway—rushing from street to street, ducking under the weeping willow on the corner of Mrs. Nita's driveway. I hid a spare set of house keys under her bathroom window, slotting them into a slit in the clapboard.

I could smell mildew and gasoline in the garage, three cans of it on the back wall and spare tires hanging from the ceiling. I left the fake plates on my car and slid the originals under a mildewed cardboard box. Once I had cleaned the glovebox of insurance papers and personal items, it would take longer for the cops to trace the car and its owner if they ever found it.

It was the black car beside mine that made me take a deep, shaking breath. I peeled back the dust sheet and squinted in through the passenger window. Keys hung from the ignition and a can of hairspray idled on the back seat.

I clenched my teeth and tried to swallow down the tears as I opened the driver's door. I leaned in and turned the key in the ignition. The engine let out a cough before purring into life. I high-fived the dashboard.

Pressing the trunk release, I swung my case over the bumper, breathing in the musty air while trying to force an image of my mom away. A younger face, an early time before her hair went gray and her mind surrendered itself to hallucinations and tremors.

The car rolled smoothly out into the driveway, gas gauge three quarters full. I let her idle as I closed the garage door, looking around the street for any witnesses.

A cat moseyed down the sidewalk and there was no Mrs. Nita staring out of her kitchen window. The rain had taken care of that.

My inheritance couldn't have come at a better time, but it also came with feelings of uncertainty. If something was too good to be true then perhaps... I didn't finish the thought.

Flooring the gas pedal, the car bunny-hopped up the street and then, as if it had suddenly found its wings, flew like the wind.

13

I didn't believe Ryan was missing. He was hiding out somewhere. After all, someone had ratted him out at work. Didn't he say he was going to rent a car?

I parked outside a bookstore on South Main and called every rental company I could think of. None came up trumps. Had Shayna driven him to Marion's? It was worth a call.

Three rings later and a breezy voice greeted me. "Don Taylor's office, Shayna Grey speaking."

I cleared my throat. It was no longer Ryan Shepherd's office. "Shayna, its Clo. It's me."

A pause. "Hi, how are you?"

"Oh, I'm fine. Good to hear your voice. Listen, I'll make this brief." I heard the clatter of a keyboard in the background. "I hope you don't mind me asking, but did you, by any chance, drop Ryan off at a car rental yesterday?"

"No. I dropped him off at the Capital One bank on Maplewood. He said he was going to get a ride."

"Did he say who with?"

"No." After a moment she spoke again. "Is everything okay?"

"Oh, yes. Yes, everything's fine."

"Listen, I'm so sorry about… the termination."

I stumbled. "These things happen. Well, thank you. I appreciate it."

"Anytime, Mrs. Shepherd."

Mrs. Shepherd now. Not Clo. It was terminal.

Poor Shayna had no idea why Ryan needed to be dropped off at the bank and likely had no idea he was missing. I had to move forward too.

Stalking Marion on the beach was easy. Following her to a bookstore was something else.

I'd parked as far up the street as I could get without losing sight of her front gate, hoping she'd get the urge to go shopping. After four long, sweaty hours, her car swung into the road and I slotted in neatly behind. When we arrived at the bookstore, I fell in behind a couple of shoppers. There were three people browsing in the mystery section and two in general fiction. The assistants weren't pushy, leaving readers to flip through magazines and entire novels. It was expected.

She was wearing flat shoes and no makeup. Just like me. A short white cardigan, buttoned just enough to cover her thirty-six Ds, and skinny jeans which embraced two pert buttocks and rock hard-thighs.

Nothing like me.

Marion, au naturel, looked like someone I used to know. Someone I had been trying to recall for the past two years. With a diet low in carbs and jogging once a day for two hours, I imagined I was within spitting distance.

She was in the kids' section wandering aimlessly between the tables, fingers trailing the bookshelves. I peered over the magazine I was holding in front of my face and noticed her hair was loose today and styled iron-straight.

Marion had been swiping through a range of web pages on her cell phone, finger stabbing the screen until she lifted the phone to her ear. She kept shifting from foot to foot and glancing around. I couldn't hear all the words from where I stood.

"I need to talk to you," she had said, creeping around a life-sized cutout of *The Cat in the Hat*. "… not to call at work but I think I'm being followed. No, I'm just saying… Well, it's probably nothing… I'm sure it was… the beach yesterday. I thought you'd want to know. Yes… yes, that was awful. They said he's at home now. Broken ribs but he's okay. Me? I'm going to Trader Joe's. I just wanted—"

There was no way of knowing who Marion was talking to or why they hung up on her. I had to ask myself who was the worst threat to Marion. The person on the phone? Or me? I was relieved about the coastguard, confused over Ryan's disappearance and I struggled to maintain a level of coolness.

I walked through the bookstore to the parking lot. Locked myself in my car and waited for Marion to come out. It was at least ten minutes before she did.

Hiding behind a flush of shame, I couldn't detect any tell-tale signs of nervousness as she walked behind a row of cars and out of sight. But what I did detect was a feeling of urgency.

I followed her to Trader Joe's on Main Street. The fragrance of a fresh garden; vibrant red beets and deep green asparagus made my head spin. My mouth was dry and I was irresistibly drawn to the cool mists of water cascading over the produce. I was about to squeeze a fat purple eggplant when I saw her double back and head for the bread.

I stood there with a thousand thoughts running through my mind. How close could I get? After all, she knew she was being followed and that made me twice as a cautious.

A small, menacing voice kept saying, *What if she calls the police? What if she knows it's me?*

But she couldn't know it was me. I wasn't swamped in sweats, hair scooped up in a baseball cap. If I had been, she would have recognized a heavy and somewhat masculine version of me. She was oblivious to my new makeover as she poked among the bins of French bread.

I saw those slim fingers reach inside her cardigan and pull a phone from under her armpit, from a concealed pocket she must have had in her bra. Hooking the basket over her elbow, she used the same hand to hold the phone and began a conversation that gave no indication she was about to call the police or that she knew I was standing behind her.

Marion seemed to float toward the spice section, free hand hovering over an assortment of wood-capped jars, her throat arching in the pastel light from the shelf.

"Hi Isla, how's it going? Good thanks. How did her references check out? Shame. What about the Southampton Press? Yes, a live-in. I really need someone. Let me think about that." She laughed and then, "I'm still thinking."

I turned my back and found frozen Sockeye salmon and a jar of tuna filets in olive oil, anything I could put in my basket. I could see she was still talking, but her voice was quieter now as she pulled a perforated bag from a dispenser and tore it off with one hand.

She finished her call and was about to slip the phone back into her purse when she changed her mind. She swiped a thumb across the screen, double tapped and then held it back against her ear.

"Hey, Frances… no, not this evening. I don't need Robert either. Can you let him know for me? Thanks. You too."

I snapped a few photos with my phone, looking behind me occasionally to make sure no one was looking.

Snap, snap, snap.

It was at times like this I wished I had my camera. Better for bringing the unreachable closer.

It dawned on me that Marion could have snuffed the life out of Ryan. Maybe that's why he wasn't answering his phone. It would have been easy for her if he fell asleep. A pillow across his face or a quick jab in the ribs with a paring knife. You always expect a killer to be strong.

As she headed for the checkout, I followed about six feet behind. There was an elderly man between us carrying a basket of duck liver pâté and a wedge of Roquefort. His face was trancelike as he scanned the shelves and shuffled in shoes that seemed too big for him.

I stood in a parallel checkout line, phone angled just enough for anyone to think I was texting. But the close-ups I took of her face revealed a doe-eyed expression I couldn't possibly imitate. My face was rounder and my eyes narrower. It would take a high-end cosmetologist to replicate the look.

I had no plan beyond taking a few videos of her in the parking lot. I last saw her yesterday and it would be tomorrow before I saw her again. I had to do this now...

I felt less conspicuous outside, tugging at a newspaper from an outdoor vending rack. The wind blew discarded plastic bags against car fenders and leaves gusted along the pavement. I wondered if I would ever forget this day.

Something different. Something new.

Her car was parked diagonally across from mine and I watched her pull out and then ease into the traffic. The car was nothing special. A four-door sedan.

Call the number, carped the small voice in my head. *You're as ready as you will ever be.*

After all, Marion needed a home help.

14

I spread the newspaper on my lap, finger scrolling down the ads until I found *Hamptons Home Help*. It gave two email addresses and a phone number. This time I called from my own phone.

After a few rings, a voice greeted me. Someone called Isla Fox, an agent handling applications. I gave her my name as Clody Turner, gave her three numbers for references. After she'd explained the job and taken my details, I understood someone would call back within a few days to set up an interview. She also informed me I was the tenth person applying.

Leaning back against the car seat, I closed my eyes and listened to the drone of the windshield wipers. I would need to stay off the streets during the day, moving from motel to motel until my cash ran out. There wasn't a second where I didn't try to untangle Ryan's words, rethinking the whole marriage to see where I had gone wrong. I couldn't go back.

It was unreal. Me out here in a black Buick and Ryan who knows where. I checked my lip in the rearview mirror. Swollen like a cyst. There had to be a better way.

I was already feeling the grit of exhaustion from another sleepless night and the weight of Ryan's disappearance, and Lieutenant Joe's blatant snooping had begun to press down on me.

I sent Ryan a text. *Where are you?*

I should have sent it last night. But if it got as far as a police investigation, I would tell them I was expecting him home late. That I had fallen asleep on the couch.

I could say he had a board meeting and dinner with his colleagues. The police would feel sorry for me. A lied-to, cheated-on wife. Even a judge wouldn't push it. Not if the police found him in another woman's house.

Then I realized what Lieutenant Joe had been gawping at when he knocked on my door this morning. A narrow figure and the hint of chocolate brown hair under the twist of a hair towel. My makeover had been noted.

I had spent weeks obsessing over my body. Lifting weights, going for runs and drinking more water. Once I started the routine I couldn't finish. Pushing a little more each day as if I enjoyed the sensation of wobbly legs and a sense of collapse. Because the thought of spending one more day without Marion was intolerable.

Lieutenant Joe would never see me again. Besides, I looked different, drove a different car. I kept turning my cell phone location on and off and without a search warrant he wasn't cleared to track me.

The squeal of the phone gave me a start. Isla Fox. Could I head down to the homeowner on Gin Lane for interview right now? Could I hell!

I took a breath of sea air through the car window as the wind tugged at my hair. There was something special in the clouds that hung low in the sky and the sun that tried to seep between the trees. No more lonely walks on the beach, no more probing behind dark glasses to see if she was there.

Today, I would be on the inside.

I was a little rumpled and bleary-eyed and I tried not to let thoughts of Ryan ruin the afternoon. After all, he was the reason I was following the white Mazda in the first place.

It appeared that Marion would be alone tonight and I was eager to see her—not in an infatuated way—more because there wouldn't be any interruptions. I had no idea how to do this, whatever *this* was. But I was determined to find out if Ryan had lied about the apartment he had rented, whether he had moved in with Marion. Whether he really had disappeared.

In our fifteen years of marriage, I can count all the nights he spent away on one hand. But last night was different. It disturbed my peace of mind. I checked the GPS and it still showed 'location unavailable'.

There were moments when I began to wonder if I was just a dull-witted housewife with nothing better to do than stalk an innocent woman. But Ryan wanted a divorce. He wanted a signature. I had sat there and refused to have eye contact, pacing around the tiny kitchen like a brain-damaged polar bear.

Now I had a sense of purpose, a sense of vengeance. It spurred me on and provided the one thing I needed the most.

Information.

I forced myself to drive up the road where the coastguard had been found last night by the emergency services. No flashing lights. No sign of the cops. The air was just as clean and fresh as I had left it.

I must have been speeding because I had caught up to Marion already. There were only two cars between me and the Mazda and—Sod's law—they both turned into a side street.

Now I felt empty and naked. Mine was the only car behind Marion's until I reminded myself I was driving the

Buick. If she ever needed a good description of the driver stalking her for the past few days, this wasn't it.

The road seemed to go on and on. Hedges flew by on both sides and I sensed a feeling of isolation, as if reality had slipped away and this was the road to hell.

Suddenly four white chimneys appeared where sunlight shimmered off the upper windows and a box hedge curled around to the right-hand side of the road. Behind it were the peaks of a pitched roof and artichoke finials, and I hunched forward, taking a tighter grip on the steering wheel. If a contemporary Cape Cod beach house crossed floor plans with a West Indies infused domicile, then this was it.

Marion's brake lights shuddered and the car rolled right at the turning. I hung back and watched her reach up to the in-car transmitter to open the automatic gate.

According to my notes, it took roughly five seconds for the gate to close. If there was a sensor to make allowances for a car pulling a trailer there would be plenty of time for a second vehicle to race in behind. Since the driveway was long and straight, Marion would see me in her rearview mirror.

I waited until her rear fender cleared the posts and then punched the gas. The car lurched forward, wheels sending a shower of gravel out into the street as I turned into the driveway. My pulse was racing. The cell phone in my pocket was buzzing.

I was in.

15

The Hamptons, New York

The house on Gin Lane was at the end of a long drive, surrounded by a seven-foot hedge. How many times had I driven past, soaked up the opulence and parked in the adjacent lane? How many times had I kicked off my shoes and felt the sand between my toes? Pretending I lived there. Pretending I belonged.

The house cast a shadow across the driveway; a long stretch of asphalt that ended in a large square. I was struck for a dazed moment at the sheer beauty of green lawns and a playing fountain. I had imagined the resident to be a dentist or an acupuncturist. A high-class call girl would not have come close.

I checked my phone. The call had been from Lieutenant Joe and I didn't feel like calling him back. I switched off the sound and toggled it to vibrate on silent.

Marion got out of her car, long hair slapping around her face in the wind. She leaned in through the driver's side and dragged a shopping bag across the front seat. The look in her eyes was bright and intelligent, the set of her mouth closed and watchful.

I opened my car door and stood there. One of us had to take charge.

"Ms. Kurchel?"

"Yes," she said, frowning first at the closing gate and then at my car.

"I'm sorry. Isla Fox called me about the job. The home help?"

Marion frowned and strummed a hand in the air. "Of course. You're Ms. Turner?"

I nodded, feeling the twisted topknot of a bun wobble a little. I was promised a headache before the day was out.

I allowed myself to be ushered through the front door, studying the slight sway of her hips and the groove of a spine visible between the cardigan and the waistband of her jeans. There was a strong scent of orange blossom and ambergris, similar to a perfume Ryan had bought me last Christmas.

Once inside, the foyer was dominated by a Rumford fireplace, framed by double entrances into a great room. Nothing like I had imagined from the outside. I couldn't help looking up at exposed beams and coffered ceilings and my mouth must have dropped at the expansive windows, all dressed with louvered shades.

Marion led me to the largest kitchen I had ever seen. Stainless steel and marble everywhere and a central island the size of a small car. There was a wrought iron rack dangling from the ceiling, boasting an array of pots and cooking utensils I doubt she used.

She dropped her keys and shopping bag on the countertop. Pulled out her cell phone and settled on a bar stool. Her skin was sallow close-up, as if she spent more time lying on her back in the bedroom and less time lying on the beach.

"Isla explained the job," she said, voice trilling upward

at the end of the sentence. It was hard to tell if it was a question or a statement.

"Yes, she did."

"And the pay?"

"$75 an hour. Is that correct?"

"Correct. It's a long day. Seven till seven. All meals included. I have a copy of your résumé. Very impressive. What made you want to be a domestic?"

A domestic… it was such an old-fashioned word but she was right to ask. My training was aligned to photographing evidence, death scenes and autopsies for criminal investigations. Nothing that would support a home help. After a four-year bachelor's degree in forensic science and three years of photography and digital imaging, it would be hard to persuade a future employer to see the merit in changing career paths.

"Perfection," I said. "It's something I always strive for. When I clean a house, I think of everything as a grid. By visualizing the space broken up this way, I don't miss anything. The longer dirt sits, the harder it is to clean off."

I didn't have much to say about the subject. If she'd asked me what it was like to be an expert witness in court, I could have rambled on for hours.

She eyed me the way a dealer would appraise a valuable painting. Perhaps it was the familiarity of what she saw. Her in me. "Two of your references were outstanding. The other was out of town."

The *other* was a criminal investigator I had once worked with—a vicious bitch—who never answered her phone. It was unlikely that particular reference would do me any good.

Clody… that's an unusual name," she said, pausing as she studied me. "Is it short for anything?"

"It's Irish." My stomach tightened. "Comes from the name of the river that runs through County Wexford. People usually just called me Clo."

Marion would be clueless about the name of the river. If Ryan had ever mentioned me, he would have used Clodagh. Never Clo.

"Oh." She gave a wide-eyed nod. "Your parents Irish?"

"My mother."

She sniffed as if she disapproved of my heritage and there was a condescension to her tone that made me despise her even more. I wondered if we would get along.

She swiveled the bar stool toward a laptop and a small black printer on the countertop behind her. Shuffled the mouse until the screen lit up. Her fingers leisurely tapped in the password.

"You would be required to live in," she said, accessing the job description and perusing it as if it was the first time she had seen it.

I briefly wondered why it was live-in.

"I may ask you to serve dinner and clean up after 11 p.m." she said. "Three times a week. You'll get overtime."

That's why it was live-in. "Sounds great."

My finger felt bare without a wedding ring but few married women applied for a live-in job. I had signed the divorce papers. I was *almost* single.

Marion pressed *print* and then whipped the cursor to the toolbar and closed out the screen. The printer whirred into life. I took the two-page job description she handed me and examined the tasks.

All tasks to be performed when homeowner is absent and at no time will they be performed during Game Night.
- *Clean house floors by sweeping, mopping, scrubbing or vacuuming. Original paintings to be dusted in situ and not removed.*
- *Clean windows, glass partitions, mirrors once every week.*

- *Follow procedures for the use of chemical cleaners and all equipment to prevent damage to floors and fixtures.*
- *Empty trash in driveway dumpster.*
- *Guesthouses will be cleaned by housekeeper.*
- *Two days off weekly and at housekeeper's discretion.*
- *All meals are included and to be taken in the kitchen.*
- *Notify housekeeper concerning any repairs or supplies as needed.*
- *Silver service required three times a week.*

If, at any time, the homeowner appears on premises, cleaning will cease until further notice. All keys will be returned to housekeeper at 6 p.m. each day.

Please note: *Some rooms will remain private and inaccessible and the responsibility of the housekeeper.*

"Game night?" I asked.

"Mr. Kimball is not only a member of the Long Island Arts Alliance but a member of The Gateway Performing Arts Center. He leads a very active life."

"Impressive."

Marion eyed my finger as it passed down the list. "Just to be clear, there is a dress code in the evenings. As the resident housekeeper, it is my job to provide staff with uniform."

Uniform? I hadn't worn one of those since school.

"Small?" she asked.

"Small what?"

"Your size?"

"Oh, yes. Small will be fine."

"You'll find cleaning equipment and hairnets in the mudroom closet. Some doors are kept locked and don't require cleaning."

Was she already offering me the job?

Something else shrieked in my brain, like the blast of an ocean liner. Marion had keys, and keys provided access to private and inaccessible rooms. If Ryan had an apartment somewhere on the property, Marion would know.

"Coffee?"

I nodded. Why not.

"If you have any questions now would be a good time to, uh, break the ice."

She wanted to break the ice? I wanted to break her neck. "Where are you from?"

She certainly wasn't from around here. The 'uh' sounded more like an 'eh' and there was a throaty mixture to some of her words.

"Originally?"

"Yes."

"New Haven."

New Haven wasn't the place I had in mind. More Middle Eastern.

"I used to be a housekeeper for a stockbroker." She drifted over to the coffee machine and filled the hopper with beans. "He was a great guy. His wife was a well-known actress. Too... how you say... glacial."

I assumed that meant distant.

"Zero personality," she said, rambling. "You know the type?"

I did. I was looking at one now.

"I don't know what he saw in her. But then I never know what men see in their wives. Too frumpy. Maybe they get like that after a few years. Do you think I'm being cruel?"

Actresses weren't usually frumpy. "Not really."

"I've never married. Never had children. Couldn't bear the lifestyle."

"Too oppressive?" I said, trying to draw her out.

"You're supposedly the legal property of a man and in some cases forced to obey them. It's a domestic violence case waiting to happen."

Yet Marion was shackled to her lifestyle which, as far as I could make out, meant benefiting from a man's success. A lifestyle from which she was unable to tear herself away. How free was that?

"Have you always been a housekeeper?" I asked.

"Yes. It pays. Very well actually. I've worked for presidents, politicians. Actors. Can't tell you their names, but well known."

I couldn't imagine Marion as a housekeeper in a tweed skirt and sensible shoes. What did housekeepers wear these days? Black sheath dresses and Hermès scarves?

"So what happened to this stockbroker?" I asked.

Marion gazed over my right shoulder and bit her lip. "You can always tell if a man likes you. Glances that last a second too long. Little gifts. Pretending he was too sick to go out for dinner. So she'd go alone and he... well, he would come downstairs to the basement to see me. Unfortunately, his wife found out." Marion turned the dial to espresso, voice raised over the noise. "I was fired."

"How sick." The words came out before I had time to stop them. I doubt she heard.

"I've always been drawn to lonely men," she said, "and he was lonely. Lived in his own world, where he didn't have to deal with her obsession. Didn't have to lie to himself about loving her. She turned one of the bedrooms into a master closet. Shoes and handbags had their own walk-in and there was a cache of jewelry in a safe. Talk about military precision, it was like a museum."

"Why screw around behind her back? Why not divorce her?" I asked.

"It was the money. Shares. Houses. He would have lost all of it."

"Were you in love with him?"

"No."

She was driving me mad with her dreamy, senseless conversation. It wasn't just the money. It was the sex. Marion certainly wasn't the type to be confined by a vibrator.

"You know what he told me?" she said. "He said she couldn't bear the thought of someone else wearing her leftovers. Fur coats, dresses, shoes. She made us carry them out to the car so she could take them to the dump. But I saved some of those clothes. Hid them in the trunk of my car. She'd die if she knew."

I noted her top lip was almost as full as the bottom and the beige lipstick a tad too glittery for my taste. There was nothing wholesome about her, nothing brassy. The word I hated to give her was *exotic*.

"Would you like to see them?" she asked.

"See what?"

"Her clothes."

"Oh."

"I can see you'd rather not. Must be strange. You never knew her."

I noticed her voice carried traces of empathy, a characteristic girls like her had in truckloads. I had to keep reminding myself she was Ryan's mistress. Not my best friend.

"When can you start?" she asked.

16

I didn't know which bothered me the most. Marion's startling frankness over her sordid past or her hiring me on the spur of the moment. I couldn't help having a violent belly churn over her affair with another married man.

I wondered if it was the bruise on my lip she kept staring at. Perhaps she empathized. Wanted to know all about it.

I sipped the froth from a cup of cappuccino, slipping from normalcy and heading into the biggest tidal wave of my career. I wanted to ask her if she hired killers and I was quite confident she would respond, we *only* hire killers. Then I'd pull out my gun and blow her all the way to Bermuda.

I signed the policies and procedures. It was my first cleaning job and I was actually quite proud of it.

"We could do with two cleaners," Marion said. "But it's hard getting honest people. Things have been stolen. Not valuable things, but things, nevertheless."

It felt like a backhanded compliment. There was no,

'We're so glad to have you, Clo. You were the best of ten applicants and boy did they suck.' Nothing that made me feel as if I'd achieved the highest honors.

"He gets mad when things go missing." Her fingers scoured her bottom lip, eyes drifting over the top of my head. "You never want to make him mad."

"Oh."

She straightened and smiled. "There's only you and me. The others come in three times a week and that's for an afternoon. Kimball's not much of a night owl. He rarely stays too late."

"What's he like?"

"Self-confident and charming. He can be a little OCD."

"What does that mean? He counts steps and lampposts? Or he has a fear of touching door knobs and using public toilets?"

Marion bowed over her coffee and actually cackled. It reminded me of a hen after laying an egg. "He's not that bad. Just a little, pedantic. Do you jog?"

"Yes."

"We could go jogging together if you like. I usually go around six in the morning."

Now that I didn't know. "Sounds like a plan."

"In the evenings, I go swimming for about twenty minutes."

"In the pool?"

"In the ocean."

I assumed it was also an invite. "I don't have a swimsuit."

"I've got loads."

I hoped it wasn't a bikini. My belly was jewel-purple with an afterglow of citrine.

The beach was the best place to chill without being disturbed, and I needed to make a schedule of how private it really was.

"Want to see around the house?" she asked.

I did.

Vast was the only word to describe it. A shingle style classic reminiscent of an 18th Century English park with eight bedrooms and ten bathrooms. Not as many garages as one would assume for such a monster. Outside were old-growth trees, rolling lawns and a pool sandwiched between two guesthouses. 2.5 acres, as Marion proudly pointed out. I could see why she was desperate for a cleaner.

Since I wasn't relegated to the guesthouse, my room was opposite Marion's. En suite and tastefully furnished, it had views of the driveway from a window seat that was scattered with cushions and wide enough to sleep on. With as many rooms as there were in the house, I was a little bummed out she hadn't offered me one with a beach view like hers.

We trooped back to the kitchen. She opened the fridge and tipped a sealed plastic bowl slightly so I could see what it was. "Salad?"

"Not too fond of celery. Or radish for that matter."

"What do you eat?"

"Fish."

"No meat?"

"Not really. If I do eat it I have to do so something physical, like jumping jacks and squats." And I wasn't about to admit how much gas that gave me.

After a tuna salad, Marion asked me if I wanted to go home and get my things. I told her I already had them.

"You're prepared," she said, frowning.

"I'm between apartments." I pushed away my empty plate. "My man went on a bender two nights ago. Came back and decided to repaint my fence. I wasn't a pretty sight after that. At least that's what he told me. So he ran off with some underage girl and I'm left with all the bills and no furniture. The upside is, he did call me yesterday.

Told me if I was a normal person he'd tell me to be careful. But since I am who I am he just wished me all the best."

"Can I see?" Marion didn't miss a beat.

I pulled up my T-shirt and there they were; garish purple splotches, knuckled like a fist and set against a sweep of yellow. If it hadn't been for one on my lip, she might have thought I was lying.

She pressed a hand to her mouth and grimaced. "Why did he hit you?"

"Because he stopped loving me."

In that moment, I couldn't remember what it felt like to be loved and desired. I couldn't remember anything but pain, the type that gutted and scorched until you evaporated into a wisp of smoke. I had a strange feeling if I looked around this house there was probably more of Ryan here than at home.

I hardly heard Marion ask me if I needed Arnica or vitamin K. But I did hear when she asked me if there was any chance my man might show up here.

"Not a chance in hell."

"I'm glad," she said. "Did you call the cops?"

"A cop did come over to my house—yes. Took a report. I doubt he'll do anything about it."

The more I ran over Lieutenant Joe's words, the more I felt as if I had taken a mental beating. He was damn smart and I was damn stupid. I didn't want to start boiling over again with suppressed hatred. It would only show on my face.

Marion took the empty plates over to the sink. Head barely looking over one shoulder, she said, "My boss won't be here tonight. Why don't you take the rest of the day off and walk on the beach?"

Problem solved. I could look around. "Thank you, I'll do that."

17

I tried not to let curiosity overwhelm me, even though I ached with a sudden visceral longing to root through the house for anything that might give me a clue to Ryan's whereabouts.

I shoved the notion aside and wheeled my suitcase upstairs. Hoisting it onto the end of the bed, I unzipped the main compartment and looked around.

There was an oil painting above the bedhead and in the bottom right-hand corner were the initials EdeB. Bold, sharp strokes of blues and greens and froth-capped waves. A boy standing in the shallows staring at a schooner out at sea, arms hovering by his sides. I caught the dark inquisitive eyes from a slightly turned head as if he knew I stood behind him and wanted me to see what he saw.

Clever how a painting could convey a feeling of being watched. As if I were the subject, not the boy.

I folded the gun between two T-shirts and took the bundle to the bathroom closet. Sandwiching it between two towels seemed the best place for it.

I took another look at the GPS on my phone. No sign

of Ryan's cheery face depicted in a circle flicking from one end of Long Island to the other. Location information was often inaccurate and I suspected a time delay. I turned off Wi-Fi in order to use data and tried again.

Nothing new.

Then I checked email. One from Match.com. *Are you single? View photos of men near you.* I deleted it and checked recent phone calls. Another from Joe. Recent texts. One. Gentle Dental with an appointment I needed to confirm for two weeks. No point responding. There was no knowing where I would be in two weeks.

I unclipped my bun and dragged a brush through my hair. The bedroom window was open a crack and fresh air streamed in, bringing with it the sweet smell of mown grass. There were two guesthouses about halfway down the drive and a rose garden adjacent to the privet hedge. I could see my car and Marion's parked at an angle near the front door. It was oddly calming.

I still couldn't quite get used to my appearance, standing sideways to admire the slender image in a full-length mirror. There was something unsettling about my face. The tramlines between my eyebrows separated two haunted eyes. I couldn't compare myself to Marion, whose indefinable beauty was typically found on the front cover of a high-end fashion magazine. But I could copy her mannerisms.

I wandered downstairs to the living room and out onto the deck. Fine gusts of wind played in the long grass and a halyard spanked against a nearby mast. I searched for my donut; a reminder of the tools of my trade. It couldn't be seen from the steps unless you were leaning over the rail. And no one ever leaned over a rail unless they were puking.

The smell of the sea was stronger here, the smell of wealth, champagne and flowers. I took off my shoes and walked down to the beach. There was a dust devil in the distance, spinning across the sand like a dancer in a mermaid gown. A group of swimmers and the screech of gulls. I almost missed the phone buzzing in the depths of my pocket over the roar of the waves. I turned my back toward the sun and looked down at the incoming call.

The same deep accented voice. "You don't have a lot of time," he said.

I decided to engage. "That sounds ominous, Joe."

"It is. I'll be frank with you. It won't be easy. The bigger the mess, the harder it is to clean up. And Ryan has made a mess."

A mess? What was he talking about? The accident? "Give him a sodding mop and bucket then."

"That's about as useless as teats on a boar. Listen, from where I'm standing you might want to watch your back. I'm worried about you."

"It's really not your business to worry about me, is it, Joe? This is the third time you've called."

"Maybe you're right. Maybe I needed to stop being a dick and caring for once."

"I'm sorry, I didn't mean—"

"Yes you did. And you're right. It's not my sodding business."

I jolted at the sound of a click. Then dead air.

Joe wasn't the type to feel sorry for himself. I began to bet he wouldn't be put off so easily. It was no use imagining he was standing on the beach or hiding behind one of the wooden struts that supported the deck. But it scared me a little.

My eyes swung out to sea, sun setting through a filigree of rigging on a distant ketch. Then at the surf where a little boy was paddling, a wisp of an arm carrying a plastic bucket.

Then I saw Jax sitting in the dunes. I couldn't help feeling he might have seen something, so I waved and said hello.

"Hey," he said, eyes scurrying up and down my body.

I couldn't tell if he recognized me without my big girl clothes or naturally assumed I was a relative. A few moments passed and I swallowed. "Seen any birdwatchers recently?"

He shook his head, eyes squinting in the sun.

I tried on a smile for size. "I was thinking along the lines of a guy with spiky hair and a pair of Oakleys."

"A cop? Nah. But after that accident, they might be doing some surveillance."

"That was awful, wasn't it?"

"My mom said it was one of *her* visitors." He hooked a thumb in the direction of Marion's house. "She has quite a few."

"Yes, well, she entertains."

"You staying there?" He squinted at me, hand over forehead.

"For now. Just helping out." I held out my hand. "Clody."

He took it. Good firm handshake.

"So you know about her?" he asked, chin jutting back to the house.

"Marion?"

"Yeah."

"What about her."

Jax flinched. "Just that my mom says she's a... well, you know."

I nodded. The statement got no argument from me.

"She has a website. Apparently." He grinned. "I quite like her actually. She's funny. I'm not sure if... if she's mentioned me."

"Marion? No."

"I deliver the eggs. Organic."

"Oh."

"Yeah. Well, she's nice and... I was told that if I wanted a successful career in law, it would be in my best interests not to associate with her."

I could see his point. "Your mom say that?"

No wonder he didn't ask if I was related. He was as embarrassed as I was.

"Maybe I shouldn't have said anything. You staying there and all."

"I'm not going to say anything, Jax. Really. I appreciate knowing."

Fear gripped me by the throat. It must have been the expression in his eyes. Dark, as if a cloud had blotted out the sun. He apologized for causing any upset, shook my hand again and shuffled off in a strip of foam left by a breaking wave.

Nice young man, I thought. But, more importantly, no stalky cops.

I found Marion sitting on the deck, face tilted at what was left of the sun and feet perched on the edge of the coffee table. She smiled, magazine open on her lap, pages rattling in the breeze. I took a seat opposite, staring at my reflection through the lenses of her Gucci studded sunglasses.

"I hope I'm not being nosy," she said, "but were you and your man married?"

I thought it best to say yes in case it all came out in a gush of verbal vomit.

"What was he like?" she asked.

I had to think about that for a moment. Ryan had given me two different lives and two different faces. Exactly when he turned into Mr. Hyde, I had no idea.

"He wasn't much of a husband. Wasn't much of anything. I just thought I needed one. Only this one had an expiration date."

"Where did you meet?" She crossed silken legs.

"I hoped you wouldn't ask. A dim, sticky bar in Queens. He signaled to a waiter to bring me a drink. Asked me to marry him that night. I thought he had something… manners. Education. Spoke nicely. A few months later, he told me how much he loved me while doing all kinds of unmentionables to me in the taxi on the way to our honeymoon. I thought he meant it. But a few wide-legged whores later, he told me life's a bitch and how he wished he hadn't married one."

Marion just stared.

"You know what I did wrong?" I said. "I gave him the mother of all words. *No.* No, I wasn't putting up with him sneaking around and polluting the sheets with his STDs. No, I wasn't going to look the other way, like some dumbass housewife who pretends it's not happening. As it turned out, he was a sick manipulator, became increasingly hard to have and to hold. If I'd had the balls I would have ejected a long time ago. Marriage scares me. All the bellyaching and the jealousy. You fall under the spell for a while and then realize you've been swindled. I guess the martyr's mantle doesn't suit me."

"I guess it's a bit late to ask if you guys did therapy."

"We went once. He was shit-scared. I could see it in his eyes. The therapist started unraveling the truth about his secret porn stash and how often he masturbated with a milk bottle. I was surprised he could stand after that."

I was enjoying teaching Marion about her secret lover and I longed for the day when the truth would split open like a sore. Killing her was a necessary evil because Ryan was obsessed with her. In some warped way, I hated myself for understanding why.

"You're a beautiful woman, Clo," she said. "Maybe he'll see you again one day and realize he's made a terrible mistake. You've got charisma. It's the first thing I noticed about you."

For Marion, it must have been like looking in a mirror, where she was the perfect half, all bright and white and I was the distorted half, all scuffed and cracked down the middle. In a few words, she got me.

Beauty was the one thing I wanted to ask God about when I got up there. *If* I got up there. Why he made some of them with the perfect ratio of mac to cheese, and others scarred and callused like gherkins. It was no use pushing the narrative that everyone was beautiful. When you compared yourself to Marion, you knew it wasn't true. She had it all; face copper in the fading sunlight and legs up to her sodding chin.

And compliments didn't work on me. I never broke into tears every time someone used the word *beautiful* because almost every part of me screamed *ugly* through a pained smile. Ugly, because of the things I've done, the things I think, the things I am. There's no real beauty in me. It's a privilege I have no chance of redeeming.

"It's so peaceful out here," I said. "You must love it. How often do people walk the beach?"

"Only us and the Jacksons. He's a film director and she's a doctor. Then further down, there's the De Beckers."

I knew she had seen me talking to Jax so I asked if he was their son.

"Jax? Yes. He's a real trip."

"There's a painting above my bed," I said. "EdeB?"

She nodded. "Elizabeth de Becker. She's a local artist. I think the painting is called *The Golden Child*. Kimball's particularly fond of it."

"What's she like?"

"Hard to tell. I saw her in the store last week. Wanted to ask her how she made those amazing things out of shells. But she turned her back. You can always tell when people don't want to talk."

I couldn't help but believe that for all Marion's stupidity, nobody would be likely to talk to a call girl.

"She married?" I asked.

"Was. Nice man. A dentist. There were rumors he was very unhappy. Found out he wasn't Jax's dad." Marion placed a hand on the fluttering magazine. "I wonder what any of these neighbors think of me."

I imagined they saw a housekeeper with a perfectly proportioned body who lived in the house alone. Three times a week she entertained a married man who had somehow mislaid his wife along the way. What they didn't know, but seemed to suspect, was that she was a cheater to the bone. A player who probably stole a little from housekeeping when the boss was out of the room.

Whatever the reason, whatever the cause, I didn't care. I was supposed to have kept my distance from her—this magnet for weak and spineless men—but somehow she had hypnotized me too.

"Are you ready for a swim?" she asked.

I didn't need persuading. Wearing a black-skirted one-piece, I walked out onto the deck. She pointed to a boat out near the buoy, port light blinking like an eye.

"That's the coastguard," she said. "They'll look out for us."

Marion pulled me down to the water, held my hand as we danced over the surf. It was colder than shit.

When we were waist deep and shivering she said, "I'll race you to the buoy."

18

My gut churned as my ankles hit water, teeth chattering as I chased after her, willing her to slow down.

But she didn't slow down. She ran faster and deeper, froth spraying between her legs. Then her body stooped and pierced the underbelly of a wave, head breaking the surface in three long seconds.

I was shaking with the cold as I swam after her, salt slipping between my teeth and scratching my eyes. The current seemed to drag and tug, breaststroke flimsy against Marion's crawl. I felt as if I was merely treading water without a hope in hell of catching up.

She was swimming in a beam of light cast by a boat, water streaming over her shoulder and trickling down the grooves of her spine. Her head turned sideways before the crest of a wave. A flash of white against black. A flash of life before death.

I kicked because I didn't want to lose the race. Didn't want to lose her. A pale shimmer of legs and arms, and for a second I wondered if she had lured me here. To show me what real stamina looked like. To show me she was the laughing demon sitting on her stalker's shoulders. I couldn't ignore those types of instincts.

I saw two things. The first was the coastguard boat bobbing in the swell, port light flashing about thirty feet north of the buoy. A man walked along the deck, hand raised in a wave. Marion responded with a flick of her fingers as one arm skimmed over her head, body rolling from side to side.

He seemed to be studying her, leaning forward as if he was feeding off a charge. He eyed the curve of her buttocks as they broke the surface, image bottled and stored, to be rewound at will.

I asked myself if he was merely flirting or was it something else. Round and round the questions went; one minute that he liked her, one minute that she was about to be the victim of a terrible accident. Then another question chased away the rest.

Was this the coastguard's evening routine? Because a male volunteer scouting for chicks was one thing, but a federal agent looking for answers as to why his buddy was almost mashed in a recent hit-and-run was a snarl-up I didn't need.

The second thing I saw was the buoy in front of me, moored by a long chain that trailed beneath the surface. I imagined a body drifting there, rope tugging at her ankles, where the water turned black and oily like a clot of blood.

I couldn't willfully close down these thoughts. They were wild and sickening. It sounded crazy but in some lurid, hateful way I wanted the murder party to begin.

Ryan had talked smack about me—depraved, twisted son of a bitch—and Marion had believed every word. She would be sorry when she realized what she had made me do.

Her competitive streak was starting to rub off on me, body cutting through water as if she had an outboard motor up her ass. I cheated the buoy of several feet and swung in behind her as she headed for the beach. It would be so easy to push her head below the surface. Harder to keep her from screaming.

I watched her through a cascade of salt water. She was kneeling in the shallows now, rear end perked up and swaying like a happy dog. Then she ran up the beach and scooped up her towel.

I knew I would have to pull the reins on my murder party until I had researched the tides and weather. It would be a bad idea to drag a body out to deep waters during a heavy nor'easter, (more likely in March) while being floodlit by a coastguard strobe.

I must be losing it.

As for a sequel—Murder Party Part Deux—it would require T-shirts and mugs.

Definitely losing it.

When my mind was less ragged and my heart stopped thumping in my chest, I touched bottom. Propelled forward by an incoming wave, I staggered up the beach, shaking and coughing as she handed me my towel.

"How was it?" she asked.

I couldn't answer. I was still panting.

"It gets colder the further out you go," she said. "You poor thing, you're shivering."

"Who's the guy in the boat?" I wasn't about to let her continue with how much of a wreck I looked.

"Larry Gilliam. His partner got hit by a car."

"His partner?"

"It was awful. The driver disappeared and now the police are looking for him."

"I'm sorry."

As she used her towel to blot the water from my hair, I noticed tight rungs on her abdomen and a ball of muscle on her forearms. No wonder she could swim so fast.

She took a deep breath. "It might have been my friend."

"What?" I almost felt my legs give way as she slipped her towel over my shoulders.

"We had an argument and he left in a hurry. Maybe it's just a coincidence. Only I haven't heard from him and that's unusual."

"Boyfriend?"

"Kind of. It's a bit of a mess really. Anyway, keep warm," she said, jutting her chin at the house. "I'm going to run in. Get the dinner ordered."

I nodded through chattering teeth and watched her sprint up the steps to the house. Tears slid down my cheeks and I brushed them away with an impatient hand.

I wanted her to know how passionately I hated her interference, hacking into my private life so she could tear it apart. I wanted her to feel my rage because it would be an epic psychotic mood swing, where she ended up begging and I ended up winning.

She was the one who had violated my trust. I had no choice but to violate hers.

19

Water jets buffeted my neck and shoulders and I stood in a stall of steam.

I couldn't believe I was here.

It was obscene—the furniture, the views, the money. There was no point drooling over a house in the Hamptons or a yacht in Shinnecock Bay. Not unless I owned both.

Marion may have been playing a game but I had invented a new one. The takeover game. Who said money can't buy happiness?

I had to learn to maintain an emotional distance. No use crying over a call girl who told every guy what they wanted to hear. Was it her fault Ryan had believed every word? Was it her fault that she passed the intelligence test with flying colors?

I needed a bigger dose of anger, otherwise I would lose my nerve. What better than to ask about her friend; the man she referred to as a *kind of boyfriend*. The one who had disappeared.

Dinner was delivered, not cooked. We sat in the dining room, salivating over sesame crusted salmon. There was a dense quiet, as if the walls were listening, waiting for the next breath. They didn't have to wait long.

"You asked about my friend? It's a long story." She ran a fingernail between her front teeth. "I suppose you could say we were pushed together."

"A blind date?"

"He was a friend of a friend."

I fidgeted and interrupted again. "What's his name, this friend?"

"Ryan."

I almost choked. "Sounds like an accountant."

"How did you know?"

"The name *Ryan* has an executive ring to it. Is he a CFO?"

"Finance manager. And no, he's not that attractive. I knew you'd ask." Marion rolled a finger at me and quirked an eyebrow. "He's funny though. Sometimes that's the appeal."

I laughed lightly. There was no appeal in his kisses. Cold narrow lips that nipped and pecked. Flaccid. Hesitant. She couldn't have enjoyed it any more than I did.

"So, let me guess," I said. "He's older, more experienced. Just how you like your men?"

"Spot on." She gave a wide smile. "So anyway, he asked me out and we've been friends ever since."

That was it? "Friends?"

She giggled, head bowing over her plate. "Well, okay, a little more than friends."

"How much more?"

Her mouth twitched for a second and then, "He's married."

"Oh."

She let out a breath, shoulders slumping against the back of the chair. "You don't approve."

I didn't and I tried not to show it. "These things

happen. He must have made a beeline for you."

"I don't know if you call it animal attraction or a meeting of the minds. It was intense. *Is* intense. I admire that in a man. Sad I can't see him more often."

"That must be difficult for you."

"It's more difficult for him. He says his wife is obese and neurotic. I can't fathom what that must be like."

"Hell, I would think."

"He's not exactly Ivy League, but that doesn't matter these days. Middle management. Probably won't go much further than that. But he's got drive. Nobody is more committed, more loving than Ryan."

"Except you," I said and winked.

"Except me." She grinned and toyed with her salmon. "I get to see him about three times a week. Sometimes four if he takes his wife out for dinner."

I grimaced. Couldn't help it. "Does he take her out often?"

"No. But when he does he'll book a restaurant—any restaurant—and he'll text me. Want me to meet him in the parking lot."

Bastard. Cheap, shitty bastard.

"He'll get in my car and... well, afterwards he'll ask me to take off my underwear." Her voice got quieter and quieter, fork hovering above her plate. "I think it turns him on that he's got something of mine. Then he tells me to leave. Goes back to his table. To his wife."

I gulped most of my wine even though my stomach wanted to reject it. She topped up my glass.

"So you never got a good look at her?" I asked.

"No. Never felt the need."

"Is he in love with you?"

"I don't want him to love me. The people you love are always the ones that hurt you. He says he loves me. I say it back. But it doesn't mean anything."

"When will you see him again?"

"Well, it's over."

"What happened?" I asked.

"Mr. Kimball happened. Anyway, I told Ryan I couldn't see him anymore. Unfortunately he wouldn't take no for an answer. Insisted on coming over, started making a scene. I'd never seen him like that. Never thought he had so much anger in him. It frightened me in a way. We think he ran over the coastguard just after he left. Awful business."

I felt disoriented, jetlagged as if I had been halfway around the world and back. "Are you sure?"

She nodded. "He's disappeared, hasn't he?"

Into thin air. "It doesn't necessarily mean…"

"I've tried his phone and there's no answer. It's not like him not to answer. I told the police he was here. That he was angry. Even the neighbors reported hearing a car revving in the road, then brakes screeching. Must have been driving like a maniac. There are security cameras outside the house. Kimball thinks he'll find something soon."

I prayed the eye on the roof, or wherever those damn cameras were, had been shat on by a thousand pigeons.

"The cops have his description," she said, finishing her meal. "They're all over the place. There was a heavy-set woman walking on the beach earlier. Might have been a reporter in disguise. There's a few of them around. Anyhow, I hope they catch him."

I shrugged. "Could have been a drunk kid driving his parents' car."

"Yes, but… you have to wonder why Ryan hasn't called."

I did wonder.

"You know what I think?" she said, tipping her glass to the bottle and filling it to the brim.

"What?"

"We should celebrate. Your new job and our new

friendship."

She walked over to the buffet and poured three fingers of Glenfiddich. I studied how she walked, leading with her boobs, weight in her heels. If she hadn't been holding two glasses of whisky, her arms would have been swinging slightly as if she were on a catwalk. The combination of alignment and rhythm sent a message that she was in control. It was no wonder she made such a kick-ass impression.

"To us," she said, ice clinking against her glass.

"To us."

I was on my side of the table, she was on hers and she laughed when I made her laugh. In fact, to give Marion her due, she aced the test. We had bonded. Ryan was a shared experience she knew nothing about. But it allowed us to move forward from a grotesque and sad story prefaced with an abusive marriage. It was a slight departure from what Marion had with Ryan.

I would be her confidant, her new best friend, until I turned out her lights for good. Until I squeezed her neck and saliva bubbled from the corners of her mouth.

Ryan, where are you? Can you hear me?

By now I was pretty buzzed. Couldn't get up off the chair without getting vertigo. Somehow, as the moonlight slanted into the dining room and I suppressed another yawn, I knew the answers lay in a sleepy house.

Secrets. So many secrets to unearth in this corner of paradise.

I could feel it.

20

Wednesday, 27th July, 2016

My first morning in a four-poster bed and I appreciated the small touches; the rose in a vase by the bed and a pair of fleece slippers embossed with the initials of the homeowner. *DK.*

I stared at the coffered ceiling and determined that there had been no nightmares, no gunmen in the closet and no knives ripping through the curtains. It was a thick, heavy sleep and I studied the walls until my brain woke up.

There was a large portrait over the fireplace; a woman wearing a swan-bill corset, hair piled high in a pompadour. The sort of girl found idling on Fifth Avenue and splayed on the edge of a couch. She had a wide-eyed innocence that contradicted her posture. I thought she was beautiful.

I thought she was Marion.

It was crazy—Ryan, the house, *her*—and I kept flipping through the years and hearing whispers and snickers.

The tears began to creep down my cheeks. It hurt so much. The soul needed to be cleansed, to go through each phase of grief until it could move on. I had grieved without restraint for the past two months before Ryan had left. Now I was tired of it.

There was only one phase left: Marion may have denied me a healthy mourning, but I would not allow her to deny me rage.

All the first-time things, like buying a new house and getting a new job would be done without toxic, vicious, patronizing Ryan. *We* were the past now. An indisputable fact.

Somehow, today, I was impatient to lay it all to rest. I wanted to kill Marion now, but there were variables outside my control. The neighbor's son, for instance. He could easily identify me, with or without makeup, because he had been checking me out on the beach. What I should have considered was a drive-by. Quick, clean and anonymous. Only I would never have found Ryan.

I checked my phone. One message from the pharmacy to pick up a repeat prescription of Xanax, and there was no change in Ryan's GPS location.

I sent him a text. *Feel like talking?*

6:10 a.m. I scraped my hair in a bun and dabbed on a little makeup. Pranced downstairs, banister smooth beneath my fingers.

I had made a few entrances in my time but this one reminded me of unexplained desertion, except for the smell of baking.

Sunlight flooded the kitchen, painting the countertops a rich shade of orange. The windows gleamed, the island sparkled and a wisp of steam curled from a coffee cup. I flexed my fingers over the waistband of my jeans, mouth agape. I had only just missed her.

There was a note on the kitchen counter. Two words. *Out running.*

I poured myself a coffee and debated if this was a good time to look around the house. Make a comprehensive list of locked doors, keys, or even a floorplan. But if Marion suspected me, this would be an excellent occasion to catch me.

I slipped out onto the deck. Sky and sea seemed to merge into one, azure blue and sleepy. I thought I caught a glimpse of her, a distant figure slogging through white sands. She seemed a mile away.

I left the cup on the banister and walked down the steps to the beach. A small boat idled in the shallows. I had seen it before, a walnut hull slouching on the beach and abandoned as if it was nothing more than a sleek ghost surrounded by a ruffle of water.

The thought was there, bubbling beneath the surface like a hot spring. A body anchored to the seabed. I was committed to the finer details and I may have just found the boat. Although I hoped those details didn't allow a resurgence of Marion along the tideline of Cooper's Beach.

There was a seagull perched on the tiller, unconcerned by the rattle of rigging against the mast. As I drew closer, it stared at me with hungry eyes, then gave a badass screech before taking off in an explosive whir of wings.

I took off my shoes and peered over the gunwale. My fingers instinctively curled around the rowlocks and I saw the oars stowed neatly in the bottom. There was a small red cooler near the stern and I waded toward it, flicked the latch and found a broken pair of sunglasses and a plastic cup. Not what you would call a classy stash.

There was a trail of dark, crimson spatters and fish scales on the boards. It was as if someone had just stepped ashore with their catch.

Flattening my hand over my eyes, I searched the beach for Marion. There was no sign of her or anyone else for that matter, only the seagull cutting a lazy circle in the sky. I paddled through a sluggish swirl of flotsam, feeling the heat of the sun on my back.

Quieter than shit, I thought, until I heard the buzz of my phone. Tugging it out of my jeans pocket, I looked at the number and rolled my eyes.

"If you prefer me to text, I will," Joe said.

"Please don't."

"You heading back home?"

"Eventually."

"Taking your time, huh?"

"Lieutenant, did I do something wrong?"

"Just a minor violation."

"What kind of violation?"

"A little deception. I'll overlook it this time, provided you're not depriving anyone of their legal rights."

Was a hit-and-run a minor infraction these days? Next he was going to ask me for my license and registration. "I'm not depriving anyone of anything."

"You sound tired."

I ignored this.

"I've been thinking about things," he said.

"What things?"

"Maybe we could meet for coffee. I know a few good places in Southampton Village. Blue Duck, Tate's—"

"You following me?" Ouch! My bad.

"Relax. It's just a coffee. I can pick you up or meet you there if you prefer."

Coffee and conversation didn't sit well with me. He'd only see the Buick I was driving and I certainly wasn't inviting him to the house. *Not so clever, Joe.*

"I miss your cheery face at a crime scene, Clo. Promise me you're not doing anything crazy."

"Promise."

"I don't want my buddies over there telling me anything—you know. Disturbing."

"Over where?"

"Wherever you are. Looking for Ryan. Stalking him when he's stalking you."

"Well, then we'll both be going around in circles, won't we?"

"You probably want to know if Ryan came home last night," he said. "As a matter of fact, he didn't. House is as quiet as the grave."

I began to sweat.

"Did you file a missing person's report?" he asked.

"You told me it was too early. You suggested he might have left willingly." A pause. "Maybe it's all in my head."

"You mean the fight you had? Which, by the way is evidenced by that shocking bruise on your mouth. I'm guessing there was a few more under that robe. Only you weren't willing to show me."

"I was naked." I let out a big sigh, the way I often did when I was about to lie. "There's nothing to see."

"It's hard baring one's soul to a stranger. In your case it's a little too close to home and far from ordinary. You'll let me know if you change your mind about the coffee."

I needed to think before answering. "Sure."

"You be safe out there."

He hung up.

Maybe it was my mind—my neurotic mind—but suddenly I felt sad and empty. I could have cried for a week. I finally added his name to my contacts.

Jogging up the steps and to a tepid cup of coffee, I jammed myself into a deck chair. My eyes were wet again and suddenly I was afraid. Maybe Joe was pulling my leg. Maybe he was protecting me from someone. It was a violent world with crazy people. No use thinking Ryan's disappearance was all a big mistake and the rest of us had our wires crossed.

Ryan had gone missing after fighting with me. Turned up at Marion's, then went missing after fighting with her. Interesting fact. But I was the one who had hit the coastguard. Glaring fact.

I found a wadded-up tissue in my jeans pocket and dabbed my eyes. I promised myself this would be the last cry.

I tapped out another text to Ryan. *Is your phone working?*

There were always options. I could drive to JFK, dump the Buick in the airport parking lot and fly to San Francisco. If I got out of the country I could get lost in Europe. I knew better than anyone that getting lost was a dream. The crows of law enforcement had circled close enough and they weren't backing off. Someone had said something. Seen something. I wasn't as home free as I had thought.

If Lieutenant Joe was watching my house he might have expected me to come home now and then. But he would never have expected me to move in with my husband's mistress.

Two figures appeared in the distance, silhouetted along the edge of the sand hills. A woman and a man. She leaned into his rigid walk. He skirted away, feet dancing a curve in the sand. I could almost make up the conversation in my head. Him pleading, her spurning.

It was Marion, I was sure of it. The hike of her hips and the pointed toe. The young man was Jax.

They stopped. Her back was to the ocean. His to the sand hills. She placed one hand on his shoulder and he lowered his head, nodding as he stared at her feet. They were close enough to be whispering.

Then he jerked his head behind him as if he had heard something, turned rapidly and jogged inland. Marion stood there for a while, staring after him and wiping one eye with the heel of her hand.

I felt like the only woman left who knew the cost of rejection. Even the Brooklyn Bridge couldn't have closed that gap.

Five minutes later, she was running toward the house. I waved. And for some baffling reason I was glad to see her.

21

"Want another coffee?" she said, pounding up the steps.

"Sure." And then as she was leaving to go into the house, "Marion..."

But she had already bounded through the French doors leaving behind a pungent scent of ambergris. I could hear the first few bars of a well-known piano sonata before she answered her phone.

I heard her talking to someone called Captain Ed. "Questions.... About what? Oh, sure. How does 2 p.m. sound?"

Then she hung up.

I was amused she assigned different ringtones to different men. As for the mention of a high-ranking law enforcement officer, I didn't find that quite so funny.

Thick roiling thoughts of death ambushed me in a vivid rush. I closed my eyes and pictured it all. The emergency services pushing a gurney up to the rescue boat. A body with a white face, weighted down with a diver's belt, and with a curl of seaweed in her hair. Then the long, reverent zipping sound of a body bag.

"Breakfast?"

I whipped my head around and grinned at the tray Marion presented. Breakfast was a plate of wheaty-looking muffins and the choice of a cappuccino or a kale shake. I chose the coffee, only my stomach had a violent spasm at the offer of country potatoes and sausage.

"You baked these?" I asked.

"Might be a little overcooked."

The muffins were a little rubbery around the edges, I hated to admit, but the cappuccino was excellent.

"Frances is coming today." I could hear the throaty bur in her voice and the occasional stress of a hard 't'. "She usually comes three times a week but Kimball's coming tonight."

I nodded as if Kimball arriving was the most normal thing in the world.

"She's a cosmetologist from the Branford Academy. Specializes in deep tissue massage. She's bringing her portable spa..."

I had never seen a portable spa and decided not to show my ignorance by asking. Mind spinning over the drone of her voice, I concluded it resembled a high-powered sheep dip. Only without the parasiticides.

By now Marion was sucking on a green shake and banging on about the chef, who had trained in some charcuterie-centric eatery in Manhattan. Forty-five but could pass for thirty-five. Faded jeans, no socks. As if no socks excused him from being what she later termed as *a strange little man*.

"There's no need to clean upstairs. Take it easy. It's your first day. If you have any questions just ask." Marion unclipped a set of keys from her keyring. "These are for the mudroom closet. You'll find everything you need."

After breakfast there was an air of excitement in the house. Marion had gone from a good-mannered host to a snappy supervisor, arms flung wide as she welcomed her staff. She took an armful of flowers from a delivery boy and began arranging them in crystal vases.

I was still studying Frances' perfectly sculptured face when I realized she was holding out a hand.

"You Marion's sister?"

"No," Marion interrupted over my shoulder. "This is Clo. Our new help."

Frances shook my hand and excused herself upstairs. As for Robert, there was nothing *little* about him. Even Popeye didn't come close.

A stubby ponytail spurted from the nape of his neck, half hidden by the high collar of a white chef's coat, which hung snugly from his tight frame. Tattered jeans and, as Marion had earlier pointed out, no socks. He appraised me with petrol black eyes that zipped up and down like a store scanner. "Welcome to the mad house."

Thick Scottish accent.

"Good to meet you," I mouthed over the clamor.

He turned and pulled bottles out of the wine rack, fussing over the merits of serving clams as an appetizer and why there wasn't a decent white burgundy to go with the cream.

"You could have at least shaved," Marion said, eyeing his stubbly jaw.

Truth was he was twenty-four hours beyond a five o'clock shadow and he hadn't even combed his hair.

"I do it once a week as well you know and that's only when my chin starts itching." Robert pivoted toward the sink and handed her a menu. "And don't complain about the pork."

"I thought we were having salmon," she said.

"The last time we had salmon, if you recall, Kimball swallowed a wee bone. In my honest opinion, it's hard finding a bone in pork."

Robert tilted his head at me like a parent with a slow kid. "Kimball—*Mr.* Kimball—claims you can die from choking on a fishbone."

"That bad," I said.

"Oh, it was. Major meltdown in the emergency room… if you get ma drift."

Any mention of death made my cheeks burn, like fingers around a throat as mine clawed and raked to remove them. Nobody knew why I was here. How could they?

The clatter of pans interrupted the nostalgia and it was Marion's fingers I felt as she took my arm and dragged me into the hall.

"Don't take any notice of Robert. He tells stories and he's a terrible flirt."

"You mean he lies?"

"I wouldn't put it like that. Bit of a drama queen really. Kimball likes him. Me… not so much. I've got a feeling Kimball will like you."

I wondered if Kimball would recognize me. The shy wife at the Christmas party. Or the flabby driver he nearly rear-ended.

You're paranoid, Clo. The words kept burning a hole in my brain.

I opened the mudroom closet. A bucket of rags and furniture polish and a pack of hairnets. I headed for the dining room. None of the surfaces needed a pressure hose or a stiff brush and I could already see my face in the dining room table.

The first hairnet pinged off the top of my head and wrapped itself around a wall sconce. The second try was more successful, especially when I pressed the edge of the elastic on the nape of my neck and stretched it over a bun.

I misted the mirrors with a good squirt of glass cleaner, gleamed up silver and vacuumed carpets. One hour. Tops.

With the staff busy and Marion dozing on a spa bed, it gave me time to get my bearings.

I sloughed off my hairnet and scrunched it into the bucket with the rest of the cleaning things. Gave myself a quick once-over in the hall mirror, to find a red welt across my forehead where the elastic had been.

Rain tapped against the crescent window above the front door. It was gray outside, clouds dropping lower and wind stirring the trees. How the weather had changed.

I climbed the stairs and glanced up the corridor toward Marion's room. Frances had to be a confidant. She would have known Marion intimately if extreme grooming was anything to go by. The door was closed and I couldn't hear much from the corridor, just muffled voices and the clunk of a box. I turned the door handle and pushed it open a few inches.

There was a rush of sounds. Wind chimes and the steady trickle of water accompanied by meditation music. Marion was talking about a new clothes store in town, how she bought a green dress there. She had somehow misread the label and tried to take it back but the thirty days had passed. Then she talked about the 'egg boy', how he had suffered a nervous breakdown after his dentist dad walked out on him and his mom. And then she talked about me. The new girl. Except for the lack of class, we were quite similar. How she hoped she wouldn't look like me in ten years' time.

#ThrowbackThursday. I didn't hear anyone laughing.

"There... right there," Marion murmured. "Big knot."

Frances extended her elbow and supported it with the web of her other hand as she leaned forward slightly. Then slowly eased up.

It seemed any conversation about Ryan had petered out and I may have missed the meat of it. Until...

"How have you been since he left?" Frances said.

"Awful. Can't stop thinking about the coastguard. He used to patrol the beach. Married with two kids."

"I saw it in the paper. It's a crazy world."

"Captain Montefiore accused me of..." Marion's voice became muffled in a towel and she was whispering anyway. Then, "He's been talking to some cop in Hempstead Village. Apparently this guy thinks he may be able to identify the driver. They're coming here this afternoon. 2 p.m. he said."

I recoiled at the words *cop in Hempstead Village*. What if this cop was Joe? I pushed my fear aside and realized it was a horrible coincidence. There was more than one cop in Hempstead Village and it wasn't always about me.

Only the coastguard *was* about me. As far as I knew no one had seen the incident first hand. I had been the ghost on the beach. The stranger in the car. The killer in the street. I had acted out quite a few parts for which I would not be remembered.

My stomach shifted and I almost gagged.

Stepping back into the corridor, I eased the door closed. It was true to say my hatred for Marion had climbed another notch.

On a scale of one to ten, it was definitely an eleven.

22

I tried to brainstorm every excuse to avoid going downstairs. But as the 2 p.m. meeting drew closer, I found it harder to resist the impulse to run.

Part of me wanted to scream at Ryan, to hold him accountable for everything he had done. I wished he'd never walked into my life. I wished Marion hadn't walked into his.

Perhaps I was the introvert everyone shunned. The person they couldn't read. The inescapable stereotype of a silent killer. It was curiously empowering.

Hand upright against the window and forehead pressed to the frame, I looked down the front driveway. My car needed a good wash. There was bird crap all over the hood and spatters of what appeared to be mud and leaves on the windshield. A bar of light from one of the guesthouses fell onto the driveway, bathing an incoming police cruiser a rare shade of gold. Two uniforms swaggered into the house. One looked up. I moved back.

I hate it when a man *lives* in every thought, no longer a transient in the street but a sublet that goes week to week. It was hard not to look at him, study his face, the tongue glossing over his bottom lip and the fingers jabbing the shirt into his duty belt. I'd know him anywhere.

Lieutenant Joe was in my 'hood and he had no idea how desperate I was. He had a damn fine haircut and he was entertaining to watch. But so are cats.

My mind had already set the scene. Lights flashing, sirens moaning. The snap of handcuffs. Would they be snug against my wrists? The paparazzi, a feeding frenzy of piranhas, nipping and smirking behind my back.

I felt a chill and the tingle of goosebumps as I walked across the corridor and knocked on Marion's door.

"I've got a stomach ache," I said, shuffling in like a Chinese girl with bound feet. "Heavy period."

"How heavy?" Marion asked.

I wanted to tell her it was *Red Tent* heavy. "I might need to lie down."

"You don't look well," she said, tightening the belt of her robe and frowning at my skin, which must have resembled poultry after the feathers had been plucked. "Let me get you some chicken soup."

It was that easy. Now I wouldn't have to explain myself to that moron Joe.

Most of me was under the quilt when Marion returned, my eyes rubbed raw so it looked as if I had been crying. If that soup tasted as good as it smelled I would be up in no time.

"Downstairs looks great, by the way," she said, patting my hand as I scooted up the bed. "You did an excellent job. Except for the hairnet. We don't usually hang those on sconces."

I winced.

"And the library looks amazing," she said.

I hadn't touched the library. It had somehow slipped my mind.

"Will you be well enough to come downstairs later?"

I nodded, feigned a sniffle and swiped at my nose.

Five minutes and an empty bowl of soup later, through the crack in the door I saw Marion stride along the corridor. It was important to get out there, to see the sights and sounds of the living room. But before I had put toe to carpet, my phone shuddered.

A text from Lieutenant Joe. "Might have some information for you. Ever seen the movie *Brought To Light*?"

I couldn't believe he was tapping out texts while taking witness statements downstairs.

"Nope. Never heard of it," I responded.

"Husband goes missing. Wife wakes up covered in blood. Her fingerprints on the knife. His blood. Did she kill him?"

I had to think about that for a moment. "She could have picked up the knife without thinking."

"She left evidence on the murder weapon."

"You said her husband was missing," I typed. "No murder without a body."

There was six seconds of silence. No dancing dots. Then he was typing again. "What about a two million life insurance? Beneficiary; the wife. Feel like that coffee?"

Piece of shit stalker! I thought. He didn't have a stitch of information. All he wanted to do was drill me about Ryan because he knew I was on a mission to find him. While he was on a mission to find me.

Psst! I'm here. Upstairs.

The other thing that struck me as odd was why Joe was outside his jurisdiction and arm-in-arm with his buddy Captain Montefiore. Was he now assisting with the hit-and-run investigation?

Only one way to find out.

I didn't anticipate any more texts so I slipped the phone in my pocket and headed for the staircase. Provided I crouched on the landing behind a decorative Mojave twill blanket, I had a good view of the living room between the banisters. They couldn't see me.

Voices. First unfamiliar. Then familiar.

Lieutenant Joe had his back to me, Captain Montefiore slightly to one side and Marion facing. The captain was ferociously critical, had a stoop to his shoulders and a permanently raised eyebrow. I could see he was just as uncomfortable as she was.

"…which at no time explains your movements on Monday night," he said. "I need you to be more exact."

"Yes, sir." Marion wiped her hands against her thighs, which in turn tugged at the neck of her dress.

"First, let's talk about the cars," the captain said. "I see four parked in your driveway… white Mazda, black Buick, gray Ford and a red Honda Civic. Can you tell me who they belong to?"

Marion cleared her throat. "They belong to the staff. The Mazda's mine."

"Staff?"

"We have a cook, a cleaner and a cosmetologist."

"Full-time?"

"Part-time. Mondays, Wednesdays and Fridays. They always leave around 5 p.m."

I noticed she failed to mention her new live-in.

"I see," he said. "I'd like you to tell me what happened that evening?"

Marion took a breath. "A friend called, wanted to come over sometime between nine and ten—"

"A friend?"

"Ryan Shepherd. He, Ryan that is, insisted on seeing Mr. Kimball but he had already left about twenty minutes earlier."

A little exaggeration, Marion. It was about five minutes earlier and Kimball was still wandering along the beach when the second guest showed up. The guest I now knew to be Ryan. I had to look at the situation objectively. Ryan was Marion's last visitor and I had to ask myself what they had been talking about on the phone.

"Ryan was upset," she said. "Pretty mad actually."

"Upset about what?"

"He was upset that Kimball had fired him. He was also mad Kimball had left. Said he was a coward and threatened to go after him. I tried to calm him down."

"And how did you do that?"

"By talking."

"So you didn't offer him a drink? A cigarette?"

"No, sir."

"Did you get the impression he was armed?"

"No, I didn't."

"Let me ask you something. What was the painting he smashed?"

"A William Bliss Baker. It was hanging over there." She pointed to where another painting had taken its place.

"So, a valuable painting?"

"Yes, sir."

"Did Ryan Shepherd know it was valuable?"

"I believe he did."

"So, he was aware that it was valued at well over a million."

"Yes, although it's not nearly as valuable as the one in the spare room."

The captain turned briefly to Joe and raised an eyebrow. "And then?"

"Then he left," she said.

"Did you hear anything after he left?"

"I don't remember." She shook her head. "No, wait— screeching brakes."

Oh, good one, Marion. That's sure to make the captain writhe and squirm with excitement.

"And what time was this?"

She looked down at her lap. "10:15 p.m., maybe later."

"Did you go outside to see what had caused it?"

"No, sir. I knew he was mad and I knew he was going to find Kimball."

"We understand Mr. Shepherd made a call to you earlier that evening. The call lasted about eight-and-a-half minutes. Was he mad then?"

Boy, the police just don't give up, do they? I was almost feeling sorry for Marion, digging through her tiny little brain and hoping to find a suitable explanation for those agonizing few minutes. But words seemed to torrent out of her mouth without as much as a breath.

"Ryan thought he could change Kimball's mind." Marion's voice broke through my thoughts. "You know, get his job back. I tried to warn Ryan not to come over but he wouldn't listen."

"How well do you know Mr. Shepherd?"

"Not that well."

"How many times has he been here? Roughly?"

Marion ran a finger along her bottom lip. "About six or seven."

"And this is to see Mr. Kimball? Or you?"

"Mr. Kimball."

"I see. What car does he drive?"

"Four-door sedan," she said. "Gold, I think."

"You don't know the make or the model?"

"No, I don't."

"You look a little red. Sunburn?"

"No, no." Marion flapped a hand. "I'm a little hot actually."

Captain Montefiore ran a finger slowly under his nose as if he was pacing himself for the next question. "Are you intimate with Mr. Kimball?"

"Oh, no. He's my employer."

"And Ryan Shepherd?"

There was no mistaking the flicker of the muscle in her neck. I was sure the captain had seen it.

"It was brief." Marion glanced down at her hands. "He's married."

"Did he pay you?"

"Excuse me?"

"It's a simple enough question. Did he *pay* you?"

"No, of course not."

Panic gripped me. It was the sudden change in tone and the way her eyes dropped to the floor. She sounded defensive. He must have sensed that too.

An eerie silence. I wondered if it was a disarming tactic the police used to make suspects nervous, but nobody spoke for at least a minute.

My eyes were caught briefly by the glare of the hall chandelier, teardrops of cut glass that spread a spidery shadow across the ceiling. Then something nipped at my subconscious and my mind began rewinding back to the question about cars. Lieutenant Joe had been at home weeding his front yard on Monday morning. He would have seen Ryan drive off in Shayna's car and he may have suspected Ryan wasn't the driver of the gold Camry that night.

I shivered, trailing my fingers through the carpet to ground myself. My head started to pound. Joe turned his head sideways, eyes flicking up the wall as if he was taking in one side of the room in the periphery of his vision. But he said nothing.

Captain Montefiore stood abruptly. "You've been very helpful."

Joe stuck out his hand. A deliberate pause as he leaned in a little without taking his eyes off hers. "Thank you Ms. Kurchel. We'll be in touch."

I wanted to tell her that cops were really good with names and license plates and Joe was the cop from hell. Even I had to remember that.

I scooted further back behind the blanket and watched the tops of their heads as they walked out of the front door.

Marion leaned against the door frame, fingers combing through her hair.

I stood, took a few steps forward and looked up at the crescent window over the front door. Clouds hung low and rain snapped like firecrackers against the glass. The hum of voices downstairs and the constant flash of Ryan's face jostled for my attention. Overcome with the enormity of it all, my knees buckled and I crumpled onto the top step.

23

I listened to the police cruiser as it pulled out, siren pulsing two beats. It sounded like goodbye. At least I hoped it was.

My armpits prickled with sweat. Joe's face loomed into my mind and I hoped he hadn't seen me cowering behind the banister. Everything felt surreal and I couldn't begin to analyze what had just happened.

They say every person is different. Some are social, independent and decisive. Some are thinkers and nurturers. I'm a thinker. I 'feel' my way through life by watching, rather than engaging. The one thing I realized was that Joe was similar. *We* were similar. Except for one gaping flaw. Joe paid attention to detail. He had my cell phone number and he could easily find my location. I must have been stupid if I didn't believe it.

I needed to collect my thoughts. The first of these was the painting above my bed. Perched on the pillows, I leaned in to look beneath the frame above the bedhead. *The Golden Child. EdeB. 2001.* It was worth Googling to see how much it was worth.

I looked up Elizabeth de Becker and found a website of all her paintings. Somehow this particular piece fell in the $6,000 category. Not *that* valuable, not as paintings go but still a sizeable chunk of change.

After splashing cold water on my face, I plodded downstairs to the kitchen. Chef Robert lifted his eyes to me as I walked through the door. Said I could do with a few fingers of Glenmorangie, all things considered.

Great. The town crier had told everyone I had a period. The dirty six-letter word.

I glanced at a smear of rain at the window, enjoying the sound of his voice. How he cracked his knuckles as if he were about to perform a magic trick. He made everything look so easy.

Frances sat on a bar stool plucking at the strands of a long bob, or *lob*, as I understood it was now called, while looking through the smoked glass of the microwave. She swiveled when she saw me, large hoop earrings brushing her shoulders.

"Marion's taking a nap," she said. "Wiped out. Those cops did a number on the poor bitch."

Frances pulled out a bar stool next to her and patted the seat. I sat.

"Apparently, and don't quote me on this." Frances' breath was hot against my ear. "Captain what's-his-face accused her of prostitution. Thinks Kimball's running a cathouse like the one in the papers."

"That's crazy."

"It's *offensive*. Anyone would think this place was an In-N-Out Burger. Remember *Redmaynes*? Biggest prostitution ring the police have ever cracked. Judges, doctors, a few well-known businessmen. Wouldn't surprise me if Kimball had shares in it. The captain will be back with some other excuse. That's how they roll here. Always snooping and saying it's all in the name of protecting the citizens. I'm sorry. I shouldn't be involving you in this."

Even I knew Marion performed the art of fellatio for a living. It wasn't any great secret. I had followed the *Redmaynes* bust for over a year and there were stringent laws all over the country against a person patronizing a prostitute. If the captain was already asking questions, the trap was set.

Frances began to sag, one hand fluttering in front of her face. "I'm sorry about her friend, Ryan."

Robert leaned across the kitchen island and stared me square in the face. "Ryan's the one they think caused the hit-and-run. Hasn't been seen since. He's the only visitor Marion's had in weeks. Oh wait, we mustn't forget the egg man."

"Delivery guy," Frances said, rolling her eyes at me. "He's hardly worth counting."

"Yeah, well it's all a bit of a mess." Robert's voice was almost a whisper. "You should know she's involved with him *and* Kimball. What's the betting they turned up here at the same time? Shit happens."

My skin was already bubbling with revulsion, stomach cramping. "Both of them?"

"I could never understand what she saw in Ryan. You know what they say? One person's trash is another person's treasure."

"What would you know?" Frances said, unhooking long legs from the bar stool. "He was charming. Bought her a set of gold bobby pins and lingerie from Provocateur. Gold chains and Swarovski crystals. What would I give to have a man like that?"

"So, she had great undies." Robert frowned and shrugged. "More fool Ryan for being parted from his wallet."

I felt the room tilt and my breakfast lurch.

"You all right, Clo?" Frances said. "She looks pale. Don't you think she looks pale?"

"I'm fine thanks. Really." But I wasn't fine at all.

My breath was choppy, pulse accelerating to heart-attack speed. If I wasn't such a damn liar I would admit to being jealous. It was no use trying to chase away every whisper of anxiety and pretend I was coping without my medication. I had been sitting on that particular fence for too long.

Frances insisted I went outside for some *blue space*. With her hand on the small of my back, she escorted me to the living room. Threw open the French windows, and walked me out onto the deck. I told her I'd be okay. Just felt nauseous from the heat of the kitchen.

She left me standing with my body pressed against the railing. The shifting movement of the sea calmed me and I became mesmerized by a shaft of sunlight that pierced through the clouds. The boat was still there, hull rippling with light refracted from the water, and I could make out a swirling shape a few feet from the stern. A dead gull.

I turned and looked up the beach. A solitary figure between my house and the De Beckers'. Not walking on the sand as you would expect, but lying on his stomach on a sand hill, hands gripping a pair of binoculars. A bird watcher?

I lowered myself into a chair and studied him for a moment. He seemed to be observing something beyond the buoy and my eyes intuitively swung out to see what it was. A fin cutting through the surface of the water, larger than a dolphin and making headway out to sea. Nothing that would interest me.

Then slowly, he aimed the binoculars down the beach to within a foot of where I was sitting. My heart thumped in my chest as I slouched, eyes aligned with the edge of the balcony. All he could see was a brunette sitting in a chair and from that distance, I could have been Marion.

Except binoculars had a focusing wheel. They magnified an image.

I sagged forward a little more. Why did the whole experience make me feel guilty? I needed to get a grip. There was no way I could walk on the beach now, check my stash and hope that tonight was the night. Not if someone was watching me.

I took out my cell phone and swiped the screen. No texts. No calls. GPS broken. Had to be.

My eye flicked to the side where I had seen the man but the image was blurry. Turning my head a little more, I focused on long grass standing tall on an empty dune.

There was no one there.

24

It was an odd day. Gray and spitting one minute and golden bursts the next. The type of day where people say they had never seen weather like this in July. The type of day my mother liked because it reminded her of home. Ireland. I had never been. But I shared her love of the sea.

I tried to pivot toward the house and almost stumbled over my feet. My reflection shimmered in the window and I caught a glimpse of someone else. A shadow barely there. Not inside the house. Behind me. I turned.

Jax.

"Hey," I said, seeing a cardboard box in his hands and a pair of binoculars around his neck.

"Good morning, Clody."

Very polite. Repeat a name and you always remember it. "What have you got there?"

"A box."

I could see that.

"I told my mom about you," he said. "She thought you might like it."

"I'll treasure it."

I peeked inside. A Christmas tree made of shells. "It's beautiful. Please thank her for me."

He nodded. He was buff. Had one of those stomachs like a washboard and there was a mildness to him I couldn't resist.

"Anyone on the beach this morning?" I asked.

A blaze of teeth; a widening grin. "Just you and me."

The answer took me by surprise. I must have sucked in a loud breath because he was looking so intently at me.

"What kind of binoculars are those?" I asked.

"Nikon. You can see for miles. I was looking for our dog. He was out there swimming, only he won't be able to paddle back when the tide turns. Black lab," he said, catching my frown.

"Can't say I've seen one."

"Well he's hard to spot."

"How old are you?" I asked, not knowing quite why I had asked.

"Nineteen. I'll be twenty in November."

I had guessed right. Almost.

"You?"

I felt weightless. Nobody had ever asked me how old I was and it suddenly felt as if I was being violated. "Me? Oh, thirty-nine."

"Nice age. Same age as Demi Moore when she met Ashton Kutcher."

"I believe she was over forty," I corrected, heat rushing to my face.

"You remind me of someone."

Marion perhaps? I didn't really look like her, not if you put us side-by-side.

"Have to go now," he said, stepping away from me. "You have a good day."

I barely had time to say 'You too' before he bounded down to the beach and shuffled through the sand. Distracted by a piece of driftwood and twine, he dragged it all the way to his house.

You can see for miles. The words scurried around in my head and I was climbing a higher notch of neurotic.

Deep in thought, I slipped back into the house and deposited my treasure on the hall table. I was beginning to doubt I could make it through the day without my medication.

There was something else that had puzzled me. A light in the guesthouse window yesterday evening. I had assumed I was the only live-in, evidenced by my car in the driveway. There were no signs to *Keep Out* and nothing to say I couldn't do a little exploring.

The front door of the first guesthouse was locked. I walked around the back of the building and peered in at a small window. A bedroom. Closet doors open. Clothes on hangers. Someone was staying there.

On the east side, the French doors were propped open by a vacuum cleaner. I was aware of the sweet smell of roses and then, just as I turned my head, a hint of bleach.

A spacious living room with floor to ceiling windows and blinds up most of the way. A half-open door to the bedroom and a dim bathroom. I noticed a computer on the dining room table, screen black and gleaming. A paper-strewn surface of graphs and tables and a log with names. My hand hovered over them, fingers flicking open as my mind tried to comprehend why someone would journal Marion's movements and those of her staff. Including me.

A time and motion study? I thought those went out with the Jurassic age. I had never been handed a card to swipe or a computer with which to sign in. How then had someone documented my arrival? My car model and registration, the time I went down to breakfast and sat having coffee with Marion on the deck. It was all there.

But what they hadn't recorded was my time on the beach. Were my movements only limited to the front of the house and to the inside?

I shuffled the mouse and the screen lit up. I needed a password. No point in trying. It was likely alarmed.

I looked across the living room at tan leather couches and a red Persian rug, damp beneath the coffee table. There was a deep gouge in the wood, comet shaped with a long trailing tail, suggesting something heavy had been smashed or dropped.

The bedroom was vacant but there was something about the clothes in the closet that made me reach in and pluck at the arm of a slate gray jacket. Trousers were hooked over a hanger, hems speckled with sand and a tie snaked on the floor, partly lazing over a tilted baseboard. My chest bucked in shock.

They were Ryan's.

Even the suit was his and the brown leather shoes. My throat closed up and I tried to swallow. This couldn't be the *apartment* he had spoken of?

I knelt to study the baseboard. One edge appeared to be angled about four inches from the floor and I levered it upward. A wallet lay in a small depression, no bigger than a shoe box and I recognized the scuffs in the leather and the initials.

RAS. *Ryan Anthony Shepherd.*

I heard my breath catch when I spotted the cell phone. No wonder I couldn't get his location. The battery had been disconnected. But Ryan had been here. I say *had* because there was a despairing emptiness to those last few relics, like I was an archaeologist brushing bones on a dig.

I allowed myself a few moments to focus on the bed. The sheets were drawn back and the pillow was dented. It was cold to the touch. I felt detached, as if I were working a crime scene, taking shots of dead things and wondering who they once were. Whether they watched me from higher ground, trying to communicate the name of their killer in a language I didn't understand.

I heard the shriek of a hinge and my gaze was drawn

to a spine of light that crept along the living room floor, widening as it joined the Persian rug.

I hesitated, feeling the old familiar tug of fear.

The French door had swung open, sunlight torching the room. First a breath of wind, then the twitch of a curtain.

Ghosts.

25

I took photos of everything, mentally diagraming and charting what I had seen.

Snapping shots of the exterior of the guesthouses against the main house were not for artistic reasons. They provided perspective to the composition, something the police would recognize.

I was interrupted by a humming sound high up in the eaves. A camera, slyer than a drone and lens protracted to enlarge me in its field of view. Just as I had taken pictures of the house, the house was taking pictures of me.

The best thing to do was to stay calm and ignore the burning in my stomach. I walked deliberately under the maple that shaded one side of the house and where the top end of the lawn met the privet hedge, there was a gap leading first to the road and then to the beach. I angled myself to one side and squeezed through.

The wind tore at my hair as I raced down the dunes and I was sure something terrible would happen. Except for a hit-and-run no one knew about, I had done nothing to incite suspicion. It sounded crazy in retrospect. Apart from finding Ryan's things stashed in the closet and no sign of Ryan, I might have assumed Marion was innocent. Would she admit to it even if I confronted her? Or would her mouth hang open in shock as she tried to take it all in?

Bile burned in my stomach and raced up my throat. Deaf to everything except the hiss of blood in my ears, I hunched over and spilled two meals into the dunes. I tried to brush sand over the puddle with my foot, telling myself to breathe.

In... hold. Out... hold.

On weak legs, I managed to walk about ten feet before buckling to a crouch. Took another deep, shaking breath and told myself to stop panicking.

I sat with my back to the dunes, flaring my hands in the sand. Didn't seem to have the necessary motor skills to go any further and if I did I'd be crawling like a slug toward the house. Moisture from the rain seeped into my jeans and I burst into tears like a kid who's just peed her pants.

Swallow it down, I told myself. Nobody's bleeding. I repeated the mantra in a steady rhythm, waiting for my pulse to slow.

Step one: Take stock of your surroundings.

The boat had been pulled further up the beach, surf bubbling gently on the sand.

Step two: Time. Time for what?

Time I pulled out my phone and sent pictures to Joe. But I couldn't.

Wouldn't.

There would be no time to fulfil my plan without police intrusion. The wallet, the driver's license, the interior and exterior of the guesthouse, weeks of Marion in front of the window, Marion on the beach, Marion in a bookstore. All this would implicate me in Marion's eventual death. The pictures I had taken would have to be deleted. No one could ever know. I was screwed. Caught in my own game. Even if I mentioned it to Marion she would know who I was.

I shuffled toward the boat. There was nothing different about it, no new lines or tackle and nothing to suggest it had been used recently. Rain pinged off the center thwart and dribbled onto the boards. The sound was soothing.

I panted out a few more tears, louder this time. I must have sensed the breeze against my cheek, the sudden change in something. I swung around.

Jax.

"Hey," he said. "You okay?"

I must have looked up and down the beach, forehead a frown.

"Oh, I was out walking," he said. "Dog's still missing."

I hadn't seen Jax earlier. He must have been searching in the long grass. "I'm sorry." I wiped my eyes.

"Come here."

I moved forward, felt his arms slip around my waist, one hand pressing between my shoulder blades. I sobbed.

"What happened?" he asked.

I spilled. Ryan. The divorce. The nameless woman who had stolen him from me. The hard-nosed callous bitch I referred to as *her*.

His hand pressed harder against my back, lips grazing my forehead. "It's not your fault. It's never *your* fault. Nobody appreciates what they've got until they lose it. I should know."

"I'm sorry," I said.

"Don't be."

"First girlfriend?"

"Yes." He pushed me back, hands pressed against my shoulders. "They say those are the worst."

"Losing them you mean?"

"Losing your virginity. It sucks. Shouldn't be like that. You leave a part of yourself behind and it's hard...

because that person has that part. Always."

"Yes."

"And you can't get it back," he said. "You remember, not how wonderful it was, but how they stole it. Laughed at it."

I wiped my eyes and looked into his. Hazel, I think. Blurred with tears. "I'm so sorry, Jax."

"I'm sorry… for you. For all that you've been through."

His shoulders slumped.

So did mine.

"If there's anything you need," he said, "anything at all. I'm here. Well… over there. But you can knock on the door. My mom won't mind."

"Thank you." I knew I wouldn't knock on his door. "I hope you find your dog."

He grinned. Nodded.

I could still feel the warmth of his breath as I walked back to the house. Empathy in truckloads. A good kid, if you could call a nineteen-year-old a *kid*.

If it wasn't for the scent of pork suffusing the house, I would have bolted upstairs to change.

"Hey stranger." Chef Robert flashed a grin from his bar stool. "You going to stand there all day?"

I searched for a witty comeback, but complaining about a wet ass wasn't it.

He steepled his fingers and studied a bottle in a wine cradle. "Did you have a nice walk?"

"I did, thanks."

My heart buzzed like a trapped fly. Robert had been watching me and for some reason that made me nervous.

"I saw you looking at the boat," he said. "A bit old, but she sails like the wind."

He must have also seen me with Jax. "Does anyone use it?"

"Kimball takes her out sometimes. For old times' sake.

Long story. Belonged to his father who was an alcoholic. Died a few years back."

"I'm sorry to hear that," I said, envisioning a back alley punch-up or a car accident.

"Fell overboard. Found his body washed up on Cooper's Beach. They said he'd been drinking." Robert sighed heavily, as if it would take some effort to explain. "Can't be easy living here with the memories. His old man taught him about the tides and the winds. Taught him how to sail."

Fear began to gnaw at me like a ravenous worm. If Kimball was using the boat he would definitely be keeping an eye on it. "So, what's he like?"

"Kimball? Not your usual suit and tie. Whiter than a computer junkie and just as reclusive. He used to be an actor."

"Oh?"

"Bit parts mainly. Played an art dealer in some crime series. Forget the name. About a year ago, he was amping up for an audition for the part of a serial killer in *Criminal Minds*. I knew this because he'd be pacing around the house visualizing and doing his lines. Didn't get the part. So now he just sends headshots in response to casting calls he finds on Craigslist."

"And he finds time to do this when?"

"Weekends. Evenings. I dunno. I've learned there are many sides to Kimball, depending on the scripts he's reading and the drugs he's on."

"Hard stuff?"

"He was in the library a few months ago when I burst in on him. Doing lines rather than practicing them. His head's a visual database of characters. He can't possibly keep up. And there I was thinking he was just a weed and whisky guy."

"You have to hand it to him," I said, eyes skimming the ceiling. "He's a self-made millionaire."

"Which doesn't compare with his dad being a fisherman."

"You have a point. But not every son follows in his father's footsteps."

"He can be an asshole but he's a good person," Robert said. "Generous. Spends a lot of time on the computer. That's how he got to know Marion. She's... well, you probably guessed, an escort."

I pretended to act shocked.

"He used to order women like Chinese food. Only this dish stuck."

Robert slowly slid off his bar stool and peered around the kitchen door, hand pressed against the frame. He listened for a few seconds and then continued.

"I saw her profile on Tinder."

I pressed my lips into a tiny 'o'.

"She's obviously looking for a husband," he said, slapping a tea towel over one shoulder. "A woman like her... *Big* threat to wives."

"What about Kimball's wife?"

"She's never been to this house. Not sure she even knows about it or the other kid he's sired."

"Kid?" I doubted Lucy Kimball was that dumb. It wouldn't be long before she pieced it all together.

"That's a story for another day." He looked at me hard. "So, how do you like it here?"

I felt a prickly heat around my ears and reloaded a breath. "It's a beautiful house. Can't complain. Not sure how long I'll be here."

"None of us know." He paused, measuring a fly with a frown before swatting it with the tea towel. "Dirty wee things."

"So what happened to the last cleaner?"

"Got married. Moved to Oregon. You got a man?"

"Divorced actually."

"I'm sorry to hear that." He turned, leaned over the

kitchen sink and opened the window. "Can't be easy. I've got a feeling this is the change you need. Good sea air. A fresh start. You'll be back to your old self in a jiffy."

"Maybe."

"Take it slow."

"I'll keep that in mind."

I excused myself from an eyeful of raw masculinity swathed in a chef's coat and bounded upstairs. I liked Robert. He was genuine. Gossipy.

The bedroom was musty, needed a good dose of fresh air. I opened the window and noticed there was one less car in the driveway. Frances had gone home. I also noticed someone had moved Jax's box from the hall table and left it on my bed. I zipped the gift into the lower compartment of my suitcase, locked away for another time.

I leaned in at the shower door, turned on the handle and peeled off my clothes. Once relieved of their soggy burden my buttocks felt like two dollops of ice cream slowly thawing in the steam. Suds streaked down my body and I spent a few minutes brooding over the fact that Joe hadn't called back. He was probably patrolling the neighborhood—a major event for an old man like him.

Oh now, be fair. He's only—what—forty something?

Snappy sarcasm, intimidation. A man who probably found shame erotic. I couldn't quite get a bead on him, who he really was. He operated by his own rules and he was experienced at tracking sleazy villains with paranoia and dirty tricks. Hard to put a man like that to the back of my brain.

I almost wanted to throw in the towel. Finding Ryan had lost its allure.

A flash of light beyond the steamy door. The wheels were turning in my overworked brain and I wiped a hand across the glass and peered out.

"Hello?"

What better way to threaten an intruder than stand naked in the shower gripping a shampoo bottle. The suspense was wearing on me. I was tired of living exclusively in my head, scared of the outside world.

Murder is real and people don't like murderers. And you are a murderer, Clo.

I turned off the water and listened. Did someone actually say that? An intangible voice oozing through the grilles of the air vent. My subconscious knew I had murder on the brain and it had a funny way of jabbing me at the worst moments.

Thinking it is the same as doing it.

Once Marion was dead, there would be no use pleading insanity at a trial. Any doctor would prove I was saner than a judge and Joe—stalky, persistent Joe—would be able to demonstrate beyond all reasonable doubt that the murder was premeditated.

I dragged a towel from the rod and finished drying in my glass cell. I had a list of things to do, specific things at specific times. If I was incarcerated, it would not be from a lack of preparation.

I stepped out on the bath mat and listened to a growl of thunder. The bedroom curtains were wind-ruffled, floor glossy with rain.

Odd. Had Marion opened the window?

And then that phenomenon when the person you were thinking about suddenly appears.

"Clo. We need to talk."

26

There was no reason for me to feel guilty at the words *we need to talk*. But somehow it brought back a flood of memories from school. The principal's office, the way she used to slant her head and squint. I could never tell what she was thinking.

It shouldn't have been a challenge for me after a lifetime of people-watching and today, Marion eyed me in much the same way.

Her hair was piled on top of her head and the gown she wore reminded me of an Edwardian tea dress—embroidered scooped neck and an empire waist—light and flowing with layered skirts. She had another dress over one arm.

"I would like you to serve us tonight," she said. "You do *know* how to serve?"

"Yes, ma'am." How difficult could it be?

"This," she said, arranging the dowdy button-down scrap of cotton on the bed, "is what I'd like you to wear. You'll eat with Chef Robert in the kitchen and then serve Mr. Kimball at 6 p.m. Don't be late."

Marion threw a look at the window and then moved toward the door. "I understand you went for a walk this afternoon."

I suddenly felt sick. "Yes. I was looking around the gardens."

"I see. Your job description does say the guesthouses are off-limits. Kimball uses one as an office and the other, well, it used to belong to his mother. She's dead now. So, you see the problem."

I didn't.

She frowned. "It would raise all sorts of hell if anything was moved."

Two dead parents. I wasn't feeling an ounce of pity as I pictured a bed covered in layers of filthy lace and cobwebs. The second guesthouse—a mausoleum to his mother—was not the one I had been in.

"I didn't touch or move anything, and anyway the door was open," I said. "It seemed to be occupied so I left."

"Sometimes we have guests." She tilted her head and looked away for a moment. "This one left in a hurry. He also left quite mess."

I was lost for words.

"Kimball will take it as an invasion of privacy if anyone goes in there," she said.

In the same way the external cameras monitoring my every move was an invasion of privacy.

"I'm not mad." She shrugged. "I mean it's not your fault. I did say go explore."

"It's quite the place you have here."

"Yes. Well, there's a lot to see." A smile twitched along the corners of her mouth and was soon gone, almost as abruptly as she was.

Apart from feeling like a punished schoolgirl, I noticed Marion didn't look too hot herself. Even after several hours of pampering, her dark eyes carried a haunted look as if someone had just given her some bad news.

I could smell pork juices and some kind of Italian seasoning as I walked downstairs. The uniform screamed modest with its high neck and long sleeves and there were a few chuckles from Chef Robert.

He pushed a steaming plate of pork tenderloin across the kitchen island and a glass of iced water. He had already eaten most of his.

"I'd give you a little something for Dutch courage but I don't have the keys to the hooch cabinet."

I pulled out a bar stool and thanked him for the plate. "What time will Kimball be here?"

"6 p.m. Not a minute later." Robert lowered his voice. "You okay?"

"A little nervous. I usually take medication for anxiety but it makes me drowsy."

"I won't take pills for anything. It's the side effects," Robert said, between mouthfuls. "And no, I'm not one of those nutty religious types who'd rather die than go to hospital. Our immune system has evolved over our entire existence as a species. Maybe it's learned a trick or two. Maybe, we should let it do its thing."

"You mean heal on its own?"

"Exactly. Why slather steroid cream on a rash when your body's natural instinct is to fight it."

"I'm not sure anxiety falls in that category."

"Listen, you might think Marion's lifestyle is bloody perfect but it's not. All that money... doesn't make her happy. She's under a lot of stress. So are you. So she exercises, meditates, eats healthy, has oodles of sex..."

He smiled brightly. I shot him a look.

"Eat up," he said. "He'll be here in a minute"

I scarfed down as much pork as my angst-shrinking stomach would allow and took a slurp of iced water. "Talking of Kimball, how am I supposed to act around him?"

"If you want my opinion," he said, lowering his voice,

"stand behind him at dinner and don't talk to him. When he arrives, Marion will greet him at the front door, take his coat and escort him into the library. In a word, she'll *manage* him."

My mind began conjuring scenes of Kimball at the head of the table. Me thrust back seventy feet from his chair and then suddenly sucked back in again as if tugged by an invisible rope. My senses were roaring, floating above the white noise and I could see pinwheels of light behind my eyelids.

A distant voice interrupted the symmetry. Robert raised his head, finger poised in the air. "He's here."

I could hear the excited timbre in Marion's laugh and the deep inflection in Kimball's. His voice seemed to imitate the clipped English of Cornelius Vanderbilt IV, failing to rid itself of the gliding vowels of the south.

A scuffle of coats. Then silence.

"Give them a good half-hour in the library," Robert said. "Marion asked me to plate up in the kitchen tonight. There's no appetizer. Just entrée and dessert."

"What about wine?"

"It's on the buffet breathing. Don't worry. You'll do fine." He pulled the dish out of the oven and let it sit. "I understand Kimball might be traveling either tomorrow or Friday. Marion mentioned something. So I may not see you again this week."

"Monday then?" I asked.

"Definitely."

Robert was at once smiling and frowning. He took away my half-empty plate and offered me a cocktail sized key lime pie.

I looked up at the clock. Six twenty-eight. Where had the time gone?

"You should probably serve the wine now," Robert said.

Two people were already settling at the table and I

waited a few seconds, while my brain twitched inside my skull. Pouring wine from a cut-glass carafe wasn't the easiest thing to do, especially a heavy carafe, and a few dribbles speckled the white tablecloth near the stem of Kimball's glass.

I returned to the kitchen and Robert handed me two steaming plates. He mouthed goodbye and good luck.

I raced the plates into the dining room. "Pork," Kimball murmured, as I deposited Marion's plate on the table before his. "A nice change, my dear."

Close up, Kimball was a disturbingly handsome man even though he was further into his twilight than I had thought. Salt and pepper hair and not much in the way of wrinkles, except a few spokes around his eyes. The whole ensemble pegged him around sixty. It wasn't hard to see how he had succeeded in business with a patented smile of complete confidence.

I stood between the buffet and the back of his chair, smelling a fragrance of grass clippings and some kind of musk. He did not acknowledge me or see me. I was simply part of the décor.

Marion kept closing her eyes and taking a breath. Sometimes she stuttered and stumbled over her words. Sometimes her laughter went on longer than necessary. She flicked her napkin onto her lap and began prattling about someone's wedding and how the groom was exactly the type of husband a lady would want. How his money would make everything jolly.

"And her father loves him," she said.

"Of course he does," Kimball said. "Aren't all daddies happy to see their daughters so well positioned? The important thing is, do you like him?"

"I think he's charming."

For a terrible instant, Marion began eating and Kimball, noticing the silence, looked up from his pork with a stricken slant to his head. "Charming in what way?"

Marion reached for her wine. "A boyish charm."

"Don't be modest, darling. You *want* him I can tell."

"Oh, he's far too young."

"And you're early thirties. It hardly exempts you from having sex with him. Look at organic-J next door. That was the romp from hell."

A shudder hit me as if someone had attached a catheter I wasn't expecting. The conversation had plunged rapidly from marriage to sex in less than a minute.

"Perhaps I don't want to," she said.

"Perhaps you're just saying that. You see, my darling, you are a fount of information on the subject. Shall I beat it out of you?" Kimball set his knife along the edge of his plate and pressed a finger to her lips. "So, who's the new girl?"

"This is Clo," Marion said, flapping a hand for me to step forward. "Our new help."

My blood began to heat and my muscles tensed. He examined me casually at first and then his eyes seemed to hunt me.

"I see. Might that be short for Chloe?"

"It might," I said. "But mom preferred Clody."

The narrowed eyes made the condescending stare all the more menacing. "Why Clody?"

"After the river, sir. In Ireland."

"I see. Have you been there? No? Well it's a cold wet place like the rest of the United Kingdom. Gets to you after a while and very soon you'll be longing to come home."

"It's not so cold at this time of year," I said, opting to fight back. "Ireland is ranked number three in the world for tourism. It's also ranked one of the top twenty safest countries to visit."

"Something against America?"

"Oh no, sir. I just support the Irish. They did make up

some of our founding fathers."

Hesitation. "That so?"

"There were four I believe. Thomas Fitzsimons, Pierce Butler, James McHenry and William Paterson. They were part of the Constitutional Convention."

It was clear to me that Kimball had never heard of these men. But he would now remember Ireland's contribution for the rest of his career.

"So what books do you read?" he asked. "Romance, self-help? Vampire?"

"I read history, politics and the newspaper, sir."

"And what have you read recently in the news that you would like to discuss?" he asked.

"I thought the court case about men shopping for sex at a prostitution-related website was quite interesting. *Redmaynes*—which I believe is a play on words since all the original girls had long red hair—boasted over three million hits last month. Apparently it's a kind of Yelp for prostitution."

Marion looked at me as if she had bitten down on a clove of garlic.

"Think about it," I said, launching on uninvited. "A man no longer has to cruise the streets and risk a date with an undercover cop. Two clicks of a mouse and he can order someone up for sex."

"And are you one of those patriotic Americans who would like to see these men castrated?" he asked.

Damned right I would. "Oh, no. I wouldn't wish that on anyone, sir."

"Oh, but you do. Let me remind you, the women are not victims. They are consenting adults. The men see it as a reasonable exchange of sex for money."

"How do we know the women weren't coerced?"

"No evidence. One man who went by the handle *Woodstock*, broke down at his sentencing hearing saying he had become infatuated with one of the prostitutes. Said he wanted to lease her an apartment in his name. She was very willing."

"It beats me how he could afford to do that with a wife and two kids," I said.

"Thank you for providing us with a layman's opinion. Let's not forget he had no criminal history and the prosecutor recommended a first-time offender waiver. He got a few months on work release. To you, that might seem a little unjust. The court system has indeed failed. Seems men may have failed you."

He met my gaze full on and I knew he was going to ask me what had brought on this recent surge of hatred.

"Have you always been so tough?" he asked.

"Not always. Just the past couple of years, really."

"A hard heart. It does well in business, Miss Clody. Remember that."

"Yes, sir."

He handed me his plate.

27

I awoke in the darkness, mind refusing to rest for more than four hours. I stared up at my bedroom ceiling, listening to a scuttle of leaves in the driveway.

4:07 a.m.

My first meeting with Kimball hadn't gone too badly, until the conversation about *Redmaynes*. Must have hit him where it hurt because he swept the few final crumbs into his mouth, checked his watch and said he had to leave.

Marion blamed me for upsetting him. Said he had left on account of my impropriety. I failed to see anything offensive about a newspaper article. The only thing offensive was Kimball's curiosity in me.

A door squeaked downstairs.

Wrenching on a pair of jeans and a sweater, I snatched my phone off the bedside table and inched along the corridor. Salt air wafted in from the balcony outside Marion's bedroom and it brought with it a stream of moonlight. The door was ajar and she was sleeping on her back, head turned sideways.

It would have been so easy. A pillow over the face and the strength to hold her down. Strength I didn't have. It didn't matter what she had done or hadn't done. There would always be cancer or a gun. None of us got out of this life for free.

Something told me I had less than twenty-four hours to come up with a battle plan. Kimball used the house three evenings a week which gave me tomorrow night now to lay Marion to rest. But if Robert's comment about Kimball traveling had anything to do with it, any plan I made might be thwarted.

I inched downstairs. My mouth went dry.

The blinds in the kitchen rattled above the sink and the door swung on its hinges. I remembered Robert opening the window to release the smell of cooking.

I must have checked every room in the house. Every drawer, every closet and behind every door. The first assumption was Ryan had never been in the main house but that was unlikely considering his relationship to Marion. He would have had access to her bed.

Perhaps I just didn't want to believe Ryan had done anything wrong. What if he was telling the truth and simply worked overtime in Kimball's guesthouse office?

Wake up, Clo. Why was his ID buried in a closet?

I opened the front door and glanced down the driveway. Kimball had left the front gate open and I could see a dog scampering down the lane.

I made my way to the guesthouse. It was locked, but there was a muted light on inside, a standard lamp on the bedside table, shade tilted toward the open closet.

There was no sign of Ryan's clothes, and since two of the hangers were haphazardly angled, it indicated everything had been ripped away in a hurry.

I rattled the doorknob and banged on the window. It

was no longer a joke. Ryan must have known I would come looking for him and had hightailed it out of Southampton. What if he had simply gone home?

An instant later, I was racing back to the main house and up the stairs to my room. My purse dangled over the back of a chair and I hooked it over one shoulder, keys rattling in the side pocket.

Marion was lying on her side now, sheet pulled down to her waist. There was a flicker on her stomach, a steady pulse that suggested she was in a deep sleep. It was hard to tell if her eyes were really closed with one arm flung over her face.

I hauled ass to the kitchen and left a note telling her I had gone out to get a prescription and would be back before lunch. The drive home gave me time to think. There was a lot I wanted to say to Ryan, but I knew better than to blow off steam. I had been worried about him. Worried that he hadn't come back to get a few things like he said he would. But I knew when I opened the door and saw him I would smile and forget about being divorced. There would be relief, a patch-up, a saying of sorrys. A cup of coffee around the kitchen island like old times.

I parked down the street near to Mrs. Nita's. She would be in bed, of course, like all sane people. The early air was thick with rain, clouds creeping toward the east and breaking away as if someone was plucking at a ball of cotton candy.

I stooped under a flick of branches, briefly hidden by the canopy of a weeping willow. I couldn't help feeling a prick of tears at coming home and I sprinted toward my backyard and in through the back door.

"Ryan!"

The door squealed shut behind me and I listened.

"Ryan?"

I was shaking now. All keyed up and needed to hear his voice to knock the edge off.

"Ryan…"

I didn't like searching through an empty house and hearing the sobs as they racked my chest. Short little spurts like hiccups and then the tears. He wasn't here and I think a part of me knew that.

No use crying. Better time spent brewing myself a cup of dark roast espresso. The blue numbers on the microwave said 5:35 a.m. It was coffee-o'clock.

I took my cup into the living room and crumpled deep into the couch. My heart ached and there was pain in my side like a stitch. Only not a stitch. Something worse.

I screwed my eyes shut and thought of the night we last made love. We had returned from a run in the park, both buttery with tanning cream and smelling of coconuts. He with his eyes bright, me clutching his hand as he pulled me onto the couch. I remembered that afternoon because the smell of cut grass wafted in through the slit of a bathroom window and you never forget a smell like that.

The incessant buzzing of the doorbell made me sit up, hand sagging with the weight of the cup as it skated almost halfway across the coffee table.

Ryan no longer had a key.

I pulled off my shoes and slinked up to the peephole. "Who is it?"

"It's me. Joe."

Oh shit. He must have seen the light on. Must have seen me. I took a deep breath and unlocked the door. He was leaning up against the porch looking down at me with a scowl.

"Can I come in?"

Just when I dropped my guard and thought there was no one else to bother me. Out popped Joe.

28

"Where have you been?" he asked, eyes grazing my legs.

"Out," I said.

"Where out?"

"Out out."

There was no sign of the bomber book under his arm. He was hoping to make a few more visits.

"What happened to your hair?"

I suddenly remembered I wasn't a redhead any longer and bit my lip. "A girl can change her hair, can't she?"

"What color is it?"

"Brown," I said leading the way to the living room.

"Looks darker than that. Well, it's nice to see you back."

"I had some errands to run."

"For two days?"

"You *are* following me."

"Not following, Clo, watching out for you. There's a difference."

"There is?"

Joe was getting to be a real pain in the ass. If I wasn't

careful he'd screw up everything. I sat on the couch. Joe sat opposite on the easy chair.

"You've been crying. Your eyes are all red and puffy," he said.

I dodged the comment with a wave of my hand.

"I'm trying to be a friend, Clo. Really. There's no need to get all defensive every time I come over."

It was hard not to when he was in uniform with a gun hooked to his waist. Must have been a long night if he had only just got off duty.

"Are you taping this?" I asked pointing at the camera module mounted on his collar.

"No. Should I?"

"I've got nothing to say."

Lazy morning sun blinked through the blinds, crowning Joe's head in a ring of glory. "Look me in the eye," he said, "and tell me you're not following him. Tell me you're not snooping."

I looked him in the eye. "I'm not."

I stared at narrowed eyes that seem to be telescoping mine. He hadn't seen me in Marion's house.

"Heard from him?"

I felt myself frown. "Nope."

"Just so you know, a colleague and I met with Ms. Kurchel. Fascinating woman."

"Oh."

"Seems to have a thriving business. Nice house too."

I was beginning to feel cornered.

He leaned forward and lowered his chin. "Belongs to David Kimball. Interesting, don't you think?"

It was. "So? He's big in aerospace engineering. Probably got houses all over the place."

"With a hooker as a housekeeper? Dangerous game. Kimball's Ryan's boss, right?"

"Right."

I bristled at the words *dangerous game.* But I needed

to quit while I was ahead. Screwing around with an ongoing police investigation could only mean one thing. I was in over my head.

"I know what Marion Kurchel is. What she does." Joe huffed out a loud breath. "And I'd arrest her, given half the chance. But she's Captain Montefiore's business not mine. She's also not your business. So don't get any funny ideas."

It became clear to me that Joe was investigating a prostitution ring with which Ryan, my erstwhile and rather dense husband, had latterly become involved. But the truth was, Joe wanted to round up this cowboy without me knowing.

"I'll think about it."

Joe stared at the TV and picked up the channel changer. "Guess I'll be waiting while you're thinking. Don't mind if I watch *Murderous Minds*?"

"You can't just walk in here and make yourself at home. Ryan will be back any second. What's he supposed to think?"

"He's not coming back, Clo. Nor is he missing. He's left of his own volition. People do."

The only thing creepier than a missing husband was finding his wallet and phone on the Kimball property. It wasn't something I wanted to share.

I had made a mistake coming home. Hadn't anticipated Joe seeing me like this and I was relieved he hadn't arrested me. I decided to change the subject.

"You should give up, you know," I said.

"Give up what?"

"Smoking. It'll kill you."

He nodded, bottom lip pushed up as if it was suddenly a good idea.

"Nasty habit," I said. "Makes a hell of a stink. I can smell it from here."

"I'll remember that. I wanted to ask you something,"

he said, replacing the channel changer. "I wanted to know how long Ryan and you had been, well… separated. If you know what I mean."

He knew Ryan had been living here but what he meant was sex, only he was too chicken to say it. "A year."

"That's a while."

"I guess."

"I understand you miss him, but people separate all the time." He seemed to be watching me like I was a rare butterfly. "I've been divorced three years."

I felt my cheeks flame, two mounds of the deepest red, and I could see he wanted me on his team. The thought repulsed me at first and then an idea pinged in my mind. I had no choice if I wanted his trust. I also had to keep telling myself that Joe had his weaknesses as a man, but he was a cop first.

"Want a coffee?" I asked.

Joe stroked his chin. "Yeah, why not?"

A few slugs of Ryan's dark roast and I was beginning to see Joe differently. The gigantic chest wasn't the work of a bulletproof vest but a billow of muscle I suddenly thought I needed to see.

I wasn't paying much attention to his questions on prostitution, whether I had noticed a large deficit in my bank account since Ryan had met Ms. Kurchel or whether Ryan had somehow been enticed by her longer than just a couple of months.

Joe kept nodding and trying to minimize the significance of my so-called research. Saying one spouse needing information on the whereabouts of the other was to be expected and how smart I was.

I wasn't going to latch onto Joe's lenient line of thinking. He was all about getting information. I was all about keeping it a secret.

"Do you have a recent picture of Ryan?" he asked.

I shrugged. Couldn't quite understand why Joe would

want a recent photo of Ryan. It's not like he hadn't seen him before.

"There's a photo in the bedroom," I said.

"Mind if I take a closer look?"

I swayed along the corridor in front of him, hand brushing the walls. "Do you think he might have grown a beard?"

"People do change their appearances. Thought you might be able to educate me about that?"

"Not sure I know what you mean."

"Looks like you've lost weight. What's the secret?" He tapped his own stomach.

"Fruit and water."

"No, seriously?"

"Diuretics."

Joe grinned and picked up a gilt-framed picture of Ryan and me at our wedding. Scrutinized it for a moment.

"You haven't changed much. Ryan? He looks older, thinner. Balder."

I would have laughed if it had been funny. But nothing about Ryan was funny anymore. I didn't want Joe to think I was the jealous wife that showed up unannounced. The wife that had to *know* what her husband was doing because she was suspicious of every tiny tidbit.

Joe's eyes locked with mine for a heartbeat, as if he had caught me staring at him with his pants down. He pulled out his gun and laid it on the vanity, swiveling the muzzle toward the wall. For some reason I was mesmerized by his hands, the tautness of his fingers.

The ceiling started to close in on me and the room began to tilt. Then he came at me hard and groping, and there was a saltiness to his lips as if he had been running a marathon. I didn't care. I liked sweat and hair.

He hoisted me up and carried me to the bed. One hand tugging at my jeans, the other pressed against the arch of my back. He was a professional.

Everything throbbed. The bed. Him. Me. While I was wondering why I wasn't counting off the notches on the ceiling, he whispered my name. I wondered if I was supposed to say something, but he didn't seem bothered about having a conversation. Just kept whispering it over and over again with the occasional grunt in between. It was comforting.

With his shirt partly slung over the end of the bed I hoped he hadn't left his lapel cam on. The sound effects were bad enough. Worse if they were eligible for public release.

He looked down at me and shaped his lips into a wide smile. "You okay?"

I must have been scowling. I smiled back. "Better than okay."

It was a good hour before I teetered into the bathroom, legs like a wishbone ready to snap. I glanced back for only a second. Joe was lying on his back, slack-limbed and snoring like a dog.

29

I found Joe's cell phone in the belt of his scrunched-up pants and briefly checked the texts displayed on the lock screen.

One about service to Joe's cruiser and one from Captain Montefiore referencing the hit-and-run.

Reviewing Kimball cams. 2001 Camry, KCM 5883 Driver descript...

Unfortunately the text overflowed behind the lock screen and I couldn't read the rest without knowing Joe's security code. The license was false. They would find that out soon enough.

I curled up in the bedroom chair and watched Joe in a streak of sunlight, the sheet covering his body at the waist and a tiny flicker of a pulse below his chest. The bed was his now. Like a dog scenting a tree, he had marked his territory and rid the home of its previous owner.

In a way, I was glad.

I reached into my jeans pocket for my phone, scrolled through my favorites until I found Marion's webpage. Her *Today* tab was brief.

I threw away betrayal. I wrote it down on a piece of paper and shredded it. Burned the shreds to ash. Threw the ashes into the sea.

What if the tranquil face of the sea asked me for a kiss? Would you be jealous then?

It threw me off guard. Had Kimball decided to terminate the assignment? Was I missing an event the rest of the world was attending?

There is nothing like your own shower. The warmth of the water, the familiar smell of your own shampoo. The only strange thing was the man who slipped in behind me, hands lathering my hair.

It was in those tense few moments I realized what I had done. Cut away the anchors of a marital bridge. A bridge that once had towers and piers and load-bearing cables. Now it was nothing more than two frayed ropes.

No chance of reconciliation. I had already stepped into the forbidden room and made myself at home. My cheeks were smeared with tears, hidden by a deluge of water and a happy, whistling man.

Joe whistled in the shower?

I chewed on that for a moment. He was too moved-in for my liking and here I was feeling wedged in and suffocated. He asked me if I was hungry and I said no. He told me I had to eat. I was getting too skinny.

"I can make you some breakfast, if you like," Joe said, handing me a towel. "I like cooking. I think I'd like cooking for you."

Oh, crap. What had I done? "That's sweet, Joe. Really. Only, I need to get going."

He slid a hand under my towel where it came to rest under my right breast. A burning sensation skimmed along the surface of my belly and I nearly hesitated.

"You could spend the day with me," he said. "When did you last go the park? Feel grass between your toes. Drink a bottle of wine. How does a backrub sound?"

It sounded rather good actually. "Maybe another time."

I inched away from him and toward the vanity, towel falling to the floor. I didn't care if he was watching me with a dribble of drool escaping from the corner of his mouth and I didn't care if he saw me bending over an open drawer, rummaging through a clean pile of underwear. I wasn't staying.

"If you married me you wouldn't have to work," he said, slipping his gun back into his holster. "With a figure like yours you could easily be a model."

"I'm too old to be a model."

I wanted him to shut up but the words kept coming. I began the inevitable landslide toward panic, mind spinning with suspicion. He was doing his best to keep me here and I was doing my best to get away.

He followed me to the kitchen where he found Ryan's bowl of roasted peanuts next to the toaster, shelled a few and threw the husks in the trash can under the sink. He had a certain dexterity I found mesmerizing, body twisting back and forth with one foot poised on the lower rung of a bar stool.

"You? You've got class," he said. "No, I mean it. A man would be proud to be seen with you. It's been weird, I can't lie. What we've just done. You know, without going out and all that. But it was exactly how I imagined it would be."

He imagined it? By the sounds of things, Joe had fallen hard.

"I've been in love with you for a while now." He accelerated. "That's why I don't like talking about Ryan. It wouldn't be fair."

"No, it wouldn't."

"I didn't do my ex-wife any favors," he said, peeling a banana. "In the end, she was as fascinated by me as she was by a car crash. Said I was larger than a walrus.

Couldn't get me in and out of the front door without greasing me up. At least, that's how she put it. I've lost weight since then."

I hoped he'd had more than a raw tune-up. He was beginning to exhaust me. "Joe, it's okay. You don't have to explain anything."

"Well I do, you see. Because I know you think I'm going too fast." He breathed deeply. "I don't see the point in wasting time. If you like someone, tell them."

I studied him as he took a few inches off that banana and then flicked through his texts, wrinkles getting deeper between his eyebrows. He was growing on me.

"Well that's a start," he said. "Got a license number for that gold Camry and a description of the driver. Male wearing a baseball hat. Ryan wear baseball hats?"

"Nope." My heart almost detonated in my chest.

"It's not his gold Camry, you'll be pleased to know. Someone registered in Southampton. So, I take it you like all kinds of food?"

"What did you have in mind?"

"Mediterranean."

I smiled. He grinned.

"I'll take you somewhere really nice, Clo. Tomorrow night. Promise?"

"Promise."

It didn't look like it was going to be easy cutting Joe out of this caper. He wasn't going away anytime soon and he certainly wasn't the type to drift through life like a skiff in a swamp.

We kissed on the doorstep. Him whistling again as he walked across the street. Me, clutching my throat with one hand and then slipping through the back yard to the Buick.

30

Driving back to Southampton gave me plenty of time to pick up my prescription. It also gave me time to think. Marion and I both had daddy issues and our fair share of men. It didn't make me any better. It didn't make me any different.

So why the heck did I feel so superior?

Marion looked up from her coffee and muffin as I waltzed into the kitchen. The scowl on her face told me she wasn't about to let go of last night's fiasco. Or this morning's sudden desertion.

"I left the front gate open for you," she said.

"I noticed."

"Was it busy out?"

"Not really." *Get to the meat of it, Marion.*

Her skin was a painter's palette of metallic shades and peachy tones that seemed to lend a chiseled definition to an otherwise bland face. Her cheekbones weren't as high as I had earlier thought and the jawline not quite as angular. But her dark eyes surveyed me from across the room like two shiny stones edged in kohl. I wondered how long it took to perfect the look.

My fingers nipped the top of a white paper bag with a pharmacy logo and I set it on the kitchen island. It was enough to confirm where I had been.

"Does that medication have side effects?" she asked.

I knew it did. Hallucinations for one. "Not so as you would notice. Why?"

"I don't take meds. Better that way."

I wanted to agree. The medication wasn't for me.

She hooked a lock of hair around one ear and sucked in her bottom lip for a moment. "I decided not to go jogging today. Didn't feel up to it."

"Oh?"

"Last night… him leaving. I've never seen him do that before."

"Maybe he was tired."

"No. That's not it." She rubbed an imaginary smear from the countertop with her finger. "Servers don't speak to the guests. It's just not done."

"If I recall, he opened the conversation. Should I have ignored him?"

"You could have answered in less words." Her voice sounded pinched. "I understand your family is not from around here."

"Is that a problem?"

"You say you're divorced."

"Barely."

"Your last name is Turner, at least that's the name every reference confirmed. I had to ask myself why your third reference wasn't forthcoming. So I tried the number. Helen Flynn, criminal investigator. She said—and these were *her* words—that you called her 'a perv sleazebag without a functioning brain'. She had nothing good to say about you."

"It was mutual."

"While I had her on the phone, I asked her if she knew your ex-husband. She said his name was Ryan only I couldn't find a Ryan Turner. So I decided to do some digging."

Digging. Never a good word when you leave your bags unattended in a bedroom with no lock on the door.

"Your name isn't Clody is it?"

Blood whooshed in my ears and I felt sluggish. She placed a familiar airline tag on the countertop. A tag that had been tied to the handle of my suitcase.

Clodagh Shepherd. 1522 Berkeley Road.

"I had to ask myself why that name rang a bell," she said. "Then I had to ask myself why you're here."

The relief I felt was palpable. No more pretending. No more lies. Just a quick slice from chest to groin to see which one of us had any guts. As for Helen Flynn, she was another woman who found it hard to keep her legs crossed.

"You're absolutely right. I'm nothing more than a bilge rat." I walked a little closer. Smiled a little wider. "Excluding steerage from first class is always a mistake, Marion. Many of the rich and famous were once poor and obscure, and rats have a marvelous capacity to climb. You should know. You've done it yourself."

Her mouth flopped open.

"We could play truth or dare," I said. "Only I've got a nasty suspicion it will turn deadly if either one of us lies. Why don't we start at the beginning? We both know my husband was lured here many times. In particular three nights ago where he was suspected to be the culprit of a hit-and-run."

Marion's eyes ping-ponged between me and a space above the door. "Your husband?"

"Oh, cut the crap, Marion. Just tell me where he is and we can get this over with. Ryan Shepherd."

Marion sucked in her bottom lip and nodded slowly. "He was here on Monday night to meet Kimball. They had a disagreement over money and then he left."

"I doubt it, Marion, not without his cell phone and his wallet. The suit he was wearing was hanging in the guesthouse closet."

Her head snapped up and her face paled under the scrutiny. "He told me he wanted to leave the past behind. To build a new life for himself. Maybe he doesn't want to be found."

I watched her fingers as they pulled the muffin apart, toying with the crumbs on the side of her plate. It was true, Ryan had bullied me for a divorce, but the part that didn't make sense was why he would leave his belongings in Kimball's guesthouse. Perhaps it was all in my mind. He had never admitted to an affair, nor had he revealed his love for another woman.

"That's not how I saw it," I said. "He was expecting a date, only you were with Kimball. He heard you on the phone."

She stared at me as though committing every tiny fragment to memory. It made me prattle all the more in an attempt to fill the silence.

"The police said he broke a valuable painting and he injured a pedestrian," I said. "Why would he do a thing like that? You can see my problem. Now he's disappeared you may have been the last person to have seen him. Why didn't you tell the police? Why didn't you tell them he'd left all his stuff behind?"

She shook her head. "I was scared."

What the heck was I doing? A nugget of guilt washed over me. What right had I to march into other people's houses and demand information about my husband? But it was only a nugget and I was tired of the lies.

I pulled out a bar stool and sat down. "Scared of what?"

"That they would arrest me. Ryan's a regular. He comes here about twice a week."

Three times, you liar. "So you were sleeping with him?"

"I don't think that's any of your business."

"He's my husband. It's absolutely my business."

"*Was*," she corrected. "You're divorced remember."

"If wouldn't have happened if you hadn't wedged yourself between us."

Her eyes bounced behind me again, climbing up the wall to the corner of the door frame. I could see the reflection of the air vent in the aluminum surface of the toaster.

"You're not going to pull out a gun, are you?" she asked.

"I wouldn't dream of it." Although there was one in the back of my car if things got bad. "So you're an escort. I've seen the website. Don't you think the police have?"

"I could call the police right now and say I have an unwelcome guest."

"And prove what?"

"That you barged your way in without invitation."

She was right. I had. "What about the ad?"

"What about it? Isla will never admit to having spoken to you. In any case, she's not a recognized agency." Marion must have realized I was gawping at her and gave the twitch of a smile. "I'll let you in on a secret. Kimball's on his way. I'm only telling you this because you might want to get the hell out of here before he arrives."

And that was a secret? Quite suddenly the lying witch had a face I wanted to punch.

"The security camera?" I pointed up to the air vent. "How long will it take him to get here?"

"Twenty minutes."

I knew a thing or two about cameras. I also knew room views could be accessed remotely via cell phone. Kimball was watching and listening, and he was probably closer than she cared to admit.

"We have a little time then," I said. "Tell me how you met my husband."

Marion set her cup down on the counter. Everything she did seemed too precise, too rehearsed. "The meeting was set up by a client with the agency. I met Ryan at Oreya. Have you been there?"

I nodded. Lush outdoor seating, Mediterranean dining. The view between a palmetto palm and a boxwood topiary two months ago had been, shall we say, *gutting*.

"We aren't given much information. The agency tells us where to meet the client and the nature of the date. Sometimes we're asked to host dinners. Sometimes the client just wants to talk or go to a movie. More of a girlfriend experience. This time, it was a valued client. Kimball wanted me to meet a friend."

Her long fingers pinched the handle of a silver teaspoon in her coffee. A whirlpool of froth. A delicate sip.

"My clients are usually celebrities and politicians," she said. "I'm assuming your next question would be how much I get paid? Five thousand an hour. Sometimes more."

Did she really say five grand?

"It was a Thursday night. Not too busy. I found him sitting by himself. He was listening to the piano and drinking wine. We got talking. I told him I liked singing. He asked me if I knew Helen Shapiro."

Figures. Ryan loved Helen Shapiro.

"I walked over to the piano and started playing. Just a few songs." Her eyes made an arc of the ceiling as if she was losing herself in the past. "I was flattered he asked. Good-looking man and stylish. I liked him from the start."

Ryan? Good-looking and stylish? Marion must have been out to lunch. He was best described as the only hobbit in Hobbiton who combed his hair.

"I didn't know he was married. Not then."

"When did you know?" I asked.

"About five weeks later. He forgot to take off his ring."

Piece of shit.

"He didn't want to talk about it," she said. "Just said he was getting divorced."

My heart was already bruised at the word *divorce*, and more so because Marion knew about it. I felt betrayed and a bit ridiculous at the absurdity of the situation. Here I was talking about my husband to a stranger. A stranger who seemed to know him better than I.

"Please understand I didn't choose to do this," Marion said. "We don't ever get to choose."

"Yet you accepted the invitation?"

"The assignment. Yes. It's a job."

Marion was beautiful. An inaccessible type of beauty enhanced by dead eyes. Shark's eyes. Her back was ramrod straight, an incredible feat when sitting on a bar stool without a high back. She reminded me of a ballerina, shoulders refined and square, and legs that curved in all the right places. I wondered if she ever knew how breathtaking she was. I also wondered why she festered in a place like this. Alone during the day and sometimes at night. I couldn't blame her. It was peaceful in a sick way.

"Did Ryan know you were a hooker?"

"I prefer *escort*." Marion leaned forward and folded slender arms against the countertop. "And no, he didn't know."

My stomach began a rhythmic pounding against the lining of my large intestine before going quiet altogether. "So you never charged him?"

"Not a penny."

31

Everything in the kitchen was quiet. Only the rumble of distant waves and the cry of a gull. No clocks ticked. Not even a digital display on the oven door. Perhaps there had been a power cut.

The smell of Marion's perfume was suddenly very noticeable and her makeup… well, there was a little too much paint on her fence for my liking. She was sweating almost as much as I was.

"I have no intention of leaving," I said. "Not unless you tell me where Ryan is."

"I understand," she said. "But he isn't here. I wouldn't lie about that."

"But he *was* here."

"Yes."

How long would it take for me to find him? I only had a weekend's worth of clothes. Marion and I were roughly the same size and an inch here or there wouldn't make a difference. It was the thought of wearing something that she might have worn for Ryan while she was grinding on top of him like a stripper.

Ryan was never her lover. He wasn't even her friend. Marion had used him.

"I understand you like coffee," Marion said, diction so perfect she could have been educated at the Dalton School in New York. "That is something he told me."

She poured me a cup. I didn't know whether to thank her or slap her.

"What else did he tell you?" I asked. "That I hate warm toilet seats and wet towels? That I take medication and drink wine excessively? That I hate pretentious people? That I hate you?"

We were both quiet for a few seconds, letting the weight of what I had just said sink in. Surely Marion didn't think I liked her? What wife ever *liked* a mistress?

"No. He didn't mention any of that."

I took a sip of fresh coffee and burned my tongue.

"He told me about his work mostly." Her smile appeared forced. "How he hoped he'd get a promotion."

I held up my hand and shook my head. "You have no idea about Ryan. He doesn't care about you. He doesn't *have* to care about you. Nor does your drug-addled pimp. On a side note, does a John, or whatever they're called, seriously qualify as a boyfriend?"

"No."

"It's one big lie, Marion. That's how you pass your time, isn't it? Screwing and lying. You let men do things to you that no other woman would. Perverted things. Then you do a little weed and get high so you can forget how he grabbed your hair and mounted you like an animal. Smiles that aren't smiles and fakely happy faces that will haunt you for the rest of your pitiful life." I listened as the walls of the house creaked in a sudden gust of wind. "These men are trying to recapture their disappointing youths and their brewer's-droop nights. They're more invested in being failures—sucking up your compliments and believing they're the biggest and the best—than they are at fixing a dead marriage. Do they know you're a corpse inside? Do they know you call them tricks?"

"I don't call them tricks."

"Oh no, I forgot. It's the boyfriend experience." I could hear Marion sigh as if I were a giant freaking shotgun she wished was fitted with a special silencer. Only I went on and on. "Did it dawn on you that Ryan had a wife? Do you know what a marriage vow means? One flesh. You… you sliced that flesh in two."

In the silence of that room, Marion's mouth cracked open and her eyes were filmy beneath the pendant lights. She tried to speak, words stumbling behind her lips.

"You have a dangerous job," I said. "Think of the risks. What do you think a wife would do? I'll tell you what she'd do. She'd load her gun and come looking for you. Now you might consider that enough, but the torture has only just begun. Then the slicing. One piece at a time. And if you ever regained consciousness, you wouldn't recognize yourself in the mirror."

"I didn't chose to go out with Ryan. *They* chose it."

"Who's they?"

"The agency—"

"My, my, Marion. Once a sucker, always a sucker."

"They would have ruined me if I'd said no."

"They lied. You're already ruined. The police know what a pile of trash you are. It's only a matter of time. Do you honestly think they give a shit?"

Marion seemed to sit perfectly still for a while listening to something. I sat perfectly still too, smelling her perfume as it spread throughout my body.

"So what did you and Ryan do?" I asked.

She swallowed and there was the tiniest hint of a twitch in her left eye that told me she was hesitant. Frightened even. I knew what she was going to say next.

"We had sex."

Out it popped as if it was the most natural thing in the

world. As if I was meant to respond with *How was it?* Like a bestie bursting with the excitement of it all.

"It didn't mean anything," she whispered.

With Ryan, I only managed to scratch the surface. Deep down, he was a loving man who had become chillingly distant. No point in pretending he harbored some kind of psychological mommy resentment or suffered the rigors of daddy deficit. No childhood is ever easy. But with Marion, he must have been different. Eager. Exultant. He must have been in love.

"Did Ryan know it didn't mean anything?" I asked.

She shook her head.

"No, you're damn right he didn't know. He filed for a divorce, that's how much he didn't know."

I wasn't going to cuss and rant and lose control. Real ladies don't cuss. Women do. There was a difference.

"You don't understand," she said, forehead lined again. "They said the client chose me out of hundreds of women. They told me if I didn't agree to do it I would regret it."

How dare she tell me she had won the bid and in a tone of voice that conveyed some pride. I made sure my face gave nothing away.

"You're nothing like I imagined," she said. "You look like—"

"You." I bet that screwed with her head.

"Yes."

"But you're nothing like me. And you know nothing about me. Nothing real."

"No."

Maybe she did know something about me. Something I didn't even know about myself. Maybe I wanted her to know how valuable I was to Ryan.

Not valuable. Vulnerable.

When they slept together was he on the right and her on the left? Just like we had been. Did he say the same things to her that he used to say to me? Or was it different?

"He said you had red hair," Marion said.

"I dyed it."

I felt the adrenaline pumping through my body and I tried to take deep breaths through my nose. Someone give me a few shots of ethanol. Just a little.

"I think it would be good for you to lie down," she said.

"What?"

"Take a rest. You're sweating and your skin's breaking out in a rash. I don't want you to get all worked up."

Why the heck did my face choose this time to break out in a sweat rash? I wanted to scream I'M NOT GETTING WORKED UP but I knew it was the coffee and I lowered my voice. "I'm fine. Really."

"No. You don't understand," she said. "None of this is normal. You… me… Ryan. Stress like this can make you ill."

"What are you all of a sudden? A nurse?"

"No, I'm just trying to help."

"Help? You wouldn't know what *help* was if it hit you in the face. You haven't helped me and you haven't helped Ryan. Where is he? What have you done with him?"

"Clo." She was pointing a finger now. "I've already told you. Ryan wasn't my boyfriend. He was a client. A J.O.B."

It took me a few seconds to reorient myself. Did she actually spell out the word *job*? "How do I know you're telling me the truth?"

"You don't. But deep inside, you know something changed."

She was right. My marriage had changed. The whole feeling of it had changed. Ryan had suddenly become neglectful, mentally absent, physically abusive. Had he hit her? Had he broken her spirit as he had mine? I remember the long silences he subjected me to more than the things he said.

"I know Ryan—"

"You don't know Ryan," I said. "Not the way I know him. I've got fifteen passionate years on your five lackluster minutes. My husband might have been an asshole, but he was getting plenty of the good stuff at home."

The compassionate frown vanished from her face and I was greeted by a blank stare. The type that resilient toddlers give when they know punishment's coming and there's nothing they can do about it.

"If you must know, I was paid to seduce him. Everything he said was taped." Marion rubbed her forehead and looked down at her coffee. "Don't ask me why. They didn't tell me."

Good God. Why did I wake up every morning only to be pinned down by the dead weight of Ryan's mistake? How terrible.

No... how terribly funny. Ryan had no idea he was the one being screwed.

"Video? Or audio?" I had to know.

"Both."

I wanted to laugh. I wanted to gut the woman my husband was in bed with all drowsy and happy. But here she was with me, sipping coffee and having a good old chinwag. I tried to fit the pieces together in my head and somehow I failed.

"Why would anyone want to tape him?" I asked.

"He said he saw something at work." Marion looked down at her phone and gave the smallest jolt of a scowl.

I was curious now. "Where are these tapes?"

Marion's eyes floated up to the corner of the ceiling again and then darted back to my face. I saw the flicker of a warning in her gaze. "I think you'd better leave."

"Listen, Marion. I want the truth—"

"You don't understand," she said, baring her teeth.

"He's on his way, Clo. I can't help you. I can't even help myself."

The sudden change in her voice gave me the chills and I wondered why there was a tightness in her eyes, where before they had been a dewy brown. She leaned over the island and grabbed my arm, pulling me and pushing me who knows where.

She mashed the garage door remote with her fist and activated the front gate. Gravel crunched underfoot as she grappled at my shirt and dragged me toward my car. My muscles were quivering as I hunkered down into the driver's seat, pulse speeding as she urged me to leave.

"The house... every room has a pinhole," she said. "You know we're being watched."

She kept looking back at the house. Her breathing was labored between each word and I thought she was hyperventilating.

This time, I knew she wasn't lying.

32

I pulled out and made a wide U-turn. The thought of leaving my gun and my suitcase upstairs left a thick knot in my stomach.

Just as I began to accelerate, the automatic gate to the property began to close. I couldn't hope to squeeze through the space without my car being crushed.

When I looked in my rearview mirror, I could see Marion wasn't alone. The man she was standing with could hardly be called homeless, someone who had broken in and held her at knifepoint.

Kimball had been there all the time.

Now a prisoner in his driveway, I felt obliged to get out of the car and assess the obvious. The words *I'm not going to get out of this hellhole* kept looping in my head and rather than stand there and listen to possible escape scenarios, I decided to confront him.

"Is there something wrong with the gate?" I shouted. It was rather pathetic in light of what had just happened.

"Not at all." Kimball shook his head and tightened his grip on Marion's arm. I could see he was hurting her.

"Open the gate," I said.

Kimball dragged Marion with him as he came toward me. "Mrs. Shepherd, isn't it?"

I hated him for trying to spin this into some sort of social engagement and my breath came a little faster.

He peered around my shoulder at the Buick. "Almost made it. I expect you're wondering why I hadn't come down earlier. To be honest, so am I. You're a good looking woman."

"Listen," I said, backing up a few paces and wishing I'd grabbed my phone. "I'd like to go home."

"Oh, really? Looked like you were in this for the long haul. As Marion said, you did barge your way in. It's all on video."

Marion looked up at him and then back at me. I could see she was trying to weigh my chances against a man whose character was stuck somewhere in the 1900s. My thoughts were firing too fast. Him. Marion. How the hell I was going to streak around the house and down to the beach. Because I certainly wasn't going to be locked up in a clunky metal cage or a basement cell.

I took a few more steps toward my car. "I came to find my husband."

"This is hardly the place to talk about it," he said, coming a little closer, "why don't we all have a nice cup of tea? Ladies."

He cocked his head to one side and stared down at me like I was a piece of art. Either he was trying to seduce me or scare me, or he was just being a jerk. His blue eyes seemed to cast a spell I wasn't curious enough to be trapped by and I looked at Marion instead.

"Maybe I've made a mistake," I said. "I must have the wrong address."

Marion shook her head. It was more of a twitch, but there was no mistaking it. I stood rooted to the spot and felt like gagging.

"I think we both know," Kimball said, passing an arm over my shoulders, "This is definitely the right address."

He guided me back into the kitchen. I say *guided*, but it was more like a shove. "A good cup of tea always loosens the tongue and I do love a good story. Don't you?"

One empty coffee cup sat where I had left it, a half-eaten cookie reclining in the saucer. Marion quickly scooped it up and dropped it in the sink under a gush of hot water. There was no sign of my prescription and no sign of the laptop or the printer on the kitchen counter.

"Oolong and hibiscus," Kimball asked Marion before taking my hand and leading me to the living room.

I shuffled beside him like a dead-man-walking. Numb and sick to the stomach. But I wanted to see Ryan. Rather more now than before.

"I want you to be comfortable, Mrs. Shepherd." Kimball pointed to an easy chair opposite the oversized couch he was sitting on. "Have a seat."

Natural light slanted in from the terraced pool area and I couldn't help studying aquamarine hues and a dark wood trim. The room had that right-off-the-beach vibe, the kind of luxury to which I didn't belong. I could hear the distant clink of crockery in the kitchen.

"Best to get it all out in the open, don't you think? I can see you agree. Now, let's talk about Ryan." Kimball loosened the knot of his tie by gently pulling it from side to side. I could hear the swish of silk as he laid it over one knee. "Ryan failed me. He failed the board of directors. Couldn't keep his eyes off my assistant. He was nervous and distracted around her. So distracted he often pretended he couldn't remember her name. That's because he was a pig, Mrs. Shepherd? Are you a pig?"

"No."

"All pigs should be in sties. Fed once a day. It would be wise of them to stay under lock and key to learn their lesson. Will you learn your lesson, Mrs. Shepherd?"

"My lesson?"

"Not to go snooping around other people's property. You see, there's always a price to pay. Ryan was snooping around my office, just like you were snooping around the guesthouse yesterday. In the case of your husband, he saw something he claimed was sexual harassment. A man leaning over my assistant on the boardroom table. He said a humpback whale would have been more subtle."

Kimball brushed the tie with three fingers and shook his head. "It gets better. Ryan wrote it up with HR and my assistant was given her marching orders. The man was never identified because the man—"

"You... You were the man." I took a deep breath and tried to swallow.

"Kerzie Waters, you might remember her. Skin like walnuts and a body... let's say her suits were well tailored. I invited her to a private reception at one of my residences. That's how it started. A little flirting, a little gratuitous sex."

"Why was she fired? She shouldn't have been fired."

"You could say that about anyone entering into an intimate relationship with their boss. She knew the risks. So did I."

"I bet she didn't know you were an asshole."

"I'd say she knew exactly what I was when she took the job."

Marion brought in a tea tray and handed me a cup. There was a slight wobble as I tried to separate the cup from the saucer and the teaspoon did a half-turn before I caught it.

"It depends how you want to play this," he said.

"*Play*? I'm sorry, I'm a little confused."

"Like you, I'm a little guilty, Mrs. Shepherd. Like you, I'm a little curious," he said, making a space for Marion next to him on the couch. "Right now, I'd say you were dying to know where your husband is. The answer? I don't know."

"How do you do it? Lie to someone's face."

"It's like the perfect hit-and-run. Oh, now, don't get all coy. I have surveillance cameras inside and out. The police were very interested in the views from the front of the house. It was the views from the side I neglected to give them. The ones of you walking down the lane to your car, my dear."

The guy was a tool. But if I continued to answer back he would take out a gun and blow off my head. There would be nothing but blood spatter on the wall behind me. Spatter he could wash away with a few layers of paint.

It suddenly went quiet.

Marion's eyes alternated between mine and his. She was as confused as I was guilty. It was no good denying it. The house and surrounding streets were rigged for sound and video. All he had to do was turn me in.

In my wounded mind I murmured a prayer. *Oh God, please don't let him call the police.* A felony seemed too vast, too massive. I felt like an outlaw in a Wild West movie, a tiny speck standing in the middle of a dust-swept town in front of a crowd of gunmen.

"Who's going to remember any of this after a few weeks?" Kimball said, hand caressing his knee.

I took a sip of hot tea. "Of course someone will remember it. People want closure. They'll stick posters up everywhere and hassle the police until they have answers."

A little light began to glimmer in my head, slowly widening to a beam that would have hurt my eyes had I actually been looking into it. He wasn't talking about the incident. He was talking about me. No one was going to remember *me*.

"Karma," Kimball said. He turned toward Marion and smiled. "We've got all the time in the world, haven't we

Lily?"

Lily? Who the heck's Lily?

"You should tell Mrs. Shepherd how we do things around here. Educate her on our great game."

I could see the word *game* excited him as if we were about to raise a few glasses to toast the occasion.

"You know the rules, Lily. No friends. Not here. How could you have let this happen?"

Marion put her cup and saucer on the table and turned slightly to face him. "The ad. She answered the ad."

"My poor darling." He brushed a strand of hair out of her face with a finger. "There's always a cost."

"Listen to me," Marion said. "Every cop in town is looking for her husband right now. They've got access to phone records and they can get a warrant for just about anything. Think about it. You want her to go to the police and tell them who I am? I've got problems. *Bigger* problems."

"I gave you my word I would look after you." His voice was low, almost to a whisper. "We'll have game night for the next three nights. You'd like that, wouldn't you? Make up for lost time."

I shivered just watching them. Kimball was a smoking gun about to become a mushroom cloud, while Marion cowered on the couch, knees drawn up to her chin and arms tucked around her shins. It was only a few steps away from a murder scene.

"P.S., I'm still here," I said.

Small fractures laced his mouth and a fake warmth showed through his smile. "And now that you are here, I would like you to stay."

"What do you mean?"

"Adults have the right to disappear. In your case, taking time off from work doesn't help. I do appreciate there would be no family to look for you and what little family you do have will think you're already dead. You don't talk to your neighbors. And the police? They'll think you have a new boyfriend. People do, you know."

He was right. No one knew where I was. No one knew I was missing. That's what came of keeping myself to myself.

"How—"

"How do I know?" He leaned forward a little. "It takes a stalker to know one. You never saw me? Ever?"

I shook my head. He must have seen all the questions rolling around in my head and all he did was smile. A big, gut-ripping smile.

"You live in a little yellow house on Berkeley Road. Emphasis on *little*. I've followed your husband there many times. And you... you seemed to enjoy parking in the lane without a permit and eating sandwiches in your car as if you belong here. It's illegal, Mrs. Shepherd."

"As illegal as trying to run me off the road into Old Town Pond?"

"It was a warning, my dear."

"Have I been abducted?" I had to ask.

"Not at all. You are our house guest. Just for a few days. And what a few days of fun and games it will be."

Oh God, get me out of here. I had screwed up. He knew. He had seen.

My car was unlocked, driver's door open in the driveway and handbag on the passenger seat. I had no cell phone. Things were going to get really bad. Really fast.

Lieutenant Joe would be returning my book soon. He would knock on my front door of my house until he got an answer and when he didn't he would come looking for me.

"I'm not going to hurt you, Mrs. Shepherd, and I know how much you want to hear about Ryan. You do want to know about Ryan?"

"Yes," I said. I could hear a shake in my voice and it was quieter than normal.

"Call it what you want. It can't have been much of a marriage. Three days a week with the woman he loved. Four with you. That's why you're here, isn't it? To meet the other woman."

Marion was staring at me like a territorial wildcat and I felt like a mouse scurrying for a rock to hide under.

"I came to find Ryan," I said firmly.

I looked from Marion to Kimball and wondered why he kept referring to her as Lily. A quick dash for the front door suddenly looked hopeful, provided there wasn't someone else hiding out in the hallway. I would have to run behind the couch he was sitting on and I didn't hold out much hope that he wouldn't try and lunge for me.

"Ryan made a fool of you, Mrs. Shepherd. He made a fool of me. It was a travesty. His smug face, his... insistence to do the right thing. Calling a board member, who, by the way, was a compulsive cheater and had just as much interest in women as the rest of us. Waters was used to the wear and tear. She was rented out, so to speak. I rewarded her for stepping up. Don't feel sorry. The judge didn't. They both enjoyed her. But Ryan didn't do his research. He was a fool. The same cannot be said of you."

I started to feel cold. Not in my feet. In my belly, where it funneled down to my groin and spread out over the top of my thighs, where I knew there were tiny little pinpricks of chicken flesh. The board of directors and a judge allowed this type of behavior? Condoned it, even.

I was scared. Really scared.

"Where is he? Where's Ryan?" I asked.

"He'll surface soon enough, my dear."

33

I wondered if Kimball was feeding me a pile of bullshit. Ryan was probably tied up in the attic waiting for me to find him.

It was a big house. Dormer windows in the roof and bedrooms with million dollar views of the North Atlantic Ocean.

I took another sip of tea and found it calming.

"Do you like plays, Mrs. Shepherd?"

"Plays?"

"Yes. Ballet. Opera. Stage."

"I suppose."

A shadow of disgust passed across his face as if he saw me as a philistine who didn't belong in the Metropolitan Opera House or Broadway for that matter. Or here.

"There's always a first time for everything," he said. "Lily has a beautiful voice and I have a grand piano."

It took me a nanosecond to reply. "I love ballet. Hate opera."

"Why?"

"Too much vibrato." Where I had heard the saying I

couldn't recall but it sounded academic enough. "It's ridiculously championed by public funds and the acting is crap."

"I suppose you agree with Twain. Wasn't it he who said it was all an incoherent noise which reminded him of the time the orphan asylum burned down? Perhaps you're right, Mrs. Shepherd. Perhaps I shouldn't believe everything I read."

What type of person looks down on another for not enjoying opera? There was no way I was going to kiss ass.

I wanted to excuse myself to use the bathroom but for some unfathomable reason I couldn't feel my legs.

Bathroom... there had to be a window in there big enough to crawl though.

"We could prattle on all afternoon," he said. "But you need your rest. She looks tired, doesn't she, Lily?"

Marion nodded without smiling.

"So helpful to bring a bag of prescription sedatives, Clo," he said. "I can call you Clo, can't I?"

I tried to stand and wobbled backwards against the chair. My head hit the backrest and all I could do was stare at him, focus getting cloudier by the minute.

* * * *

I couldn't figure out what had woken me. The open window and a set of white drapes billowing out like two giant spinnakers, or the fact that someone was playing the piano in the next room.

I tried to wake up and all I could do was lie there mesmerized by the fact that I was wearing a night gown. Someone had undressed me. I hoped it was Marion. But it certainly wasn't her who had carried me.

I threw off the quilt, legs dangling off the edge of the bed. I wasn't weak, nor was I going to collapse at any moment. I put it down to being amply caffeinated before the sedative.

My clothes had been laundered; shirt and jeans pressed and hanging over a button-tufted chair. I tugged at both and noticed they were still warm. Someone had left them recently and it gave me an indication of how long I had slept. Long enough for a full wash and dry cycle and not long enough to have been fully drugged.

I slipped into the en suite bathroom and opened the closet to check my gun. It was still snuggled between two face towels and I moved it down a shelf.

I gagged a few times and held my hand under the cold tap, taking small sips. I squinted at hardware that gave a nod to feminine beauty and mother-of-pearl inlay. The white pedestal sink was equipped with just about every fragrance of soap known to man. This was how the privileged lived.

Pulling on my jeans and shirt, I crept back into the bedroom. The bathroom was likely wired for sound and video, and it was pointless thinking I wasn't being watched, even in the closet.

A soft swish caught my attention and I whipped my head toward the window; a two-panel slider was closing all by itself. It took me a few seconds to grasp that someone was operating it remotely and a few more seconds to identify a gray sheet of metal beyond it, rolling downward like an eyelid.

I held my breath and tasted the bile in my throat. It was as if I had been sealed in the hull of a large ship, where soon I would hear the groan of metal and the popping of wrought iron rivets before the water gushed in.

I gave the blinking fire alarm the finger, the only place I could conceive a hidden camera. If Kimball was watching I wasn't apologizing.

The door was unlocked and I peered out into the corridor at walls as smooth as they were thick. The sound of the piano came from the landing, a familiar waltz I had heard many times before. Couldn't place it. I was never good at names but it was one of those tunes you could hum along to.

I was about to go back and get my gun when I saw Marion, hair tied in a knot and a waterfall of curls swept over one shoulder. Elegant fingers stopped tapping the keys as she turned to look at me. At any other time she would have been the essence of grace and nobility, but her corset had been ripped open at the back and blood glistened between the laces.

"Marion?"

She looked like she was about to collapse into a fog of depression and the bruises on her wrists told me everything I needed to know. Kimball was a sicko. If this was how he had punished Marion, I dreaded to think what he had done to Ryan.

"Where is he?" I whispered, feeling oddly detached, as if my emotions weren't firing right.

"He went out to get something. I don't know what, so don't ask."

"What happened?"

"Nothing."

"Oh, *please*. Something happened, otherwise you wouldn't be sitting here in a…" I waved my hand in the air, "whatever it is you're wearing all covered in blood. Was it him?"

She nodded.

"Well, that's great. That's really great. Something to be proud of," I said. "You know something, Marion? You're pathetic. First, you slip me a Mickey and *then* you take off my clothes and put me to bed. Why? So he could beat the crap out of you without a witness."

"Yes."

I stood perfectly still and stared down at two watery eyes and a girl playing dress-up. It made me wonder if she was a flat-out pansy or just plain stoned. I thought I had problems.

There was a distant possibility that she was almost as incapacitated as I had been a few hours ago. It was about time I did something.

"Marion, where's your phone?"

"He took it. He took all of them." She stood and took my hand, folded it over her arm just as Kimball had done. "He's watching us. He can hear us too."

I could hear the rolling mechanism of the hurricane shutters downstairs as each dropped in unison, blocking out the only light we had. All operated remotely and at the press of a button.

I struggled against her arm, broke free and raced downstairs. Lurching from one room to another, banging on windows and doors and flicking every switch I could find. She was right. There was no way to open the shutters and there were no phones.

I searched the kitchen for the laptop. The cupboards, the drawers, the mudroom. He seemed to have taken that too. I returned to the sitting room a panting mess of frustration and sweat. She was sitting on the couch.

"What about the doors, Marion. The front door... the French doors. What about them?"

"All doors are wireless—"

"There must be a key... to override the locks. A switch."

"There's no way out."

I understood electronic access was to keep burglars out, not to keep people in. The system had to oppose every residential fire regulation in New York. Now every window was a blur of shades. No light.

"You see how it is?" she said, sobbing. "I made him mad."

I slouched next to her on the couch and locked eyes with her as she perched on the corner, back straight so as not to stain the fabric.

"You need a doctor," I said. "Those cuts will get infected. They'll scar."

"Bleeding cleans out the wound," she said, blotting the corner of her eye with a handkerchief. "Best to let it dry."

Best to get to urgent care, I thought. Get a good dose of antibiotics and gauze to stop the wound from chaffing against her clothes. But there was no way out and every view was a gray wall. The gun was the only thing that stopped me going stir-crazy. Still snug in the bathroom. I had already checked.

So Kimball had web-based video. Ran audits on all locks and lock times, where updates are sent to his phone regularly.

I had to think of something else.

34

"Listen," I said, feeling a little burnt out. "Got anything to drink?"

I wanted to make Marion feel comfortable and to give Kimball a false sense of security. After all, a full-throttle breakout wasn't out of the realms of possibility. Not if I could pick a lock.

Another idea did spring to mind. To hold her at gunpoint and yell at the nearest camera. But something told me Kimball wasn't as invested in Marion as she was in him. Blackmail like that never had a happy ending and the thought of being blanketed in hours of non-stop night were hours I'd rather share with another human being.

It was easy to forget the nightmare in such lavish surroundings and somehow it felt like a vacation. There wasn't much choice but to relax, even if I was hermetically sealed inside a house controlled remotely by a raving lunatic. I had to draw Marion out and socializing was the only way I knew how.

She poured two glasses of gin and set them on the coffee table in front of a nest of decorative pots. I had never drunk the stuff to be honest. But now seemed like a good time to get better acquainted with my threshold. Was I a lightweight? Or a heavyweight? I suspected the former.

I smiled a warm smile and lifted my glass in a toast. "To you and me and all this craziness."

Craziness? The whole thing was insane.

"I'll drink to that," she said.

I looked around the great room. There had to be a pinhole camera somewhere, concealed on a shelf, behind a parlor palm or inside an air duct. Kimball had to go to sleep at some point and whether or not the lens had some kind of night vision capability, it was possible to disarm the place after dark.

"I'm sorry," Marion whispered, putting her glass on the coffee table. "I had a bad feeling this was going to happen. Thing is, he gets aggressive when he's crossed."

"And that's supposed to make me feel better?"

"It makes him feel in control. Wait until morning. He'll open the shutters and the windows for the house plants. He likes to think he's a horticulturist."

A professional plantsman. That was good to know. For a crazy moment, I wondered if the CCTV reached as far as the hole I had dug on the beach. I seized a breath.

"Why does he call you Lily?" I asked.

"It's a long story."

"It's going to be a long night."

I angled my glass to my lip, smelling berries and the warmth of holidays. Kept her in the periphery of my vision as she leaned back against the couch and closed her eyes. She can't have felt any pain because her lips moved as if she were in a trance.

"When I first started out," she said, "I never cared about any of them. The boys at school, the one night stands. Then I got to thinking. Why do it for free? There's all sorts on the streets and they want a large piece of you.

A piece I wasn't prepared to give. There was something different about this opportunity. I had visions about the client. Unrealistic visions. It turned a blank face into serious money. A big step up from the occasional pleasure seekers." She opened her eyes and turned her head toward me. "I was told this man was a hobbyist. Required a girlfriend experience three nights a week."

I topped up her glass.

"The agency also told me that he needed a certain type of pleasure, that his appetites were, well… singular." Marion took a sip of her gin, bottom lip sliding slowly off the rim of the glass. "What they didn't tell me was the unimaginable suffering he enjoys inflicting on people."

I took the glass away from her and set it back on the table. I wanted to hear this and I wanted her sober enough to tell it.

"He has fantasies about chorus girls. Five in particular. Maude Fealy, Julia James, Ethel Warwick, Lily Elsie and Evelyn Nesbit. I have played nearly all of them. Shall I tell you how it goes?"

"Tell me," I said.

"Two days before a meeting, he sends me a music score. He expects me to be perfect. I have to sing and dance just as they did. Sometimes I get it right. Sometimes I don't. When I don't, he breaks me down with a slap. Or a choke. But never this."

Marion wasn't Kimball's brand of crazy. He didn't accept her passions and her flaws. Instead, he demeaned her, pointed out every fault. He was probably a master at it. I knew Frances and Robert assisted Marion in setting each scene but they were gone by the time Kimball arrived. They couldn't have known the suffering.

"Does he have fixed days, fixed times?" I asked, trying to get a better picture of my jailer.

"Not always. Sometimes he likes to surprise me. He says suspense is good for me. Keeps me on the edge of my seat. Of course, those times are unscripted," she said. "He's tender then. More affectionate."

Kimball didn't know shit about suspense, unless he was alluding to the horror movie type of suspense, where you didn't see the axe murderer hiding behind the curtains. But what if I was the one hiding behind the curtains? The loner, the girl with no friends, no family. The stereotypical serial killer reinforced by the media and forensic investigation shows. The type of killer he should have been afraid of.

"And the other times?" I asked.

"He says cruel things, words I don't want to hear. I shut my ears, pretend I'm that woman... the woman he wants me to be."

Every time she dropped her eyes I examined her. Why was Marion everything I wanted to be? Classy where I was crass, graceful where I was awkward. When I looked in the mirror last week, it was her smile I saw, her elegant hands reaching for fruit in the produce aisle.

"How long have you been doing this?" I asked.

"Since I was a teenager. I worked on the front desk at The Mill House Inn on North Main. It was my mom's idea. She told me I'd meet a lot of people that way. Especially men. I guess I did because my boss found out I was dating one of the residents. He told me I was a slut. I began to wonder if I really was."

"A slut? You dated one guy and you're a slut?"

"I broke one of the cardinal rules. No dating residents."

"So what happened to this guy?"

"He wasn't as single as he made out. His wife was a plastic surgeon, a good one. Only he liked his women thin. She was... stocky."

Love, the unscratchable itch and a wife who was starting to pork up. Why did this man have to go out for milk when he'd got two perfectly good jugs at home?

"How did you know he was married?"

"I followed him home once. A perfect house with a private beach and a Juliet balcony on the third floor. He didn't look unhappy, Clo. Not from where I was standing."

"Where were you standing?"

"In the woods… at the back of the property. Saw four kids diving into the swimming pool and her in a floppy hat on a sun lounger."

"So you admitted defeat and walked away a wiser woman?"

"I walked away with blood on my hands."

Shit! Did she say blood? I tried to put Marion in a category—give it a name—but for some reason I couldn't come up with anything suitable. She was a runaway and a throwaway. The man she once loved had seen to that.

"I really loved him," she said. "He was my first. You never forget your first. I swear to you, the way he dated me, the way he loved me, I had no idea he had a family."

"You said blood."

"I said *blood* because I killed her."

My heart missed a beat. Two. Three.

"I followed her early the next day," she said. "I remember the sun was really orange, creeping through the trees along 7th Avenue. Blinding enough to put on my sunglasses. I must have driven for about a minute before I called her cell phone. She picked up and listened to what I had to say all the way to the Tennis Club. Then just before the bend, I accelerated. My front bumper caught her rear fender and her car did a full circle before skidding off the road into a wooden fence. I parked a little way up the road and ran back. There was blood all over the windshield and the airbag. I couldn't get any closer because of the flames and the smoke. Lights came on in the house behind the fence, the one by the tennis courts. I knew they'd heard the crash and I knew they'd come out and help her."

How achingly familiar. "So you ran."

"Yes." Marion wiped one eye. "I never loved another man after that. I know what you're thinking. You're thinking I should leave this house, leave Kimball and his stupid games. The answer is, I can't. He knows."

Sadomasochistic bastard. He'd trapped Marion as well as me for a hit-and-run and now we were locked in a fatal game. It was play or be played.

"Two months later I had a phone call," she said. "One of those private unlisted numbers. It was a man's voice. He told me he had witnessed the accident. Said he wouldn't go to the cops as long as I went out with him a couple of times. Wanted me to see the tape. He gave me his address and I went over. Only it wasn't his house. It was a rental. He told me to go in, make myself comfortable. There was a bottle of wine and a glass in the kitchen and a note. It told me to press *play* on the remote. There I was on the TV. I have no idea how he taped me."

"Did you meet him?"

"I found him in the bedroom like he said. Naked. Wearing a mask. I did what he asked me to do and then left. I didn't hear from him until a few months ago."

"Until this particular assignment," I said.

"Which is why he chose me. Not because I was one in a hundred on the website and he just had to have me. But because he wanted me to pay for what I had done. It's a small world, Clo. The woman I killed was in the newspapers. Her name was Anna Schellenbeck. She was Kimball's sister."

Oh crap. It would be just my sodding luck if the coastguard I had hit was his long-lost cousin.

"Does he have any more relatives?" I asked.

"A younger brother in San Francisco. His picture was in Forbes two years ago." She shook her head. Bit her lip. "And I thought Kimball was smart."

"Did you meet him?"

She nodded. "Xander. He's a psychologist."

We could all do with one of those.

"Between you and me, he has a share in this property. Kimball wanted to buy him out but Xander wouldn't hear of it. Emotional ties."

"Were you more than friends?"

She smiled. "*More* means *better*. More money—plus more status—equals handsome. He's got all of it. So, I'll keep whether or not I slept with him to myself."

Marion clearly wasn't looking for a match. She was looking for a jackpot. Xander could have half his face burned in a fire and here was Marion who couldn't find Paris on a map but really wanted to go there because it was economically hip. "Good memories, huh?"

"Memories? I don't have many good ones."

The type of memories I could see Marion having were those that sliced into her flesh and clung like limpets to each layer of her brain. Memories that every now and then caused an explosion of pain so sharp it was as if Kimball had just struck her all over again.

I wanted to ask how many times she had been slandered and choked in order to pay for the murder. The pain must have been beyond her worst nightmares. She was already fractured and numb and if she didn't get out Kimball would kill her before I did. Now only one voice penetrated in my head, one clear thought.

Marion would die.

I couldn't feel sorry for a woman whose tomorrow would only bring more misery. Here she was hoping there would be no tomorrow. I wanted to give her that hope.

"I'm sorry." I said, even though I wasn't sure I meant it. "You're going to need every ounce of strength to put up a damn good fight."

A sound came from somewhere at the other end of the house. I held my breath.

"He's on his way," she said. She stood now with her

back to me, eyes fixed on the lamp like a moth drawn to its beam. "Tie my corset, would you, Clo?"

The pathos of her voice made me want to smash her head against the wall. "Marion! Don't you want to get out? Don't you want to get away from this home-made hell? How difficult can it be? You have your own car, for crying out loud."

"I want you to go back to your room and lock the door. Don't come out, no matter what."

I stood behind Marion and tied the laces, folding the stained portions of the chemise inside the corset. She hardly flinched.

I leaned over her shoulder and whispered, "You don't have to let him blackmail you. Go to the police. Tell them it was accident. They can't prove you rammed the crap out of her. We'll find the tape and destroy it. Both tapes."

"I signed a contract."

"Contracts can be broken. There must have been a termination clause. Negotiation over illness, other party breach, that kind of thing."

"Yes, there was."

"Good. Because a contract isn't valid if you're being abused," I said. "Come on, Marion. It's not even legal. I have friends in law enforcement. Do you want to get out? Because I can get you out."

I said it loudly for the benefit of the eye in the sky. If the asshole was listening then let him hear. Let him think I was alerting the cavalry.

"I mean it. I have *friends*."

The only friend I could think of was Joe and he was expecting a text. Since I had stood him up, there was less than a twenty-five percent chance he would want to help me.

Marion turned to face me, hands straightening a diamond choker at her neck. "How do I look?"

I groaned.

"Do you know what distinguishes a real lady from a fake?" she asked. "Class. You either have it or you don't. Do you know who I am tonight?"

I shook my head.

"I am Lily Elsie. The Merry Widow. It's a beautiful operetta."

I didn't want to think of her acting out some sick fantasy for Kimball to play, dressing the way he wanted her to dress. But there was something about her voice, a resignation that gave me the chills.

We both heard the wheeze of the garage door, the only part of the house unsealed by shutters. Marion placed two fingers against my mouth and shook her head, motioning for me to get back to my room. I would have made a dash for it but the garage door came purring down. Then a rattle of keys in the connecting door to the kitchen.

I could feel the buildup of adrenaline inside me like the fizz of a soda from a freshly opened bottle. I ran upstairs. I knew Kimball would subject her do all manner of humiliation but what I couldn't imagine was Marion forcing herself to smile demurely and wantonly, whether or not her mind rejected it.

I can't have been in my room for more than a minute, before I heard his voice in the corridor.

"You're drunk. You filthy, disgusting whore. You're drunk!"

I heard a crack and then a loud thud. My heartbeat thrashed in my ears and I almost passed out from the lack of air.

It was about to start all over again.

35

I was a prisoner in sicko-land and I had no idea what time it was. Kimball had either removed or disarmed every clock in the house.

There was no time to fawn over hand-crafted pieces, one-of-a-kind deco and silk rugs worth well over seventy grand. Instead, my hands were pressed against a closed door, listening to every breath of air as if it were my last.

I gazed up at the ceiling, to the air vent. Too small to crawl through because houses were rarely designed with the large industrial conduits associated with businesses. There was no way out and my mind churned over and over. There had to be a computer around here or some way I could access the internet. The whole place was a technological marvel and since Kimball clearly loved secrets, it was time to reveal a few of mine.

I was thankful my gun was still where I had left it. If there was a camera hidden in my room, it would have focused on the wad of shirts I had taken out of my case. No way would Kimball have seen I was unpacking anything other than clothes.

I paused at a scuffling sound in the corridor followed

by a squeak on the hard wood floor. As if someone was dragging a mattress across the carpet, shoes taking the corner too fast. I wanted to go back for my gun but I was afraid of the cameras, afraid to show the ace in the pack before I was ready.

I curled my fingers around the door handle. The corridor was empty except for three brownish red streaks on the carpet. I took off my shoes and padded along the corridor to the stairs. The stairwell was lit by a pendant lamp, which cast a halo effect along the hall walls.

It was deserted.

My fingers made swirly patterns on the smooth banisters, while my eyes absorbed every shadow, every detail so I would become familiar with my new prison.

Then a distant click. A creaky floorboard. Not from the bedrooms behind me or from downstairs. But from somewhere above my head.

There. Another click.

Twisting my head back to listen, I felt my breath come faster.

Slowly, I told myself. *Easy now.*

I took a swallow and waited.

Over the next couple of seconds, I heard a familiar sound. A rumble high up in the vault of the house as if a picture vibrated against a wall from a heavy tread.

There was a way in, if I recalled, a staircase accessible from the mudroom behind the kitchen. A butler's pantry, if you will. But I knew before I tried the door that it was locked.

I ran from room to room, staring at grayed out and sealed windows. There was no way to manually override the storm shutters and no light switches with which to operate them. It was the sound of breathing that turned my head. Soft panting as if someone was jogging.

A bar of blue light seeped under the library door and I made my way unsteadily toward it. Propping myself against the frame, I tapped away a metal doorstop with my foot and pushed down on the handle. It griped and whined. If there was anyone in there, my presence had been duly noted.

Worn leather couches and chairs. A coffee table. An open file. White painted shelves lined three walls, books regimented within each frame. There was no one there.

The flickering lights had come from a TV hanging on the far wall, where sounds throbbed with a deep pulse. Lovers' limbs, like muscular snakes, writhed on white cotton sheets. Perpetually ravenous.

Who… But I knew who.

Sobs threatened to choke me and my hand instinctively reached out for support. The room warped and waned and I felt my breath coming faster. Ragged. Unlike anything I had ever heard.

A voice sounded through an intercom. Kimball, loud and whispery, like a defective train station announcer.

"You wanted to know what happened to Ryan, Mrs. Shepherd. Why don't you sit down and watch?"

A feeling of emptiness welled up in my chest and I almost collapsed on the couch. He would have walked past my bedroom and seen the open door, knew I was downstairs trying to get out.

Oh God, oh God…

"Mrs. Shepherd," the station announcer said, "there is a file on the coffee table. I think you should read it."

I sat down then. No sooner had I opened the file than the video paused, where limbs were too grainy to make out.

There were two letters in the file. The first was more of a memo, informing Ryan the house he frequently visited to receive sexual favors belonged to David Kimball, president of Kimball Aerospace. The same company Ryan had been finance manager for the past seven years.

The second letter, referencing the words *Termination of Employment* was addressed to Ryan and copied to the board of directors.

Dear Mr. Shepherd,

This letter references our discussion during the April Board of Directors Meeting and subsequent discussions we had with you regarding your claim against the CEO, Mr. David Kimball and his assistant, Ms. Kerzie Waters.

Having conducted a thorough and impartial investigation into the report of sexual harassment against Ms. Waters, we found no witnesses or any X-rated material in both audio and visual form to substantiate this claim.

We regret to state that despite giving sufficient opportunity to resolve this misunderstanding, there has been little or no effort on your part to reconcile. Moreover, your claim was considered by the company as untrue and unwarranted.

In order to reduce the adverse impact on team members, the management offered to relocate you twice. First to Kimball Aerospace in Texas and second to our office in Washington. We also warned you to abstain from any further rumor that might endanger or defame the reputation of the company. However, despite giving sufficient opportunities it has been observed that you still wish to sue the company for sexual misconduct and abuse.

Considering the seriousness of the matter, it has been decided by the company to terminate your employment with immediate effect.

You are hereby advised to return to the company any property that was handed over to you during your tenure.

Thank you.

Milo Franklin

Chairman of the Board.

c.c. The Law Office of Kuykendoll & Mayle.

So Ryan had been fired because he saw Kimball screwing his secretary. The pinhead.

"I expect you have a few questions," the speaker sniped. "You can talk to me. I can hear you."

Great, I thought. The bastard could also see me. How else would he know I had finished reading the accusations my husband had brought against the company?

"I remember now," I said.

"What do you remember?"

"The Christmas party. You were playing dice."

"And?"

"You lost."

"That's very observant," he said. "There must have been something about me that fascinated you."

There had been something. Hair a mixture of black and white and a keen stare. Or was it the wink of his cufflinks, the cut of his suit, the money laid out on the table? There had been so much of it. No, it was the women, pandering, fawning, groping. Women in tight dresses who couldn't wait to get near him. Women on offer at a company party. I had to agree there was something absurdly striking about him.

"Was Marion there?" I asked.

"Yes. It's where Ryan first saw her. A trail of dazzling crumbs. Bait for a hungry wolf."

Hungry? What part of Ryan was hungry? "So you hire Marion to fulfil your sick little fantasies and in return video her having sex with my husband?"

"It's the pot calling the kettle black. And as you've already figured, undermines his claim against us. Visual association tends to jog a few memories in the courtroom, Mrs. Shepherd. You of all people should know that."

"Were the tapes of him and Marion dated?" My eyes reluctantly skimmed over the television screen, which was fortunately still paused.

"I think it best to assume they were. We do our best to make sure all loose ends are tied."

"So where is my husband?"

"All in good time, my dear. Please make yourself at home. Have a pleasant evening."

There were too many similarities, too many coincidences. It was making my mind whirl.

The TV livened up after that, more grunts and groans and then Ryan made that noise he always made. A loud exhalation of breath before he lay face up on the bed beside her. Marion rolled over and placed one thigh over his belly. She was smiling as they talked about mundane things and then whispered things I didn't like.

"I love you," he said.

There was something about my husband saying that to someone else that made me ball my fists. But I couldn't tear myself away.

"So," she said, "I should ask you about work but you never want to talk about it."

"I don't mind talking about it. It's just… Listen," he said, leaning over on one elbow. "I don't want anything to happen to you."

"Nothing's going to happen to me. I don't know any of your work colleagues and they don't know me."

"I was threatened." He dragged one hand over his head. "I was told if I asked any more questions I'd be fired and if I hired an attorney I'd be sorry. I don't know how they knew. They always *know*."

"You did the right thing coming here. You're safe. Isn't it better to be safe than sorry?"

He took a handful of her hair and rolled it around one finger. "I guess."

"So, what happened?"

"I think my boss caught a whiff of something." Ryan made a sound as if he didn't want to go any further.

"Such as?"

"Such as I think his admin was assaulted. I told a few others. Probably shouldn't have."

"Maybe it's nothing."

"I'm serious. I think he's following me."

"Did he follow you here?"

"No, I don't think so. But I need your help. I need somewhere to stay."

"You can use one of the guesthouses."

"Just a couple of weeks. My apartment will be ready then. I need to lay low. Until this whole thing blows over."

"You mentioned you told a few others?"

"Yeah. My neighbor. Flat out told him. Lawsuits can be tricky before you settle. I hope he kept it to himself."

"What's he like, this neighbor?" Marion asked.

"Joe? Nothing to tell really. But he's discreet. I can trust him."

Good old Joe, I thought. Never told a soul. Never told *me*. Here I was thinking he was snuggling up to me to buy information, when all along he might have been trying to help me.

"Listen, Mo," Ryan said. "I don't want you repeating anything, okay? The CEO's crazy. They're all crazy."

Mo? He had to be kidding. He called her *MO!*

I watched him stand up and walk toward the shower. He turned and put his hand against the doorframe. "Got anything unscented? It's just that my wife keeps sniffing the back of my hair and... well, she's gotta know something's going on. We haven't had sex in months."

Bastard! I could have clawed that TV screen to shreds.

"You still sleep together?" she asked.

"The couch gets old after a while and the spare room's full of her photography equipment. Wanna know about Clodagh?" he said and didn't wait for Marion to say *yes*. "I'll tell you about her. Dull wife, dull life. Well, shit, of course life is dull after... what is it? Fifteen years? She's overweight and thankfully over there," he said, pointing in the vague direction of the western horizon. "I can't take it anymore. Her psycho crap."

"Does she take medication?"

"Hell, yeah. That's the problem. Alcohol *and* medication. If she wants sex she can find some creep in a homeless shelter. She can't promise to make it fun anymore. She tried her damnedest last week to jack up the heat. Asked me to take her to dinner, which in Clodagh-language means something else. Only I didn't fancy something else."

"Come back to bed," she said, patting the mattress.

He started forward and then stopped. "There's something magical about you and me. Do I sound crazy?"

"No," she said, eyes floating over his body. "I feel the same way."

She gave a soft croon here and there, and her eyes were fixed in a salacious stare, kind of blank, if that's how it's done. She was sitting on the bed with her knees tucked under her chin and then, very slowly, she let one knee drop.

Ryan walked back toward the bed and grabbed her by the hair. I must have flinched when she did. But then her contorted features relaxed into that same blank smile and she sucked on her bottom lip.

I got the chills watching them and I tried to erase the image of limbs entwined as they purred and writhed like cats in the sun. But I couldn't.

I began to sob.

36

I tried to battle another wave of disgust. A porn movie starring my own husband. It was probably all over YouTube.

I wanted to shout at him. To tell him that call-girls always fake orgasms and any cheap-ass mention of the wife was an act of sheer cowardice. But I knew he would only stare at me in that way he did. Inappropriately unemotional. Unstable. Guilt-ridden. He was like a cloud of bad weather you couldn't avoid.

Love.

If he was watching me on some monitor in a tight crawl-space, I was his nightmare come true. Different on the outside. Sanded. Polished. A guise of sexual spontaneity. A threat to his masculinity.

Honor.

But on the inside... a sociopath. A killer. Two words so poisonous when said out loud. So who gets the last laugh now, Ryan?

Obey.

I should have licked my finger and drawn a *one* in the air. No longer a rose shriveling against the noise but a prickly thorn bush. Bristling. Stabbing.

No point mentally poking the bruise, Clo. Because you are poking and he's not here to poke.

I turned my mind to the house. There had to be a way out. The only person who had any inkling of where that would be was lying in a bloody heap upstairs.

I was sorry. I really was, because Marion was my only answer to freedom. Best be nice to the bitch and heal her wounds. Because tomorrow Mo-the-Ho would die.

Kimball was suspiciously quiet. He could ignore me all he wanted or be entertained by the glossy eyes I kept wiping. But if he was the gentleman Marion claimed he was, then the next move was mine.

It was then I understood the meaning of dumped. Kicked to the curb. Most women would have freaked out by now. Not me. Isn't it desperation that makes a person dangerous?

I hightailed it upstairs to where I had heard Kimball dragging something across the floor. Followed the smears to Marion's room and tried the handle. It was locked.

"Marion!" I rapped a knuckle on the door. Then I began pounding. "Open the damn door!"

I could hear the sound of a groan, punctuated by a few sobs. She must have been really banged up this time.

"Hold on," she murmured.

I could hear bare feet against the floor, no longer slinky and carefree like the girl in the *J'Adore* commercial. I was shocked to see the once bouffant bun had spilled over one ear like a liquefied cottage loaf.

"Marion," I said. "You look like shit."

She pulled me into her bedroom and almost hurled me across the room. "Keep your voice down!"

I don't know if it was the combination of her snapping at me and finding myself thrust against the bed, but I shrugged her off.

"Don't touch me. Don't *ever* touch me!"

"Stop it!" she hissed, grabbing a pillow and pushing it against my face. "Just stop it."

I threw the pillow across the room. My first kick caught the side of her hip. The second sent her back against a chair. The howl when it came should have hindered me but I came on like a wildcat, scratching, biting. Slapping.

We both must have let out synchronized manic grunts as we punched and tugged on clothing. There was no stopping me until I yanked her hair and she knelt on the floor begging me to stop.

I stopped.

Let her drop into a crouch as I ran an agitated hand through a mop of my own hair, thoughts whirring through my mind.

"I saw the tapes. You and Ryan." I glared down at her and tightened my lips. "Are you going to deny that too?"

"No, no." She was clutching her waist, breath coming in gasps. "Clo, please."

Her voice dripped remorse and beneath it I caught a thread of terror. I wanted to punch the fear from her face and the words from her mouth. But the bitch raised a hand to ward me off.

"You don't understand—"

"You were screwing my husband! Look at you? Filthy bitch. Did he know what you were?"

It struck me for the first time that I not only had the capacity to kill Marion, but the desire to do so. What would Lieutenant Joe say to that? Except that I had worked with law enforcement long enough to know there was no way to hide a bloody mess. I couldn't risk a homicide. No, Marion's death *had* to look like a suicide.

"It wasn't like that…" Her voice trailed off as she struggled to stand. "I didn't…"

I tried to fight off a wave of nausea. Ryan was actually going to marry this woman? Over my dead body.

No. Over hers.

She kept hugging herself and trying to catch her breath over the sobs. I could see she was in agony.

Between the braless slouchy sweat shirt she was wearing and a pair of low-slung yoga pants, were the raised ridges of fresh cuts. Some were still bleeding.

"He really beat the crap out of you this time." I said, scanning her tears with satisfaction.

"I told you," she said, stooping slightly. "He likes surprises."

"Well, *surprise!* At least you're still alive."

She nodded. She *actually* nodded.

"You can't love him," I said. "And if you say you do, I'll assume you're tolerant of his bullshit and actually quite enjoy it."

"He broke one of my ribs." She rolled up the sweatshirt, where a brown gauze bandage was wrapped tightly beneath her bust. "Do you think I enjoyed it?"

I knew it wasn't the first time she had taken full hammering, unless the scars on her belly were from an operation. A person rarely sustained injuries like that from falling into furniture or in the shower, which begged the question of how abusive Kimball really was.

"Why?" I asked.

The upside of her injuries was there was no easier target than a victim sorely disabled. Kimball got a pat on the back from me.

"Kimball doesn't… doesn't like me drinking or smoking. Hates it."

I took one step toward her. "So he just beats the crap out of you to teach you a lesson."

"Yes."

My smile would have widened if I hadn't caught it in time.

"From now on, things are going to change," she said, hands spread in an open gesture. "We're going to work this out. Together. I want to get even. You want to get even. We're in the same boat."

"Bullshit, Marion."

"I'm serious. I'm sick... of being used. Sick of being pushed around. Sick of him holding a... shotgun to my head and threatening to blow my brains out. And now... now we can't get out. This is his house, Clo. He's the only one with a key."

Yes. The house. I scrubbed a hand over my face and studied the bedroom. Another exquisitely furnished room that ran from the front of the house to the back. There was a giant TV hanging on the wall above a dresser, which was covered in a glass forest of perfume bottles. A terrace that would have looked out onto the front driveway and another facing the sea. Easy to jump if you'd done a skydiving course.

Did Kimball have a shotgun? Probably and it was likely one of those pump action thingies that just went on and on. I didn't fancy a face-off if his was bigger than mine.

"It's gone too far. This wasn't my idea. It was *his*." Her chest bobbed a few inches and tears glossed her chin. "He said he was coming back."

"He's not coming back from anywhere, Marion. He's upstairs. I heard him."

"He's gone *home*, Clo. He's got a wife."

"Where's home?"

"Beach Lane. Wainscott. I don't know the number."

Taking NY-27 east it would take about thirty minutes or so to reach Wainscott Main Street and a further ten depending on where he lived. I just needed a phone to Google it.

"There's got to be computer. Something," I said, trying not to let a slide show of bruises contaminate my mind.

She closed her eyes briefly and sighed. "I told you. He's taken everything."

We should have been more alert. Shouldn't have lost the only communication we had with the outside world. Then I saw the bloody corset draped over the bed. I almost pitched forward and gagged.

"I'm going to need my pills, Marion." I made a show of rubbing my head and pacing a little. "Any idea where they are?"

"He took them upstairs. That's all I know."

Her eyes suddenly swerved to the wall opposite her bed, where a streak of light flashed across the room like a strobe.

"What is it?" I whispered.

"Some kind of motion detector. I've never seen it before."

I saw the light fading into the darkness. It was mounted too high on the wall to be infrared or one of those photoelectric light beams they used in museums. There would have to be a second detector on the opposite wall and more effective when several were aligned in a checkerboard pattern throughout the whole room. I wasn't sure you could see such a thing through the naked eye.

What I did determine was the direction of the beam. It was trained on her bed so Kimball could watch her sleeping. Only tonight she had a visitor. Tonight, she was very much awake.

"Listen, Marion. There's a computer in the guesthouse. Where's the key?"

She brushed her forehead with the back of her hand and gave a small sigh. "It doesn't matter where it is. We can't get out, Clo. Use your head."

She had a point.

I watched as she dragged her fingers down her cheek, hand trembling as she circled the room. Was she having second thoughts? Or would she choose her employer over me? Everyone had their loyalties—a code of silence, a mafia style omertà. I just hoped Marion hadn't been promised a magic carpet of a Ferrari to keep her quiet. I hated her just a little more because I wasn't convinced she had the balls to break away.

She sank to the floor and began crying again. "There's no way out."

"Don't be such a wuss. There's always a way out. Don't you want to get out?"

"Of course I want to get out. But he's... he's so—"

"Stalky? But he's not here, is he? He's not in the house."

"He's watching," she said, shoulder peeking out from that slouchy sweatshirt like a porno slut.

"He can't be watching twenty-four-seven, unless he's watching through his sat nav. You said he was driving home."

"I don't know. He could have been lying. He could be in the guesthouse." More tears leaked from her eyes and she swiped them away, legs buckling beneath her. "He even knows what I'm thinking."

I wondered if she was making it out to be more dramatic than it was and I didn't care to dignify the word *thinking*. The horror stories Marion had already spun about Kimball's abuse, his weirdness, his utter indifference toward human life were frightening. So was the fact that she was under his spell. There was no way he knew what we were thinking.

But sometimes I wondered.

"Listen, Marion." I sunk down to a crouch. "I'm fully aware he has video of us and of this house. Videos he can record and rewind for up to ten days. He can see us from almost anywhere from his cell phone. But what I don't know is whether every camera in the house records video and if he can switch between cameras. Because as far as I know, video recording supports four cameras at a time. It's a question of which four."

She looked at me as if she couldn't figure out the logic in any of it. The camera thing was beyond her, although she wasn't as simple as she wanted me to believe.

I remembered seeing two long range night vision cameras outside the house on the way in. How long range they were was anyone's guess. Inside? There had to be some perched high up in the corner of each room. It seemed like that kind of house.

I stood and looked down at her. She was so useless, so fragile, I could have killed her right there and then. I had come here for that very reason. But now I needed her. How ironic.

"I want the keys," I said.

"I don't have the *damn* keys."

Her words clotted in my ears and I wanted to shut out the white noise. I felt utterly defeated.

She gave me her hand and I pulled her up. "You've got to get your shit together," I whispered. "What about the attic?"

"What about it?"

"*Think*, Marion. Just think, okay?"

While she was thinking, I was studying that pigsty of a face. I doubted any skillful contouring could cover up a half-closed eye and a split lip. The smooth happy-hour look had been replaced with broken veins around the tip of her nose and there was a red blotch in her right eye that had started to bleed around the iris. She was a road-wreck.

"I don't know what to do." Her voice was so brittle it began to break again. "I really don't know what to do."

"During your wanderings, did you at any time notice a side door, a back door, a secret door?"

"No."

I caught sight of myself in a gilt mirror above the vanity and blew an errant lock of hair from my eyes. The face I saw was young, tortured. Pushing thirty-nine with no particular style. Marion's skin had somehow evaded the passage of time with a frank disregard for the scorching summer winds that blew in off the sea. It was all so unreal. So unfair.

"Would it make you happier if I just smashed a window?" I asked.

"What with?"

"That nude statue over there," I said, pointing at a heavy looking Grecian figurine.

"I already told you, the windows are alarmed."

"Exactly, and if we're lucky, all the way to the police station."

We weren't whispering anymore, which was dangerous if the eye-in-the-sky was listening and watching at the same time. If I did throw the figurine, there would be all kinds of noise forwarded to Kimball's phone. He would stare at the screen bleary-eyed and it would be just my luck if he hightailed it over here in under twenty minutes.

I must have looked as miserable as I felt.

"You need an icepack," I said, hoping to steer her to the ground floor. It would be safer if we broke a window down there. "Are you okay?"

Her eyes welled up and she shook her head. "I'll be okay."

Her eyes skated around the room and finally landed on the door. "You're right. I need an icepack."

37

"Might be a good idea to get some music on," I said, slipping an icepack beneath her bandage.

"Music?"

"Yeah. Got anything light-hearted?"

She must have thought I was mad and then one eyebrow lifted so subtly I could see she was on the ball. Although not quite on the ball if you consider her bottom-of-the-barrel taste in music.

A man's voice began to hiss from a state-of-the-art sound system, something about a couple in a coffin which slowly began to plunge me into a suicidal despondency. It was doubtful the singer found much traction with a serious hit afterwards. It was shit-awful, but Kimball would be hard pressed to hear anything over the noise.

I wanted to take a look around. Although it seemed a little callous right now, what with her looking all sad and mental. But I needed my gun.

I bounded up the staircase to my bedroom, picked up the gun and checked the rounds were seated properly before slamming the magazine up into the well. I nestled it in my waistband. Listened to the sounds of the house.

There was no one upstairs, no movement, no creaky floorboards. I was dead tired and my head was pounding from Marion's whiny attempts at conversation. So I decided to take a look at the front door. It was a hell of a lot more productive than staring at the ceiling.

It was made up of a panel likely thicker than the standard 1 and 3/4 inch and with no view from the peep hole. Whether this was because the storm shutters extended to all doors, I couldn't tell, but after processing the simple fact that the front door was Kimball's likely access point when he returned, I decided this was where I should hide my gun.

There was a cabinet under the stairs, where the beam from a small lamp carved a faint circle in the wood. I opened one of the four door panels and found two empty shelves. Crouching, I slipped the gun from my waistband, racked the slide to chamber the round and tucked it as far to the back of the cabinet as I could.

I would be ready.

Marion's voice brought me to the kitchen, where the smell of fried onions surprised me for a moment.

"Want something to eat?" she asked.

I didn't but I nodded anyway. Told her I needed to use the bathroom. Slipped through the hall and made a detour to the library, which faced the front of the house. I recalled a metal doorstop in the shape of a crouching monkey with a ring in its head. It was light enough to lift and heavy enough to make a dent in one of the windows. I closed the door.

The smash was loud, glass splintering onto the carpet. No sirens and no matter how much I pounded on those rigid, gray shutters, they wouldn't budge. It would be the same all over the house. I could try over a million times and I couldn't make it happen.

Had I waited too long? Had he heard my intention earlier and disarmed the alarms?

There were cuts in my fingers when I returned to the kitchen. But they didn't deter me.

Rummaging through the kitchen drawers, I was hoping to find something thin, long and solid and found a kebab skewer. It would have been easier to shoot a few rounds through the door to the garage but I didn't want to reveal a weapon to Marion this early in the game. Having no idea how far away Kimball really was, any alarm would be the invitation I didn't need.

While Marion was railing on about her abuse and how much money Kimball owed her, I twisted the doorknob and jabbed the tip of the skewer every which way. I felt a little movement but not enough to give a whoop of joy. How many more benign zones were there?

Marion turned on me with a raised hand. "Whatever you do, don't break the lock."

"Who gives a shit?" Lucky she didn't know about the library window. "We're both trying to get out, aren't we?"

"If he comes back and finds it broken there will be hell to pay. Don't you think I've already paid enough?"

Not quite, I wanted to say. There was the larger issue of screwing my husband and for that she would pay dearly.

"You were talking about food?" I asked, trying to distract her from the spanking daddy issues.

"Chicken and rice?"

I nodded as she pulled a dish from the fridge and a knife from the block.

"You know he owes me money," she droned, slicing cooked chicken into small cubes. "Thing is, he owes me nearly a grand for the chef and the stylist, and a few bottles of Chateau Coûteaux. Here I am trolling around in a Merry Widow corset and cami-knickers and I'm getting nothing out of it except this." She pointed at her face with the knife.

"Is it worth putting up with his crap for a few thousand bucks?" I said, taking the knife out of her hand.

"No." She shook her head, poured the fried onions over the chicken and put the plate in the microwave. I could see she was struggling to lift her arm. "He blew a few hundred grand on his wife. I saw the receipt. An antique choker from Sotheby's."

I fed the point of the knife between the door and the frame and jigged it around a little. No give. "I wonder if she knows he's cheating."

"Sleeping with an escort isn't technically cheating though, is it?" she said. "Especially if he's playing under a different name."

"Don't be stupid, Marion. Of course it's cheating." The knife bent at the tip and I slammed it onto the countertop. "There are videos of you and Ryan which means there are videos of you and Kimball."

Marion's head flinched back slightly. "You're brutal."

"I'm practical. Let's face it, Kimball could easily share video clips online. Aren't you worried about that?"

"Hardly. He's in most of them. You're being judgmental," she said. "Not all *hookers* are scum."

"I didn't say that."

"You implied it. Just because every guy wants to bang me doesn't mean I'm a celebrity."

"I think you mean a *nobody*." I sat opposite her and smiled.

She handed me a steaming plate and a fork. Eating was a blur from then on and my attention was on the tiny corridor that led to the garage. How was I going to ram the door with a chair if I didn't find a tension wrench or a paperclip?

It would be daylight soon and we had no way of seeing the sun come up or Kimball pulling into the drive. What a relief it would be if I could get back to my old world with or without Ryan. That pin-thin punk.

I continued to push a piece of chicken around on my plate, while chewing on a mushroom. "Marion, I just need to clarify something. He said he was coming back three nights in a row. Sounds like punishment to me."

She was holding her breath, teeth continually tugging at her bottom lip. "I don't think he'd hurt me again. Well, not *kill* me."

"I wouldn't be so sure. You haven't factored me into the equation. After all, I am Ryan's wife and I wasn't expected. Kind of changes everything, doesn't it?"

"Yes. I suppose it does." Her eyes were focused on mine as if the thought had only just occurred to her. "There is a way. If you're willing."

"What do you mean," I asked, twisting a spray of pepper onto my plate.

"It's quite simple really. I can't entertain him like this. But you can." She stroked the curve of her throat with one hand and gave me a long hard stare.

"Me? Listen, Marion, I didn't come here to take your place—"

"That's not true. Look at you. Your hair. Your clothes. Did you have a particular look in mind when you changed your appearance?"

My heart was thrumming against my rib cage and I could hardly breathe.

"I know what you really look like underneath all that *me*. Your photograph was in his wallet. I took it out when he was sleeping. It was you on the beach, wasn't it? You... following me. Watching me."

I listened with a blank face, unable to think of something to say. It wasn't a dream but it was one hell of a mistake.

"I know what you want," she said, recoiling as she took a breath. "You want the video he was talking about. The one of you driving into the coastguard. So I'll tell you what I'll do. You take my place when he comes for dinner and I'll get you that video. You really don't have a choice."

It was true. I didn't. But how naïve of her to think it was the video I had come for. Unbeknown to her, taking her place as Kimball's lover would never happen, considering his brains were about to be blown out before he reached the hall.

"Do you know anything about computers, Marion? Because if you don't, it's really going to screw this whole thing up."

"I've got my own website, haven't I?"

"Do you have his passwords?" I was trying to think outside the box.

"Only to the laptop. He does have an iPad. I think he keeps it with him."

The videos implicated Marion in prostitution inasmuch as they implicated me in a hit-and-run. According to Joe, the driver was likely Ryan. According to Kimball it was me.

I kept thinking about the gun in the hall. So near and yet… I talked myself out of using it to pry the six-digit password for the security system out of Marion. Two reasons. One: The bullets were for Kimball and let's face it, he was the only one who could open every door.

Two: The cameras recorded every scene and killing Marion would give Kimball more ammunition with which to incriminate me.

A rich dude like him probably had a vast array of covert cameras and several DVRs that gathered and amplified faint sound waves like a massive space telescope. I had a strange feeling either way that I was shit-out-of-luck.

The more I thought about Marion's offer, the more I liked it. She was quite clever when she wanted to be, only she wasn't out of the woods yet. A bullet through the brain, nice and quick, because I was still going to kill her whether she helped me or not.

Her idea of a costume was a good one. Especially if a witness heard the shots or someone in the house next door happened to be walking their dog. The description they would give to the police would match Marion's. I decided to play along.

"I don't know anything about hookering," I said.

That made her smile and grimace all at once. "We'll go over it together."

The speakers overhead spewed out another miserable ballad and I was beginning to feel claustrophobic. I knew Kimball could be back anytime. He valued the element of surprise.

"I won't have to have sex with him, will I?"

"Promise," she said, moving the icepack over her right side. "Sometimes all he wants to do is talk."

Promises weren't my thing and I suspected she was still a little woozy from the booze to be giving them. *Gin o'clock* was a while ago and thinking of gin gave me an idea. If I could find my pills, Marion would be history tonight. The thought gave me quite a thrill.

"What's he really like?" I asked.

"In bed?"

"As a person."

"Well, you've met him, he's successful. Independent. Unlike Ryan." She twitched a little and then settled back down. "I shouldn't have said that. But Ryan is a little needy. Always calling. Was he like that with you?"

I nodded. Couldn't help myself. Truth was, he never called me unless he had to.

"He talked a lot about how he wanted to get remarried and have two kids," she said. "Honestly? There's no way I'm pumping out kids or marrying him. I hate guys who include you in every life decision without asking you first. I'm not in love."

"He doesn't know that."

Marion rubbed her rib cage with both hands. "It bites sometimes," she said, misreading my frown as concern.

"Got any painkillers?"

She shook her head.

Marion must have been the loneliest person I had ever met. Probably the type to top herself if left alone for too long because she needed people, needed skin to touch. I felt queasy whenever I imagined life through her eyes; a bunch of tarnished memories and pity cases she was paid to listen to. At the same time, she was willing to help me escape this nightmare. It was big of her to take the load.

"You haven't eaten your chicken," she said, head bowing toward my plate.

I tried to take another bite but something was nibbling at my mind and then it was gone.

"I'm not hungry," I said, spitting out a piece of gristle into my napkin and wedging it under the rim of my plate. There was something disgusting about reheated chicken. Too chewy.

"I've got some Pinot in the fridge," she said.

I decided to pass on that too. She was Pinot-obsessive, talking wine 101 for the next two minutes as she led the way into the living room, swinging a bottle in one hand.

Suddenly, the world was on my side.

38

Friday, 29th July, 2016

I could imagine stars hovering above the house and lights flickering in the front yard. As I recalled, there was a rank of black lanterns along the driveway and I bet they looked beautiful in the dark. It had to be sometime in the early hours.

Depending on wind current, they say you can detect salt in the air up to five miles inland, especially if waves and wind kick up spray. I couldn't hear the ocean over a seventies disco beat thudding through the entire house. But I could smell it.

I lay on the couch for a few moments and closed my eyes. The sound system kicked up a notch and if it hadn't been disco I probably would have been in a deep sleep.

My eyes snapped open. Not only from the surge of hope but from the strong smell of marijuana. Marion was sitting bolt upright, smoking a roofie. One bare foot rolled an empty bottle of Pinot back and forth and there was a halo of smoke above her nose, which she sucked back in through her teeth.

"It's just a cigarette," she said, flicking what was left into an ashtray. A third grader would have known she was lying. "It's a painkiller."

She gave me a sad, glossy-eyed stare, foot propelling the empty bottle across the carpet. I heard the clunk as it came to a stop against the leg of an easy chair. I wasn't in the least bit sorry and my sense of envy had escalated since staying in the house. She certainly wasn't living on beans and tea.

"Listen, Marion, you want to cut down on the drugs. If you keep going like this you'll end up with brain damage."

She gave an involuntary shiver and then regretted it. The *oohs* and the *ouches* were exaggerated and I didn't feel like falling under her spell. Or should I say being swindled by it. Facts are facts. Marion was playing me in the same way I was playing her.

I crouched down and pulled up her sweater. The bandage was firm and the icepack was still cold. There was nothing else I could do for her.

"Will I need stitches?" she asked. It was her temple she was tapping now.

"You'll be fine. No cuts, just bruises," I said, examining a spreading rash of purple. "Can you stand?"

She pulled against my outstretched arm and wobbled a little on her drainpipe legs. I was surprised she hadn't handed me a bobby pin from that rat's nest of a hairdo. I could have used a few to pick a lock.

"I need to take another look around," I said. "There has to be a phone."

"There was a landline on the wall in the mudroom," she murmured. "My guess is he took that too. You'll find jacks in some rooms but nowadays everyone has a cell phone, so…" She gave me a heavy-lidded stare and shrugged.

If Kimball had taken Marion's phone there would be no communication between them, no knowing when he would show up, *if* he showed up. I wondered how that made her feel.

"Do you get any deliveries out here?" I asked.

"You mean food?"

"I mean anything."

"We get a delivery of eggs every Thursday and Saturday afternoon," she said.

I had to cast my mind back. Friday was today. A missed opportunity. But there was always tomorrow.

"Jax," she said, lowering her eyes. "His mom used to bring baked goods."

"What about Robert and Frances?"

"I would need to call them."

"No point hoping they'll show up then."

"No."

"Right."

I wedged myself in a wingback chair and watched her as she padded to the windows, hand pressed against the glass. There was nothing to see, except her own reflection against the storm blinds.

"These, for instance," she said, trying the handle of the French doors. "They're all locked and bolted."

"There's a keyhole." I wagged a finger.

"What use is it when we don't have a key?"

I waved her off because she looked as frazzled as I felt.

"What if there was a fire?" I asked. "We'd have to get out then. I've never seen heavy duty storm blinds like these. Have you?"

"What other types are there?"

I didn't know. But these reminded me of commercial store shutters. Effective against hurricanes no doubt but I couldn't help feeling they served more than one purpose.

"It's been a while," she said, "since he locked someone in the house. Her name was Katherine. Stockbroker's daughter. She was here for almost three weeks."

I let out a big sigh. "How do you know?"

"He threatened me with it. Said if I was disobedient…" She didn't finish the sentence. "Made her dress up as five different girls. I saw a photo."

"Did he hurt her?"

Marion's eyes welled up and she looked at me as if she was about to bawl. "She disappeared. That's all I know."

"How did he meet her?"

"Montauk Models. Thing is, she didn't keep any records, dates, photographs. There's no proof she was abused."

"But there's proof she was here. The agency sent her."

"Yes. But they rarely follow up with runaways."

"Do *you* keep records?"

Marion's eyes tilted to the ceiling. I noticed they floated around, never quite finding a spot to settle.

"Yes," she whispered.

"Are they safe? Your records. Because if Kimball has access to everything—"

"He doesn't."

"When he hit you a few hours ago, did you record it?"

She nodded.

"What with?"

Marion pouted and picked at her fingernails. Her voice even lower. "A camera. And no it wasn't a cell phone camera. One of those old SLR things. I can show you if you like."

"It's good that you record everything."

"Yes."

"I only ask because… because if anything should happen to you, anything at all, you might want to tell me where it is. So I can show the cops."

I smiled inwardly, hugging my knees and rocking a little. I didn't want any pictures of black-and-blue Marion any more than Kimball did. He and I had a few things in common.

I looked at the mantel. There had been a clock there. I had dusted it.

All in good time, my dear.

His voice was like a burst of static in my head. I chewed on a thumbnail and wondered how long we would have to wait until we heard the jangle of a key. Whether it was worth standing at the foot of the stairs with my gun.

Marion lifted her eyes from beneath those perfect brows. "Did I mention Kimball has a fishing business in Mattituck? True story. It's the same as a Montauk charter, tons of porgy and bass, only his is the best fishing of the summer. You won't believe this but he's also been on TV. That's why he talks the way he does."

"Really," I said, flatly. She was blathering.

"Ever chartered a fishing boat?"

"No." I let the lie hover in the air.

"You'd love it. It's peaceful. The seabirds, the waves. Sometimes you can hear the wind…"

My mind zoned out as she described the fishing boats, the cargo ships, the restaurants that served the best seafood. She was trying to calm me, make me forget I was a prisoner. But the locked-in syndrome had already set in and I was preparing for a tailspin. The room started to look narrower and my heart was racing.

Think. Think of how you could get up into the attic, climb out onto the roof and slide down… just far enough… How many times had I run up and down stairs and into every room? I must have lost pounds.

I was fed up with being derailed by my anxiety, a disorder the psychiatrist trimmed down to a catch-all category that described any worry lacking a discernable cause. My brain, it seemed, was hardwired to worry, anticipating future scenarios that were destructive; clench-jaw negative scenarios that left me with a three-day headache. I had assumed worrying was effective, an internal receiver that protected us from potential harm. Dr. Howarth, on the other hand, disagreed. He said I responded to the perception of a threat and not actual danger. He wanted me to study where a usual response to anxiety left off and a disorder began.

As I fixed my eyes on Marion's body, I was afraid of it. Why? Was it a threat? Arms smooth like butter, an exotic brown. Legs slender and compact and calves toned like a dancer. Alive she had threatened and destroyed my marriage. This was a common anxiety. A usual response.

Was I afraid of drowning her? Absolutely. There was no point in thinking I could merely push her head under water and wait for a minute or two. Those legs would thrash and kick until her head broke free. Although she had a broken rib, I would still need to sedate her before dragging her out to the fishing boat.

This was a disorder. An unusual response. I think.

I shook myself from the filmic image of Marion sinking beneath the waves and illuminated by a single shaft of sunlight. If we couldn't get out of the house, death by drowning would not be an option.

39

I had been fumbling in the dark for long enough and listening to the drone of Marion's voice. Something had been gnawing at my mind.

Fear—that was it. Or the lack of it. Why wasn't Marion afraid? It did occur to me that she might be humoring me before the big reveal. The experience of a lock-down hadn't deflated her in the least and here was I thinking prostitutes had street nous; that extra piece of intuition the rest of us lacked. Perhaps I was wrong.

Her lips formed the chorus of a song that was blaring from the speakers, head rocking from side to side as she made her way into the kitchen and clinked a few more china saucers in the sink.

There is a dishwasher, Marion.

Naturally, I was concerned as I headed for the hall. I didn't want Mo-the-Ho wearing herself out like a toddler because there would be a downward slide when the Pinot wore off. She still needed to teach me the rudiments of role-play rather than futzing around in there, peeling and scrubbing things.

This is what got me going on the bobby pins. Marion had a drawer full of them and it seemed there was a better use for them than pinning up hair. What Marion didn't know was that I had no intention of playing dress-up. I was hoping Kimball would be mugged by drug addicts before he got here.

I ran up the main staircase, where crystal balls topped the newel posts and where the landing opened up into a reading room. The music was just as loud here as it was downstairs and I didn't have to be quiet as I opened every closet and every drawer.

I was starting to lose my patience and went for broke. There were only so many times I could go through empty bathroom vanities before it got old. Dick-wad Kimball was probably watching every move and laughing, and the more I thought about him, the angrier I got.

Where would a king keep his crown jewels?

It was a no-brainer to assume they were in the master suite because it was off-limits. Instinct told me to call down to Marion and ask her if it was okay, but instinct was an obstacle. What if she said no?

The en suite bathroom caught my attention first and so did the toilet; a wall hung, self-flusher I needed to use. I studied the floor as I sat there; marble and mother-of-pearl flowers so sheer each petal looked like glass. There were spots of blood beneath the sink and dried smears on the pedestal, and a soiled wash cloth where Marion had tried to clean herself up.

A central oversized tub would have provided a shimmering escape if it looked over the rear pool and terrace. I was so disoriented I had no idea which way I was facing.

Creeping back into the bedroom, I noticed a king size bed which seemed to float against a built-in headboard. Vases of fresh flowers framed a portrait of a Gibson girl, this time with a towering coiffure and a tightly cinched waist, which I felt was unlikely for someone of her height.

Beyond the bedroom was a small sitting room and a mirrored closet with a brassy colored keyhole. Was it a fur coat locker, climate controlled with low humidity? Or a sealed vault full of dead people?

I searched through two jewelry boxes and found no keys, but more bobby pins; some double pronged and wavy and some straight and flexible, many of which I pocketed. And a letter. Typed to preserve the writer's anonymity and unsigned.

My eyes skimmed over the first two paragraphs. A picnic in a secret place. A favorite song. A cherished rose.

Do you know how beautiful you will always be? Do you? And you say you're so unhappy. So unloved. Why? I love you more than he does. You're right. I can't prove it. You will never see it as I see it. Please know, there's no earthly reason why I would want to live without you.

A painful few seconds where I wondered if Ryan had typed it at work or at home. Where I realized he had never written a letter like this to me. Then shame at the thought of him baring his heart to a woman who had no love to spare.

Idiot! I folded the letter and put it back. *Pathetic, stupid idiot.* I let my eyes roam the room, berating myself for interfering.

Until I saw between the fireplace and a faux topiary, a coffered wall panel which didn't match the others in the room. Instead of lining the lower third of the wall just below the chair rail, it fell all the way to the baseboard. As far as I could make out, one side was hinged.

There was no handle, no lock, just a gentle push should have done it. But the frame only budged about half an inch and no amount of clawing at the gap would open it.

I found two gold bobby pins decorated with rhinestone butterflies. I straightened one into a pick and the other into an 'L' for a tension wrench.

I had no idea what a pin tumbler lock looked like inside but I remembered Joe telling Ryan how it could be done. How one could be shaped and used as a lever and the other a pick. About key pins and driver pins and how each had to be lifted to the correct height. I was certainly no master of picking locks but I had watched enough to understand the pins had to be set before the plug would fully rotate.

As the two bobby pins clicked and scratched inside the lock, the vision of a man's face seemed to hover behind a windshield, teeth grinding against metal. I couldn't shake off the coastguard's face.

I suddenly felt sorry. He wasn't smart enough to know how frightened I was, how desperate I was. That's why killers kill because they're paranoid freedom will be a thing of the past. Freedom will end. Even for me.

Pick, pick, pick.

The first bobby pin snapped, but the second remained intact as the door soughed open. Either the lock had never been engaged or I had successfully picked my first one. I decided on the former.

A narrow staircase.

I climbed the steps slowly as if there was something at the top I needed to be afraid of: a dismembered body, a bloody carpet. But there was neither.

The first thing I noticed was the silence. The second was the moonlight. Blinding. I nearly choked out a sob at the sight of it.

No music in the attic, as if the speakers didn't reach that far. The second was the green draperies, partially drawn against the moon and where a nimble beam revealed one long room that stretched almost the entire length of the house.

At one end, there was a red swing suspended from two hooks in the ceiling and beneath it a cherry blossom parasol lolling on the rug.

Through two large dormer windows, there was a view of sparkling water, a secret place the storm shutters couldn't reach and on the other side, a panoramic view of the driveway and the road beyond.

There was no sign of my car, which included my handbag and phone. It also included my driver's license still in the name of Clodagh Turner.

Don't sweat the small stuff.

I exhaled. Eyes flicking to the window sill where I saw a paperweight—a humming bird darting through a bunch of violets. I imagined it smashing through the glass, falling like a rain drop and shattering into a spray of colored shards on the driveway below.

I took a deep, cleansing breath and set that notion aside. Studying the angle of the roof, I pictured myself sliding ten feet from the dormer, heels jabbing the gutter before going over the side. My knees almost buckled at the thought. I was sure to break something.

The windows were locked and as far as I knew alarmed. What if the alarm only went through to Kimball's phone? What if it wasn't audible from the house, like a dog whistle wasn't audible to a human?

Through the trees I could make out a knot of lights, hazy through a slant of rain. People doing normal things like sleeping with no idea where I was.

I heard rolling waves and the clarion tones of a buoy bell, close enough it could have been a wind catcher hanging from the terrace. There was no distant rumble of traffic and sadly no headlights streaking up the road. My mind began to sink further as I sought out a neighboring house, although I couldn't see much over the saddle of a nearby skylight.

I studied a pedestal desk at one end of the room and settled in Kimball's leather throne of an office chair. Turning on the lamp, I ran my fingers along the surface, fingernail picking at the gilt tooling. I tugged at a brass lion head handle on the top drawer and found five files neatly staggered and labeled.

Maude Fealy: 1883 - 1971
Julia James: 1890 - 1964
Ethel Warwick: 1882 - 1951
Lily Elsie: 1886-1962
Evelyn Nesbit: 1884 - 1967

It was Evelyn Nesbit that fascinated me, partly because Marion resembled her and partly because I did. And partly because she was the last on the list. Inside her file was a photocopy of a 1906 newspaper cutting which had been pinned to the left side with the words *Harry Thaw Kills Stanford White On Garden Roof!*

Evelyn had attracted the attention of Stanford White, a New York socialite. He invited her to his 24th Street apartment where he gave her a tour of rooms including one paneled entirely in mirrors. What disturbed me was Evelyn's description of White's apartment above a toy store. The article claimed that after lunch, Evelyn and her mother were taken upstairs to play a game. Stanford White introduced Evelyn to a red velvet swing that hung from the ceiling of one of the rooms, strikingly similar to the one in Kimball's attic. As White pushed Evelyn back and forth, her foot targeted a parasol her mother held, a game that ended when the rice paper canopy had been successfully shredded. Nothing inappropriate was said to have happened that day, but I was sickened by the picture of White. Kimball could have been his brother.

But on another occasion when Evelyn's mother had left her unattended, the girl had fallen prey to White's charms. After drinking several glasses of champagne, she lost consciousness and was sexually assaulted. She was only sixteen.

A few years later Evelyn married Harry Kendall Thaw, a man with mental illness and, by all accounts, a lavish spender. His picture bore a slight resemblance to Ryan. The same nose, the same mouth, the same sideways look. I was floored.

Due to the sexual assault, Thaw became obsessed with White and latterly killed him in Madison Square Garden. It was dubbed by the press as *The Trial of the Century*. There was never a happy ending to a mess like that.

I looked around the room, surprised not to find computer monitors displaying rooms section by section. Instead, the attic seemed abandoned and the surfaces were coated in a light covering of dust.

I opened the top left-hand drawer and found three medium-sized padded envelopes and a lined pad with handwritten notes. As far as I could make out they were meeting transcripts with a note to Katherine Ainsley.

You are Evelyn tonight. Fly, my little bird, fly. Poor girl. She should have been more careful.

I reached into the drawer again. Stuffed at the back was a white bag with a pharmacy logo.

My pills. I punched the air. As far as I could see only two were missing.

The second drawer held two identical keys. It would be a miracle if they matched the pin tumbler on the mirrored door in Marion's room. I stuffed them in my pocket and gripped the white bag.

Looking around the room, I tried to imagine the house from the outside. Were there other attics attached to this? If so, how were they accessed?

I rubbed the back of my neck, allowing my eyes to scan the room one more time. The empty shelves, the swing, the parasol, the drapes and the bookcases. Was this the ultimate skit he played with each girl, before making them disappear?

I wasn't surprised I had missed something. A book on the bottom shelf that didn't quite look like a book, skinnier than a book and hard like an iPad case.

I lunged for the bookshelf. The cover was soft leather and better yet, the iPad had no security lock. I scoured the apps and found what I was looking for. A well-known security logo that led me to a blue screen labeled *Kimball Home*. I scrolled through a range of cameras, shifting between views, clips and activities.

The entire house read *Armed* and there was only one way to clear the status. I needed six digits to access the passcode.

40

With the house armed, surely the police were on their way? Unless Kimball had cancelled the call soon after I had smashed the library window.

It wasn't my lucky day. The only thing the brass keys matched was a jewelry box and there was nothing valuable inside, except a typewritten note with no signature.

Meet me by the boat at 1:00. Don't let me down.

1 a.m. or p.m.? I guess it didn't matter. It was the despair in Ryan's voice I couldn't stand. I closed the jewelry box and locked it.

Marion started singing scales downstairs and the extremes in vocal range left me wondering if she was a little too far gone. I wanted to shout at her to shut up but I didn't want her hating me just yet. She had to teach me everything she knew about Kimball so he would dine with me long enough to taste real trust.

Never underestimate the power of surprise, Kimball. Because you will be surprised when the time comes.

There wasn't enough time to dwell on how depraved and twisted my mind had become, or how much anger I was carrying around. I kept telling myself there was no moving forward without full disclosure, and Ryan's face kept coming out of a hopeful mist, only to disappear again in segments.

I perched the iPad on my knee. I had no hope of learning the passcode to shut down the system, but I could scroll through each room and determine the location of the cameras. There were two in every room; one fixed on the wall to encompass the entire layout and another camera aimed at the door. What struck me as odd were no cameras in the attic. Nothing to record what Kimball did up there.

In most cases, the cameras were set at eye-level. Some in dimmer switch plates, others on shelves disguised in ornaments. Luckily, few were placed high up in the corner of each room, where they could only be reached on a chair.

I scrolled through the main part of the house, checking the iPad for any cameras I might have missed. I had seen a movie once where an intruder used a flashlight to scan the rooms where light bounced back from a hidden lens. I could have done the same, only I didn't have a flashlight.

I hid the iPad and the keys behind a set of white fluffy towels in Marion's bathroom cupboard. My head was throbbing and I felt oddly detached from the danger I was in.

I could hear Marion's feet tripping up the stairs and when she skirted the corner her eyes were pug-wide. She was holding a cushion against her injured rib.

"What are you doing?"

I pointed at the mirrored closet. "Any idea what's in here?"

She walked forward and stared at her reflection. "Oh, I look a fright!"

She sauntered over to the dressing table and I could hear bobby pins bouncing into a china dish as she brushed out her hair.

"Marion. The closet?" I asked.

"Gowns." Her hands were fast. The cottage loaf had gone and in its place was a low ponytail. "Old dresses."

"Show me."

She pulled out a chain from her décolletage and unclipped a dangle of keys. Two, to be precise and both identical.

Pushing back the mirrored slider, I could see she was right. From the Gibson girl to tea on the Titanic, there were dresses with tulle and ruffles and the wink of sequins everywhere.

"I sometimes wish we still wore them," she said, dropping the keys down her front. "The shoes can be a little hard to walk on."

I didn't answer. I was a jeans girl myself. You could run faster in jeans.

She walked in and reached for a large leather-bound box. "It's a necklace. Belonged to a lady called Charlotte, one of the survivors on the Titanic."

"Have you ever worn it?"

"Once."

She unlocked the box and opened it. A three-drop cluster of rubies interspersed with diamonds.

"It's beautiful," I murmured, wondering what other keys she had squirreled away in that big old bra.

"I need to start doing your hair. It can take a while."

"My hair's not going to make any difference. He's still going to recognize me."

"Contouring and makeup will change your bone structure, Clo. You've already done most of the work." She snapped the box shut and set it back on the shelf. "He loves the red and black beaded dress. It's his favorite."

I say we get out of here so I don't have to play Rose Dawson to his Cal Hockley. It didn't seem right to defile something so beautiful. "Who will I be?" I asked.

"Evelyn Nesbit. Girl number five."

"But she was only sixteen."

"It's called acting, Clo. Haven't you ever acted?"

"Not really."

"Just talk to him. Make him feel at ease."

"What am I supposed to talk about? Golf? Old school reunions? Bitch about his chubby wife?"

"This isn't a bitch-fest, Clo. It's a dinner scene from a play he wrote."

"So now he's William sodding Shakespeare?"

"Don't you write?"

The question threw me for a loop. "Shopping lists."

"George Orwell once wrote: When I sit down to write a book, I do not say to myself, 'I am going to produce a work of art.' I write because there is some lie that I want to expose, some fact to which I want to draw attention, and my initial concern is to get a hearing."

I was suddenly very frightened of Marion. She wasn't nearly as wasted as she had been an hour ago, and there was something very *cavalier* beneath that artificial veneer. Someone who could remember an entire paragraph and deliver it without stumbling was someone to watch.

"It was in a script he once gave me." She arranged the dress on the bed, fingers plucking at the beaded lace.

"How much will I have to learn?"

"A page or two. Remember, call him *Mr.* Kimball and don't speak unless you're spoken to. And don't cuss."

"Oh."

"You'll shower and shave. Just in case."

She looked at me for a long time and it was then I saw the crêpey lines around her eyes, accentuated by the powder she wore. She was right. Contouring made a big difference.

"Deportment," she said, walking behind me, hands lightly resting on my shoulders. "Don't slouch. Chin up a little more, eyes forward. Keep your legs tightly together, never crossed and hands on your lap. Your diction will be, how you say, faux-British."

"Transatlantic," I corrected. "And when's he going to twig I'm not you?"

"He won't. I'll set the dimmer switches on low and light the candles." She stood in front of me now. "Your legs are shorter than mine."

Don't remind me.

"But you'll be sitting or lying most of the time so he won't notice."

Emphasis on the lying because I would be lying. Through my teeth.

Her eyes roved around my body as if following a buzzing fly she was about to swat. Her fingers curled around the collar of my T-shirt and she peered over the top.

"What cup size are you?"

I patted my T-shirt closed. "Thirty-six."

"Those aren't thirty-six."

"Yep, they're thirty-six." Boundaries. Where had they gone?

"No, you're a thirty-four. Maybe a B."

"Does it matter? Don't corsets fit all sizes?"

"We might need some extra padding. You know, something to hoist them up a bit. Don't take this the wrong way, but Kimball's all about size."

Were my two little specks on the horizon worth hoisting? "Marion, are you sure you can't do this? You being so good at it and all."

"Quite sure."

"I assume he doesn't realize he's broken your rib? Because if he does, I'm going to have to hobble around a bit."

"Just chill, okay?"

It was hard to chill when Marion kept dangling bits of jewelry against the dress to see which one she liked best. The only thing creepier than a woman admiring a red dress was a woman stoked enough to know she wouldn't have to wear it.

"Maybe something a little less revealing?" I said.

"It's perfect."

"I'll need a petticoat. Several actually."

"Clo, do you want to do this or not?"

I'm ashamed to say I had to think about that for a moment. Time began to slow. Probably like squeezing the trigger before killing someone. Or being strapped to a gurney before the lethal IVs were inserted.

I gave a rapid nod.

41

I helped myself to more bobby pins. Stripping off the rubber knobs with my teeth, hoping I had a shot at freedom.

While Marion was arranging one half of the bedroom with makeup and studio lighting, I slipped the pins in my pocket. There was no knowing when I would need them.

My mind wandered off course in another squall. It had been almost two years since Ryan had paid any attention to me. It was my birthday and we drove all the way to Cowfish, a restaurant on the waterfront with panoramic views of the canal. I had jumbo diver scallops and he had baby ribs and if I thought about it long enough, I could still smell the cologne he wore.

These weren't the usual people we ran with or the restaurants we could afford—glamor-girls in tight white dresses and men in suits, so squeaky-clean you could smell the soap—but Ryan really wanted to try it out and in a way, so did I.

His eyes strayed to every table, never once taking in the small black dress I wore or the new lipstick I had bought. It was the waitress who served up a platter he couldn't ignore. A boob-tube of a skirt that revealed two dollops of flesh every time she stooped over the Mimosa and Bloody Mary bar.

"I'll love you forever," Ryan had said, eyes flicking sideways as he said it.

I felt the remnants of a tattered love and a warning shudder like the time we first met. I should have paid more attention to that shudder.

When we arrived home that night, the overhead remote for the garage door failed to work. Ryan opened the driver's door and dropped the keys which, due to the drainage in our driveway and a natural camber in the concrete, rolled under the car. His cursing would have launched a rocket from NASA's Kennedy Space Center.

He left me sitting in the driveway while he tried to find the spare. I don't recall the confluence of circumstances, how Lieutenant Joe suddenly appeared from his house earlier than the end of his usual shift. It was only 11:55 p.m.

He was like a Springer Spaniel bounding along the front path, ears shaggy and flapping. I looked up at the rearview mirror and instead of talking to Ryan, Joe crouched down by the open passenger door and asked me if I was okay.

I told him we had locked ourselves out. Joe said he had a lock pick set in the back of his car and he'd be happy to help. Before he left, he whispered a question.

"Are you happy, Clo?"

I had recoiled. Tried to fob him off with a yes and a fake smile. But deep down I knew he had seen a deeper despair, saw the prickle of tears in my eyes.

I remember watching him pick the lock and I asked him why he wasn't working late. He said *undertime* was the new thing now he was a lieutenant. Got enough money to retire. I laughed at that. He said some people had to work a private security detail at Yankee Stadium during their police shifts to supplement their pay. Although conning taxpayers didn't interest him. Nor did felony grand larceny.

Easing back to the present, I half wished Joe was here to help me. Perhaps his sentient transmitter had honed in on my distress. Perhaps he realized I hadn't come home.

Perhaps he already knew I was the perpetrator of the hit-and-run. If there was a way out of this mess, would I be able to find it in spite of what I had done?

"Here it is." I heard her cheery voice as she opened a drawer, hand flapping a DVD.

"Here's what?"

"*The Merry Widow*. We should watch it."

"What if he comes early?" I asked.

"He never comes early." I saw the quirked eyebrow and understood the vulgar innuendo.

I asked to be excused. My bladder was twitching up a storm, or so I told her. But the fact was, I didn't know if I would have another opportunity to get away before she dressed me.

The question was how to sedate Marion. I had replayed it over a thousand times in my head, through a rising fog of panic.

Once in my bathroom, I reached for the canister of sedatives, snapped off the lid and locked eyes with the pills. On the side of the sink was a porcelain soap dispenser and, using the rounded edge, I crushed several tablets into a fine powder. There was a small notebook in my suitcase and, peeling off a sheet of paper, I made a sachet.

I had to be close to it at all times and the silver condiment tray on the dining room buffet sprung to mind. If Kimball passed out in the library soon after he arrived, it was there I would make Marion a celebratory drink before calling her downstairs.

Where to leave the canister… The recessed sanitary disposal wouldn't invite curiosity. I picked at the pharmacy label, cursing as I tore away at my name, the date and pharmacy address. I washed the shreds down the sink, hot water jabbing the drain and steam coating the mirror.

I slipped the sachet inside the side seam of my bra and walked back to Marion's room. We sat on the bed like a couple of teenage girls, reading a Cosmo magazine and drinking Evian. My stomach was a swill of acid.

Then Marion turned off the surround sound and slotted the DVD into the player. She pressed me into a seat at the dressing table and I watched the 1952 musical of *The Merry Widow* while she did my makeup. I wasn't sure I could move like Lana Turner, let alone speak like her. But Marion insisted I learn best angles and etiquette. The way I had to stand in the frame of an open door when Kimball approached the house.

"He'll open the shutters remotely as he's driving in," Marion said, and then pointed at the TV with an eye pencil. "Look at the way she's standing, slightly sideways with her hands on her hips. Can you do that?"

"I think so."

"The way she asks him for a light. Her fingers… the way she plays with the strings of her purse."

"How she lets him guess at the subtext of her words."

Marion nodded eagerly. The movie was frothy and fun and she was as smitten as I was. But to me it represented a darker side of married life, how women were once dependent and viewed as property.

"If he asks you to sing, Clo, you'll say you have a sore throat."

"I could tell him I have a broken rib and can't breathe. It's the truth."

"Don't, and I mean it."

It would have been easier to take aim with my gun. But he'd only see me and that would be like Elmer Fudd saying, *Psst, I'm over here* to Bugs Bunny before shooting him.

"Wouldn't it be quicker to beat him over the head with an ornament?" I said.

"You love pushing my buttons, don't you?"

"No, Marion. It's this. He and I don't exactly have the right chemistry and what we do have is hardly going to erupt into a boner-inducing porno session. This whole thing's cheesy. Can't you see that?"

"Calm down."

"I am calm. I'm just asking you to rethink the whole thing."

"No."

"Fine."

I was already planning an early murder—dare to dream! I could persuade Marion to have a celebratory swim with me in the ocean after a few glasses of wine. Accidental drownings were endemic, especially if Mo-the-Ho died with a gut full of pills and booze. It was a two-way street. I would see to that.

"You'll take his coat and hang it in the cloakroom," she said, painting my lips. "Men love perfume."

"Are you sure I need to wear any?" I asked. "I'm allergic to most of them."

"You can't be allergic to oil. Nobody's allergic to oil."

"We won't be kissing. I don't kiss."

Terror had already wound its arms around me. What if the gun jammed? What was plan B? Should there be a plan B?

"What if he knows I'm not you the minute he opens the door, Marion? It's a valid question. I don't sound like you. Not one hair on my head has your DNA. He's going to know."

"He'll do most of the talking and you'll be a gracious hostess."

"He's not likely to plop me on his lap in an overstuffed chair and lick wine off my décolletage?"

"Clo, stop overthinking this. He's only coming here to talk."

Damn right he is, I thought. Two seconds to pull out my gun and one to aim.

I was getting stage fright. As with all plans there had to be a backup and if for some reason I couldn't get to my gun there were the sedatives. Ten minutes for the drug to take effect was a hell of a long time when a man's all revved up and your gas gauge is on empty.

"Marion."

"What?"

"Look, I don't know anything about lace dresses and I don't look good in them. My waist is the same size as my hips and my breasts, as you helpfully pointed out, are smaller than what he's used to. He's hardly going to want a beer and celebrate."

Marion held the dress for me to step into. "He doesn't drink beer."

"I don't care if he drinks Dr Pepper. He's not going to fall for it. Any man would rather be balls deep in excrement than go out with a look-a-like." I hated to admit it.

The grin on her face was too wide. Nobody grinned like that when they were under house arrest.

"No sense trying to get ready on an empty stomach," she said, buttoning me up. "How about fruit and yoghurt?"

I pretended she had won me over with her words. But the truth was I couldn't see myself lounging artificially on the couch with my stomach sucked in. I hadn't done myself any favors and time was running out.

42

I felt sluggish as Marion did my hair. Teasing and blow drying as my mind crawled from the gray haze of Kimball's world, where it had been trapped for the past two days.

It was possible I could crush several pills into Kimball's wine. A glass would send an elephant to sleep, although I wondered how long it would take to send this particular elephant to dreamland. Hopefully, not more than ten minutes, otherwise he and I would be fusing in the bedroom.

What took a while was my brain. It whirred in and out one minute and went blank the next. I tried rebooting but kept coming up with chunks of Joe, hard-muscled and lean.

I had unwittingly put a marital wedge between me and Ryan and I had to ask myself, who sleeps with a work colleague and a neighbor?

Me apparently.

Had I been attracted to Joe subconsciously for all these years? Men, sex and bullets. Everything had suddenly become penetrative.

It was a crazy weekend with crazy people and maybe, just maybe, Joe and I had got our emotional wires crossed. Like survivors of a plane crash, we were only huddling together to keep warm.

Marion pinched a strand of my hair in the curling irons and there it was. I was finally Marion. On the outside.

On the inside there was a marrow of evil. I could see it prowling behind my eyes, threatening to burst through an open zipper in my face. A scene that looked like something you might expect from a nightmare, where Marion's body teetered and twitched over the deck of a fishing boat.

I wondered if she saw what I saw. Wondered if she despised it as much as I did.

"Textbook," Marion said, standing back a little. "Like a true Gibson Girl."

I turned to the mirror and saw upswept hair and curls, where my face had somehow caught the aristocratic air. Although it appeared as if the dark circles under my eyes had migrated to the gap between my nose and my upper lip. While I couldn't hope to rival Marion's mystery, I could mimic the elegance and style.

"Youth and purity," she said. "That's what he likes."

My skin might have been smooth and flawless but any resemblance to youth and purity ended there. Concealer, contouring, and some kind of lip-plumping gel. There were cosmetic marvels in that box of hers.

I couldn't begin to describe the dress. The beaded lace, the rhinestones and the red satin underlay. It was the inflatable breast enhancer Marion slipped inside the cup of my bra that made me feel like I was a fraud. It was a stroke of luck the sachet remained trapped in the seam.

"Is this dress too tight?" I asked.

"It's supposed to be."

"You don't think it's too glam? I don't want Kimball sweet-talking me out of my underwear."

"Here, read this." Her dead eyes contradicted a broad grin. "It's only two pages."

The script was, as she pointed out, two pages long and there were more stage directions than dialogue. I was scared at the thought of being seduced by a stuffed shirt. What I needed was an industrial-sized can of pepper spray.

A wave of heat broke over my crown and surged down the back of my neck. Taking Marion's place was dangerous. If Kimball asked me the same type of questions he usually asked her, was I supposed to prattle like hostess or should I be intellectually succinct? You could toss a coin.

"He's never hit you before?" I asked.

"Never."

Liar. I had seen him hit her through the window from the beach. "So cruelty isn't part of the agreement? I'm just asking because I am taking your place tonight."

"It's not in the script, is it?"

I ran my eyes over the sheet of paper I was holding just in case. "Nope."

"Then why worry?"

My mind was numb. This would either be a success or a dead loss, and I was confused about which. Or what, if anything, I could do about it.

Marion said I needed a shoulder rub. I flinched her off.

"It's messed-up, I know," she said. "But I wouldn't have accepted this assignment if I thought Kimball was dangerous. He can be overpowering when you first meet him. But he grows on you."

She wasn't kidding. He was Rasputin-scale overpowering and I didn't want any part of him growing on me. As far as I was concerned Kimball was erotica non grata.

"Is he likely to take those videos to the police?" I asked.

"Who knows? He's made a few porno pics of me. I can't let those get into the wrong hands, can I?"

I shook my head. They were probably the reason for the three million hits on the *Redmaynes* website. "He's not likely to video me?"

"It's a given," she said.

"That's encouraging."

"Listen, I admit I obsessed over Kimball when my agency first told me about him. I was stupid. Satisfied?"

I was. It gave Marion the incentive to leave and it gave me hope.

"Trouble is, Clo, there are cameras everywhere here. This is elite-ville, remember?"

Never mind the absurdity of a prostitute worrying about sex tapes. Maybe it was the stalker in me, but facts were facts. There had to be something far worse on hers than just a bunch of dirty talk.

"Relax," she said, hands resting on my shoulders. "I have just as much to lose as you do. Let's have some wine."

We walked downstairs to the kitchen and Marion uncorked a bottle of wine for dinner and set it on the kitchen counter. She excused herself to use the cloakroom.

This was my only chance. My hands were shaking. Fumbling at my bra and plucking at the sedatives. I tiptoed into the dining room and angled the corner of the sachet into the mouth of the empty mustard pot. It filled halfway. I crept back over hardwood floors to the kitchen, listening to a distant flush and the squeak of a faucet. When Marion returned, her voice was silky and strangely hypnotic as she poured the wine through a filter, a process I watched with interest.

Bile rose in my throat. The enormity of the risk struck me as tragic. This could be the beginning of something bad.

I pointed at her necklace and asked her what the keys were for. I knew one opened the bedroom closet. The other two, she said, were for the guesthouses. Her choice of the guesthouse was brilliant, seeing as neither of us could get to them. I would never know if she was telling the truth, assuming, of course, that she wasn't.

"Since there aren't any switches to operate the storm shutters," I said, "there has to be a security room somewhere in the house."

She nodded and went to the freezer to replace her icepack. "Upstairs. It's the only place."

"Have you been up there?"

"A few times. But I didn't see any computers."

She wasn't lying about that. I patted my stomach. "Got anything to eat?"

Her eyebrows shot up and the brain behind them seemed to tick over. "A spoonful of yoghurt? It'll be dinner soon."

A pause. I shook my head. I would have preferred steak.

"You're nervous, aren't you? He can be very charming. Very loving," she said over the silence. "Sometimes he brings flowers. Sometimes bruises."

There was an odd light in her eyes when she thought of him, the way a seventeen-year-old would view a crush on a boy a few years older. But I could feel the sharp-edged regret dangling on the last word.

"He won't hit you," she said. "Not unless you say something to upset him."

"Like what? Like he's a shit-for-nothing narcissist?"

"Something like that."

I exhaled. If she was right, Kimball had already meted out enough punishment in the past twenty-four hours. That is, as long as I kept my rebellious trap shut.

"I'll prepare Oysters Bienville," she said. "It's one of his favorite dishes."

I asked her if she had studied acting at school and she said yes. She also told me you had to be great at acting to be an escort, pretend to be excited over a molehill *and* assure every client it was a mountain. No wonder Kimball had an inflated ego. I was starting to get the picture.

"I don't want to keep replaying the record," I said, recalling the guesthouse and Ryan's wallet, "but did Ryan mention an apartment recently? One he wanted to rent?"

Marion nodded. "Yes, but he didn't tell me where."

"On a scale of one to ten, how mad was he on Monday night?"

"A good ten. He was all fired up and disoriented. I thought he'd been drinking."

"Ryan doesn't drink and drive."

Marian took two quick breaths. "All I know is that he left, slamming the front door and cursing Kimball."

Could be true.

After Kimball's brief 'date' with Marion, I had seen Kimball exit through the rear of the house to the beach, kick up a little sand before headlights announced a car in his driveway. He veered rapidly toward the lane and likely accessed the house between the privet hedges. There had been ten minutes where Marion disappeared into the house. I could only assume this was when Ryan entered, became aggressive and was told to leave.

"I know it sounds lame…" Her voice trailed off, fingers massaging a hitched eyebrow. "But I didn't want to get caught in the middle, so I went for a swim."

True.

She angled a practiced ear toward the front door and patted me on the arm. "He's here. If he asks where Mrs.

Shepherd is, you'll tell him you've locked her in her room."

I braced my feet against the tile and hauled myself up. Why did I feel like a rat in a maze, scurrying from one dead end to another? I could hear light drops of rain popping against the shutters and my flesh began to creep as I shuffled towards the front door.

Marion made a few adjustments to my stance, throwing her head from side to side. "You look like me."

A dead ringer. The voice in my head went on and on, coaxing, encouraging but for some reason I wasn't convinced.

"I'll be right here," Marion said, as she walked back to the kitchen.

"Right where?"

But she was gone.

A raw clunking sound caused a ripple of dizziness. The hurricane shutters at the front of the house powered up just as Marion had predicted. I gagged and swallowed a bitter reflux of Evian.

In those precious few moments, I reached into the cabinet under the stairs, hand patting the shelf where I had left the gun.

I swayed—body listless, as if my blood vessels had become clotted with glue—because now he was here.

And the gun was gone.

43

I slanted a glance through the open door and saw a car. Sleek and gray, parked by the curve of the fountain.

I drew a breath. Then another.

Shit-scared didn't come close enough. If the dress I wore hadn't been tapered at the ankle, I would have hitched it around my hips and streaked out of the front door. But my feet were fastened to the floor. Helpless.

Guns didn't disappear by themselves and I could only conclude that Marion had taken it. She was my enemy and now I was twice as vulnerable.

It was clever dressing me as Evelyn Nesbit. I would take her place, while she devised a way to ruin me. I felt a fool, hair swept on top of my head and decorated with a large mantilla comb of baroque pearls. I should have shot her while I had the chance.

Kimball swung polished shoes onto the gravel and shook out a set of keys from the pocket of a dark coat with slim-cut lapels. Head angled, he seemed to be assessing the gleaming satin I wore. He did not wave or smile. It was those liquid black eyes I was afraid of because they hid the sharper edges of his cruelty. But what frightened me more were his striking features. I hadn't accounted for any appeal.

Taking my hand in both of his, he stooped, moustache sandpapering my skin.

"Bit dark in here, darling," he said.

I was grateful he didn't look me in the eye. Under the beam of a few candles, such a simple gesture would have given the game away. He draped his coat over my outstretched arm, brushed past me to the candlelit living room and hurled his top hat across the room, where it alighted on the arm of the couch.

I was distracted by his choice of room, having been earlier instructed that he preferred to take drinks in the library.

"Mrs. Shepherd locked in her room?" he asked.

The words *of course* slithered out of my mouth, disjointed words that could have been whispered by someone else. Just as he turned his back, I dropped his coat on the floor and kicked it under a chair.

He took out his phone and tapped the screen. A distant humming. The automatic blinds opened beyond the French doors and there was no point hoping they were unlocked. They weren't. Instead, I sat on the couch, eyes drawn to flickering candles on a dark wood sideboard. A trickle of wax traveled down the shaft of the candelabra, collecting in a puddle at the base.

Marion had been busy.

"What's for supper?" he said, slipping the phone back in his pocket.

"Oysters Bienville," I said, trying to keep the pitch of my artificially constructed voice as low as possible.

The texture of oysters always made me heave, never mind the *bien* or the *ville*.

"I thought we were having prime rib?" he said, off script.

Life was getting shittier by the second. I decided to downplay the faux pas. "Chef said he could only get choice cuts. Apparently, restaurants aren't serving prime as much as they used to."

"That's a shame."

There was a stiff silence as he stood in front of the window, studying a fuchsia sunset. His mind seemed to float in a dark limbo as if he wasn't properly awake. I could feel my heart rate rising as I fixed my eyes on a rigid back and square shoulders.

"Evelyn, my dear. Haven't you forgotten something?"

I was briefly thrown by the sound of the name. I shifted my weight, saw two empty glasses on the sideboard and felt a tingling in my fingers. How could I have forgotten?

"Oh, the wine. Yes, the wine."

"The Chateau Lafite," he said without turning. "You do have it, don't you?"

"Of course, Mr. Kimball."

I had no experience of good wines. A slug of the cheapest plonk was velvet in my throat. According to Marion, the bottle had been set upright for the sediment to settle. I had watched her pry the cork out and decant it through a wine filter. I would have used a tea strainer. Too ghetto perhaps.

"Much sediment?" he asked, barely looking over his shoulder.

"A little."

The Waterford decanter stood on a dark wood sideboard, where the diamond cuts threw a prismatic effect on the mirror above. Beside it stood a set of silver salt and pepper shakers and a mustard pot filled with sedative. I poured the wine into a glass and deposited three heavy spoons of the ground powder, occasionally keeping my eyes on Kimball's reflection. Stirring with a finger, I held the glass briefly to my nose. A hint of blackcurrant.

"Quickly now," Kimball said, snapping his fingers.

The beaded hem of my dress rustled against the hardwood floor as I walked the glass over to him. But he stood looking out at the ocean, his mind elsewhere.

"Will you sing for me tonight?" He took the glass, nose hovering over the rim before taking a tentative sip.

"I have a sore throat. It wouldn't do to spoil such beautiful music."

"No, indeed."

"How's the wine?" I asked.

He seemed to be trying to make up his mind. A shiver of unease tossed around in my belly as I followed him to the couch.

We sat.

He turned to face me, eyes scanning the silver bugle beads and ribbon embroidery on my bodice. His lips were slightly parted as if his eyes needed to adjust to the new costume. I wondered if insanity ran in his family because tonight, it positively stampeded.

"Tell me about your day," he said.

"Lonely."

"Are you always lonely?"

"I would have liked to have gone for a walk."

"I'm sorry. The extra security is to protect you. Things are different now she's here. You're so precious to me."

"Am I? I sometimes wonder why you keep seeing me." If Marion was watching, she would be cringing by now. Wishing I would shut up for her sake.

"You know the answer to that," he said. "I'm obsessed. I can't stop thinking about you."

"Then why do you hurt me?"

"I don't like hurting you." His voice was whispery, his gaze distant. "It's not because I'm grotesquely rich or because I can. It's because you don't listen."

"Do you hurt your wife?"

"You know the rules." He drank again. "No wife-talk.

Why are you not drinking?"

"You don't like me drinking. Besides," I patted my stomach, "I have, how you say… a little complaint."

"So many complaints, my dear. Perhaps I should leave."

"Oh, surely not. I have been so looking forward to this evening."

I really had. Kimball lying on his back from a knife wound in his chest, legs twitching like an upturned cockroach. No point in thinking it was going to be easy. He was a big man playing a daring game.

"Cigarette?" he asked.

I shook my head and stared out of the window at the ocean; a rare privilege. "Coffin nails."

"I am impressed. You've given up?"

I managed a nod and grin at the same time. *If you are listening, Mo-the-Ho, now's the time to quit.* Because cigarettes may be excellent nerve-busters but what man enjoys a tongue full of ash?

"There's something I want to show you." He rolled the glass in his hand and then set it on the coffee table. "Thing is I would like you to change."

"You don't like my dress?"

"I like the dress. I prefer more of you."

"Me?"

"Yes. Why not skin the rabbit, my dear?"

I hadn't heard that expression since I was eight and all I could think of was my mother yanking a school sweater over my head. I almost clapped a hand over my mouth. He wanted me naked? I stared at him, insides riddled with fear and instinct.

"Are you afraid?" he asked.

"A little."

"How delicious."

He looked at me as if I were a plate of crab legs he'd like to crack. It gave me the creeps.

"Something different." His face was serious, except for his mouth, which jerked upward at the corners as if party to a secret. "*You're* different."

"Oh."

"Prettier. It's the makeup, isn't it?"

"I suppose."

He put his hand on my shoulder, thumb tracing my collarbone to the tender hollow of my throat. Then, leaning in a little, he whispered, "Sea air suits you."

Again, I said nothing. Panic had taken up residence in my blood, like a chronic disease refusing to leave. My mind, now achingly acute, knew that whatever happened this evening would be critical to getting out alive.

He lifted the glass and stared through it, then took another sip. I watched his Adam's apple as it bobbed in his throat, wondering how long it would take. It had been eerie watching him. Fit and formal, at least that was the exterior he imposed on the outside world.

"Would you get me another glass?"

He was so close I could almost feel a current of air from his eyelashes when he blinked. My fingers brushed his as they hooked around the stem of the glass and I took in his scent.

I made my way to the sideboard. This time he was watching me with torch-lit curiosity. For some reason I thought of the portrait in Marion's room, the lofty coiffure, the tiny waist, eyes blandly flirtatious. I wondered how the girl in the picture walked. Slowly perhaps. Tiny feet pointed out deliberately and a sensual hike to her hips.

Glass kissing the decanter, I eyed the mirror long enough to see his head down, thumb and forefinger pressed against his eyelids. I took a spoonful of that precious powder and left the little bone ladle in the mustard pot.

As far as I recalled, one camera was hidden behind a

dimmer switch and focused on the door. The other was fixed inside an alabaster statue of Venus on the mantel and trained on the couch. In the distance, it would be possible to see my back as I angled myself against the sideboard. If Kimball was taping the scene, he could pinch it later to enlarge the view. But I doubt he would detect the slight tremor of my right hand, after I had set the decanter back on the sideboard.

As I turned, I tried to take in the periphery while keeping my eyes on Kimball. If the cameras had no panning ability, I was in the clear. It wasn't until I was halfway across the floor that I realized I hadn't stirred the wine. Tiny granules floated to the bottom, resting in the curve of the glass like sediment. If he noticed, I was screwed.

He didn't see me leave the wine on the coffee table, but he must have felt the cushion subside a little as I sat beside him. His eyes flashed open and he appeared to be focusing on my throat.

I set my hands on my lap, wound my fingers around each other and pressed my knees together. "Are you hungry?"

He didn't answer. Instead, he took a sip of wine, longer this time, rivulets forming where his lips met the rim. Then raising the glass to the light again, he shook his head.

"I thought it was bitter," he said. "Too much sediment."

"Can I get you something else?"

"I have all I need."

He slid the wine glass back onto the coffee table. Cupped my cheeks with his hands and tilted his head. Before I could think of something to say his mouth was heavy on my mine, tongue cutting through my lips like a high-speed drill bit.

My gut instinctively retracted and instead of a twist of

tension, I couldn't help feeling a forbidden ecstasy. The deliciously heinous thing about Kimball hoisting me on his knee was the mental clang of a sculptor's hammer as it chipped away at Marion's self-esteem.

Sliver by sliver, minute by minute.

It would prolong her agony. Make her regret filching my man just as much as I was enjoying hers.

44

Pressing his cheek against mine, his lips grazed my ear. "Do you want to know about Ryan?"

"Ryan?"

"Her husband."

I did. "Oh, no."

"You deserve to know. You worked so hard, my darling. Was he a good lover?"

"He wasn't you," I quickly pointed out.

What did he want? A swell of applause? A trumpet flourish?

"But he was in love with you. All those texts. Calls. Emails. He couldn't get enough." Kimball sighed faintly. "What did you do to him?"

"Everything you asked me to do," I said.

"I think you did more. You see, I wasn't here."

"The videos—"

"Are so revealing, my dear."

My skin began to itch. Where was this going? I suddenly felt like a naughty child he was about to spank.

"I wanted him to find us together," he said, drawing

back a little. "To know I had already set the flag on Everest. He was buckling under the weight of his misery, especially the part when I told him about the video. He said I was a sick pervert. Maybe I am. But I'm not the type to go down without a fight."

When had he told Ryan all this? After he had arrived that night? Kimball's muscles trembled beneath my thighs and I wondered if I was too heavy on his knee. Whether he had noticed any difference in my weight and Marion's.

"He threatened to call the police. I told him he was too late. The videos had been emailed to my attorney, the board," Kimball cracked a smile, "the employees. He was sobbing like a baby. I told him he needed to get a grip."

I couldn't imagine Ryan sobbing but then again I had never imagined him being in love with someone else. For an instant I closed my eyes and saw Ryan in the kitchen for the last time. How he had told me about Kimball and his assistant, and now the poor girl was pregnant. Had she really disappeared? I remember Ryan saying, 'Lucy doesn't know. He doesn't want her to know.' But Lucy will know, I thought. I'd make sure she knew.

"I couldn't let him poke about in my business," Kimball said. "It was blackmail. And you know how I reward blackmail."

I did and I knew he would remind me.

"He was fired, in a manner of speaking." Kimball tugged at the corner of his moustache. "The man was a pariah."

He said the last word with so much venom I didn't know if we were supposed to slap palms or dance a jig to the proverbial gramophone.

"I could have walked behind the couch," he whispered, fingers stroking my throat, "and wrapped my hands around his neck."

Oh, God... Had Ryan gurgled his last words? Had he

called out to me while his fingers plucked at Kimball's hands? I tensed.

"But I didn't," he said. "Even though he would have ruined me. You. Us. I'm not a murderer. You must understand that everything you have seen and heard here is confidential. You have played your part well over the last few weeks and I have played mine. There'll be no talking to the police or anyone for that matter."

"Why would I talk to the police?"

He stared at me as if the question was not mine to ask and the slap was so swift I had not seen him lift his hand. The walls seemed to sway around me, a blur of shades and I could hear the steady pulse in my chest. I wondered if he could too.

He seemed to sense my horror as I pressed a hand against my cheek.

"Do you hate me now?" he asked.

The *no* that came out of my mouth was throaty as if spoken by someone else.

He kissed me again. "I love you too much to lose you."

He ran two fingers down the inside of my arm. It made my flesh tingle. It made me sweat.

"I'm going to stay with my brother for a few days. It will give sufficient time to put this horrid incident behind us and move on." His chest swelled behind the white shirt and his eyes kept flicking from side to side. "It has contaminated what we have."

"Of course," I murmured. "May I make a call to the agency? They'll need to know."

"That your assignment has been extended?"

In truth, I would dial a three-digit emergency number and get the shit out of here.

"There's no need. I've already called them," he said.

I wondered if the time was a means to prolong Marion's torment and then I withdrew the idea. It would be my torment, not hers. But it would also buy me time to subject Marion to the end she deserved. Nobody ever believed a call girl. They would say she had been asking for it.

Kimball's eyes flicked back to mine. "Let's not be miserable. Let me see how well you look in your dress," he said, urging me to stand.

He seemed to take time inspecting the drape, the symmetrical pattern of the lace. Every second felt like one big ulcer growing inside me. Ready to burst.

I waited like a good dog for a tidbit. But the compliment never came, and my mind kept begging him to show signs of collapse.

"Tonight, you are my special guest," he said, swiveling me around. I could feel his chest against my back.

According to Marion, it was customary for a gentleman to make the first move so I waited. His hands were already picking at the hooks and eyes of my gown until I was standing in chemise and stockings. It was the whispering I couldn't stand, the obscene words and the smile in his voice.

In movies, the heroine fainted right about now and I wondered what Evelyn would have done. Placed a hand over her brow and made a feeble groan? There's no telling what would happen if I didn't do what he said.

Whatever grotesque act he had planned, I knew he would want it to last.

45

My mother always said that if I kept worrying I would tear a hole in my stomach. If that didn't happen, I would get cancer by the time I was fifty.

She always had a gin and tonic at 5 p.m. My sister would tease her about the ratio of gin to tonic, especially in her last days. Even the nurses didn't care about a food plan.

"Give her what she wants," they'd say. Because it didn't matter anymore.

She lasted four more days after I had bought the last bottle of gin. Poured a measure in a plastic cup and watched her down it with a smile. I wondered then if I had killed her. Sown the first seed to my *serial-ness*.

Nothing mattered now as Kimball led me like a jailer to my execution. Walking me upstairs to Marion's bedroom, he fumbled in his pocket for a key to the attic door. There was a satisfying clunk as the key engaged the lock but the very sound of it tripped an alarm in my brain.

As far as I knew, I was the last person to have opened the door. If I had not managed to pick the lock successfully, had it been unlocked all the time? Could it be remotely triggered by a cell phone?

He seemed to slide in and out of his part. Sometimes mentioning my mother—not my real mother—Evelyn's mother. How he had persuaded her to leave for Pittsburgh two days ago to visit friends and how he had told her not to worry about me. He was my benefactor. I was well looked after.

When we reached the attic, I was surprised at the wall sconces; cylindrical tubes sitting atop cut glass bobeches that cast a pink flush. Again, the light was dim but not enough to keep my curves and features a secret.

Kimball took my hand and led me sharp left to an access door, bracing it open for me. I hadn't noticed it on the way in, partly because it imitated the paneled walls and sloped to the angle of the ceiling, and partly because there was no door handle or lock. It was a push latch design I wouldn't have had a hope of finding.

I almost gasped at the interior. Again, the same soft glow from concealed lighting and a few candles scattered here and there. An antique gramophone in the corner, a green velvet couch angled in front of a wall of mirrors and a rosewood coffee table with a floating glass frame. Everywhere, my reflection and his.

I noticed a yellow kimono draped over the arm of the couch and tensed at the thought of wearing it. Had it been laundered? Or was it stained with the tears and blood of Kimball's last casualty?

On the table was a lint roller, a packet of antiseptic wipes and gold bottle of champagne rammed into an ice bucket, where frost had already formed on the sides.

In which case...

Marion, you sick bitch. Had she staged this room? Or was it him?

My mind began to unravel the scene he was trying to recreate: the champagne, the green couch. Evelyn's last memory. She had survived, even though her benefactor had sexually assaulted her. The lint roller and the wipes were to remove all evidence. But this game didn't belong to me. It belonged to Marion. A game she was supposedly too ill to play.

"Sit down, will you?" Kimball stood above me like a stag with a ten-point rack.

I sank into the couch, and it felt unexpectedly snug. I took a deep breath. The air tasted of seaweed.

Kimball threw an envelope on the coffee table; a donation, I assumed, and several thousand if Marion had calculated correctly. He moved toward the couch, spread his coat tails before sitting beside me. His chivalry was oddly out of place in this mirrored prison and I tensed as his thigh touched mine.

He eased downward to the ice bucket and grasped the bottle. "Ah, the ace of spades. It has the assemblage of Pinot and Chardonnay. Good choice."

Pinot. Figures.

I stared at the bottle, studying it for a moment. Then, like a pop-up toy, a thought sprang at me. Marion couldn't have shifted a bucket of ice up several flights of stairs with a broken rib.

"Thirsty?" Kimball took off his coat and loosened his tie.

I said I was, even though I needed to stay alert. One slug of champagne wouldn't hurt.

He set it on the edge of the couch between his thighs and untied the wire cage. Draping a napkin over the bottle, he twisted until the cork eased out with a soft *pop!* I hated to say I was impressed. Nothing like Ryan with his clumsy hands fumbling over a bottle of prosecco one Christmas. It was like shooting a rocket indoors.

Kimball poured two glasses and handed one to me. "To you. To us."

"To us," I mimicked.

He seemed to like that and in one rapid sip, downed half the glass. I barely sipped mine.

"Do you know what I thought, the first time I saw you?" He shook his head. "I thought you were the most beautiful girl I had ever seen. That's why I invited you and your mother for dinner. Not for her, you understand. For you."

He drew breath while eyeing a picture of a young girl I hadn't noticed in the corner of the room. "It's hard gazing at you in black and white now that I have you in color. You're mine at last."

His eyes seemed to coast over my body like the voluptuary he played. The words *mine* and *beautiful* kept spilling out of his mouth and I felt roped and tied like a calf to a quarter horse. Me, beautiful? Hardly.

My sister was the beautiful one. She had made her way through life because of her looks, or so my mother said. In her opinion, a girl should never marry for money. But let her heart go where the money is.

Kimball took my hands. I crossed my legs.

"There's something so different…" His voice slipped in and out of the act as if it didn't matter. "How are you so different?"

"Because I'm not her. Not really—"

"Who… who are you talking about?"

"Evelyn." I looked at my shadow as it stretched along the carpet toward the picture he was so in love with. "The little fourteen-year-old."

"Sixteen. Quite a woman."

"Quite a child," I corrected.

Taking both glasses, he set them on the table. Then he coaxed me back against the headrest, lips grazing my collarbone, moustache prickling my flesh.

"*She* is you," he whispered. "And you accepted my invitation."

Not strictly true. It was Marion who was paid to satisfy Kimball's eccentric tastes, only tonight she insisted I take her place. I would be taking her *donation* whether she liked it or not.

He dipped his hand into his pocket and pulled out a gold locket. "Shall I give this to you now or later?"

Later. After. What did it matter? It was a sorry-assed reward when I considered the jewelry he had given to Marion.

He threw it on the table and patted my knee. I knew I had to say something but I'd forgotten the words. The script had only made a brief appearance since he walked through the front door and now it was positively passé. Since I wasn't taking the lead, there was no 'I used to be a massage therapist so I know how important it is to take care of your needs'. This was a subservient role. An education, if you will.

"Dance with me," he said.

"No."

"No?"

"I don't dance."

"You know what I mean."

So dancing was his word for foreplay. I was more interested in hacking into his computer and digging up the files relating to Ryan. There had to be another room.

He must have read my restlessness. "You're hiding something."

"Why would I be hiding something?"

"You're a quick-fingered little slut. You understand the meaning of value. I've seen you dragging a finger over the porcelain, admiring my paintings. Incidentally, did you get a police report for my William Bliss Baker?"

I remembered Marion saying she had. "Yes."

"Well done, my dear. So, what are you hiding?"

"Charlotte's necklace."

It was my turn to smile. I knew about mirroring, making someone trust you by focusing on what you had in common.

"You took it—"

"I'm afraid so. Let's say it's mine until you pay your debts."

"Debts?" I heard the rattle of a laugh. "What debts?"

"You owe me for the chef, the wine, I could go on. I have the receipts."

"Don't be the worm in the apple, my darling. I'll make a deposit tomorrow, several actually, if that makes you happy."

"It does."

"If you want the truth, I always thought you were vain and greedy. Now I know you are."

"Then we have a lot in common."

"I wouldn't want you to think you were any less desirable. I like vain and greedy."

Pity, I thought.

"Perhaps you're the type of person who doesn't give up until a puzzle is solved. Persistence," he said, fingers gently trailing my thigh, "is the one thing I admire the most. I sensed it the first time we met."

"How did you know?"

"There's a certain satisfaction in knowing intimate facts about someone. I watched you for several weeks. Asked about you. Aren't we all a little curious? Falling in love with you never crossed my mind."

"Have you?"

"I have."

He took both my hands and looked into my eyes. The room was stuffy and the air had gone flat. He kissed me again, getting off on a game of two warheads tapping noses to see who would detonate first.

His warm palm pressed against the curve of my breast, fingers barely skimming over skin. Most guys go insane about breasts. Not mine. That's just the way it is.

His hand found its way to my belly and lower, circular motions and not the fierce goring I had come to expect from Ryan. Ryan always touched me in the dark as if he somehow didn't want to look at my face or remember it. Obedient to his obligations, nothing more.

This man, this Kimball, whose first name I never uttered, barely looked at me either. I doubt he heard each catch of breath as I closed my eyes. Then a flash of madness. I had no desire to end the amatory warmth that had been dead and buried for almost a year. Strumming fingers, bursts of lust. There would be no crying this time.

If I said to myself I wasn't painfully stirred by an older man, I would be lying. This was deliciously special, as if I now embraced this secret insanity rather than feared it.

Would Kimball ever stop acting out twisted, perverse games? Could he ever be normal? Was this normal? Lips soft and hard at the same time, a moustache lolling over his top lip—and now mine—like a hairy caterpillar. I almost giggled.

He studied my neck, his hands mining in unchartered territory. I felt him hesitate.

"How would it be if we were married?" he slurred.

Terrifying, I wanted to say, but Marion would have said something different. "Exciting."

He squeezed his eyes closed and opened them again, tongue running along his bottom lip. I could tell he was straining to keep his focus.

"Last week you said I could tell you anything," he said, "anything at all. I'm taking you at your word."

"Of course," I said, longing to know what it was.

His eyes locked on mine and then he smiled. "I have been keeping something from you."

"Oh?"

It was now I was beginning to regret filling his glass with a sedative. It was a foolish thing to do in light of his confession. I could feel a drain of energy as he studied my eyes.

"I was fired last week. Partly the harassment scandal and partly due to a bonus pay out." His clean accent had been replaced with his own, deep and grating and startlingly different. "Ms. Waters said that throughout her employment she was subject to a sexually hostile work environment. Filed a complaint with the board of directors against me."

"Did you harass her?"

"Yes. No. Not really. The allegations were extensively investigated and found to be without merit. A flirtation that went too far. She flirted. I went too far."

"Mr. Shepherd's allegations?"

"Yes." He rubbed his eyes.

"Then there were bonuses paid out to the executives. Three million dollars based on premium growth and performance incentives. But our employment agreements were found to be illegal. They had never been disclosed to the board or any department for that matter."

I remembered Ryan telling me we wouldn't be having a bonus one year. I was disappointed. We counted on it. For four years after that, none of the employees benefited from any pay out and we naturally assumed the company had fallen on hard times.

"Who's *we*? Who received the bonuses?" I asked.

"Myself and three others."

"So none of the employees." I was trying to get a picture of where Ryan fitted into all this. A brief show and tell.

"No." He stared at me, deep lines etching into his forehead, mouth ajar. "You're not... you're..."

"Where is Ryan? What have you done with him?"

He tried a flicker of a smile but his face was numb, as if he had been given a shot at the dentist. He lay back against the back of the couch, hand flopping onto his lap with a thud. I caught the cast iron look in his eyes before his head snapped back and his mouth gaped open. I couldn't stop staring at rawboned cheeks and a thick moustache and wondering why it had taken him so long.

I tried to shake him awake, begged him to tell me where Ryan was. When he didn't, I set to work, using the antiseptic wipes to clean all signs of me from his hands and fingernails, and the roller to dust away hair from his suit. It was what he would have done if it were him.

Wrapping the napkin around the neck of the bottle of Armand de Brignac, I positioned it next to him on the couch, where the dregs glugged onto the floor in a pool of froth.

Then his body tensed, hands and arms jerking rhythmically. His head slammed back against the couch, mouth filling with a froth of spittle. It went on and on. Silent spasms he couldn't fight, throaty groans no one heard.

At first I was afraid of what I saw, struggling against the temptation to let the seizure go on without calling for help. If no one helped him he would die.

He started gagging, like someone was spitting after cleaning their teeth, while I stood there like an idiot holding a lemon scented wipe.

Then a sick gurgle. He was trying to scream.

I groped in his jacket pocket and found a key fob to his car. Checked the other pocket and found nothing. Wrapping the fob tightly in my hand, I screwed my eyes shut and inhaled the cold tang of disappointment. What concerned me was why Kimball's key ring lacked house keys, shed keys, keys to his safety deposit box. Hell, most people had a bunch of them.

While his head sagged over his chest, teeth clenched, I swiftly came to the conclusion there was nothing I could do for him. So I waited. After ten long minutes it went quiet.

Feeling no pulse at his throat, I had to assume the stag with the colossal antlers had finally croaked.

46

I snatched up the locket and the envelope, and all the cleaning things, and hurried to my bedroom.

My hair was a sculpture of hairspray and bobby pins and I picked and pulled, until I had dismantled it in favor of a ponytail tied with a thick toweling headband. Pulling on jeans and a T-shirt, I jammed Kimball's key fob into my pocket.

Car lights rushed down the lane and I pressed my face against the window, hoping it wasn't a cop. My hand instinctively covered my cheek. I was conscious of a slight burn where Kimball had slapped me.

It was still dark outside and the string of lights along the driveway revealed a closed gate. I just hoped I could get that far.

I stuffed my washbag and my clothes into my suitcase. The 'donation' envelope was thick in my hands and I ran a thumb under the seal and looked inside. Five grand? It looked like more, but I didn't have time to count it. I jammed the money in the upper compartment of my case.

Something had been left undone. The lint roller. I ran it over the sheets and pillow case and made the bed. Dropped the torn-off adhesive wipes down the toilet with the soiled wipes. Watched them circle the bowl before rushing down the pipe. No regurgitation. Must have been a high-power flusher.

I carried my case to the downstairs cloakroom, wedging it between the open door and the wall. Then I heard a noise. Heels twanging on tile and heading toward the kitchen. Marion. It reminded me of a lead-in to a thriller, where the viewer only saw two feet before the victim was overpowered.

I stalked toward the kitchen doorway and leaned against the jamb, while she gave the glittering ocean an objective survey. It was the first time in hours I had seen the blinds open, the first time I wondered why she hadn't made a run for it.

Dark blotches spined her gray sweatshirt, perfume suffusing the air. She pulled a knife from the wooden block, began slicing radish and celery on a board, cuts so perfect she could have put a gourmet chef to shame.

Radishes and celery. Two things I hated in a salad. Two things Kimball loved. She hadn't been expecting me.

Then she turned and froze, glaring with dark-ringed eyes. "Clo. Where's…"

My cheek still stung from Kimball's open hand but I gave her my best apple-cheeked smile. "Didn't expect to see me, did you?"

"How—"

"How did it go? Smoothly, thank you for asking. Did you find the videos?"

She shook her head and mumbled something about having the wrong key. Then she looked over my shoulder. "Where is he?"

"Had a little too much to drink. Passed out."

I didn't feel inclined to share how I had drugged the wine. It was more fun to watch her face, brows flickering as she tried to work it out. Eyes skimming up and down my body, expecting me to be naked under a yellow kimono and preferably passed out on the couch. Instead, I was wearing the clothes I came in and very much in control of my mind.

"Where's the gun, Marion?"

"What? I-I don't have a gun."

"Bullshit!" I yelled. "Give me my damn gun."

She dropped the knife and held up both hands. "Clo— please, I don't have a gun."

The fact that she was not coming at me with the knife was either the result of brilliant acting or someone too naïve to know she had the upper hand. I couldn't exactly threaten her without a weapon. In spite of myself, I grinned. Who was she fooling?

"So he slapped you?" she said, looking at my cheek.

I shrugged. It didn't hurt.

"You know what would help?" I said. "If you could show me where the security monitors are."

She graced me with a disappointed smile. Apparently, she had no idea where the security monitors were.

According to the iPad, there weren't any cameras in the attic so I could not be implicated in Kimball's death. But I could be accused of aiding and abetting. Was that a misdemeanor or a felony?

I wriggled free from her touch, didn't hear her voice, syrupy and concerned. "How much does he weigh?" I asked.

"Who? Kimball?" She saw me nod. "Why do you ask?"

"He drank most of that bottle. Left a shocking mess. Do you have any rubber gloves?" Her face knotted in confusion. My breath caught in my throat. "For cleaning," I said.

She plucked a pair of purple Marigolds that had been reclining over the faucet nozzle and handed them to me. I snapped them on and escorted her upstairs.

Kimball was a ball of fun; eyes closed and head wedged against the back of the couch.

Marion knelt at his feet and tried patting his hand.

"Darling, it's me. Wake up." She grasped the ice bucket, then the neck of the bottle just as I had hoped. "He's never drunk this much. What happened?"

A mixture of Xanax and wine, and then a little champagne happened. But why tell the truth to a liar?

I wanted to drag him down several flights of stairs—a Christopher Robin and a Winnie the Pooh—*bump, bump, bump* all the way down to hell. I wanted to bury him in the ocean with Marion's help. Then I could bury her too.

She kept asking me why there was foam on his chin and tie. I palmed her off with how he glugged down several glasses and how it couldn't have been good for him.

She grabbed the napkin in an attempt to wipe the snot from his nose and I barred her hand with my own.

"Don't touch him."

"We need to call an ambulance," she said, wincing as if I were about to slap her.

"What with? Neither of us have a phone. Do you honestly think I'm going to call an ambulance just because he's drunk? He's not doing anything wrong, Marion. Not in his own home."

She shook her head, long sighs snaking out of her mouth.

"Put that napkin down. He's going to come to in a few hours," I said, "and when he does..."

I didn't bother finishing the sentence. I knew she was scared enough to see the sense it. Just too stupid to know why.

The air conditioner soughed on and whistled through the air vent, tugging at his hair and the tips of his moustache. It was sicker than sick.

There were two choices. Finish what I had come to do or make a run for it. If only I could get to my phone.

"Are we going to just—?"

"Leave him here? Yes, I think so," I snapped.

Marion started crying again and kept tapping Kimball on the knee. "Darling, please… wake up."

"Shhh… keep your voice down, Marion. Do you want him to wake up suddenly and have another seizure?"

She gave me a hangdog stare. "I didn't know he had seizures. I knew he had asthma."

Shit. Why hadn't she dropped that little clanger earlier? I could have pepper sprayed him.

Marion was getting paler by the minute, hand slapped over her mouth. "He ought to be in bed."

He ought to have been lying down but I didn't fancy touching him.

"I'll get him a blanket," she whispered.

"What?"

"A blanket. He needs a blanket."

"He doesn't need a blanket. It's seventy-two degrees up here."

"He looks cold."

What part of him was she looking at? He looked fine to me.

"He looks… I don't know," she said. "Really sick."

"All drunkards look like that, Marion. There was this guy at Walmart the other day, hunkered over a shopping cart full of empty bottles. I wanted to give him my sandwich but he gave me a stare. You know, the 'sod off or I'll cut you' stare. But his skin." I made a face. "It was white. Like he was the walking dead."

The fact that man I had seen was redder than a fox's ass and had welcomed that sandwich with a smile and a prayer, was nobody's business.

"How much did *you* have to drink?" she asked, eyeing the second glass.

"Not as much as him, it seems."

She was now pacing in circles, gaze shifting. Her whisper had a rasp to it. "He's going to kill me. He will. He'll kill me."

I pointed with a rubber finger. "He's not going to kill you. Look at him."

She looked.

"Sleeping like a baby," I said, my eyes flicking to the window where streaks of rainwater slid down the glass. "Better he wakes at his own pace. How often does he have asthma attacks?"

"What?"

"Asthma. How often?"

"I don't know."

"Does he have an inhaler?"

"He keeps one by the bed."

Not only was I going to make this whole thing look like a terrible accident, but the coroner would latterly find large traces of Xanax in Kimball's system. It would be Marion's prints they found on the champagne, the ice bucket, the glass table. Boy, what a buzz that was.

"If he doesn't wake up in twenty minutes, you better call a doctor, okay?" No normal person would leave someone in a postictal state in the attic and I waited for the words 'I can't, Clo. I don't have a phone.'

"It's your decision," I pressed.

"Yes. Yes, I will."

I felt a strong urge to leave the room. Marion's hands flat against Kimball's forehead were making me uneasy.

"Come on," I said, taking her arm.

I dragged her downstairs to the kitchen. The only way to keep her mind off it was to keep her busy and the whole place had suddenly taken on the odor and appearance of a downtown squat.

She turned to face me, finger vertical against her lips. "Shhh, he'll hear us."

47

Kimball couldn't hear a dog scratching its ass.

"He'll be out for an hour at least, Marion," I said. "If he comes downstairs all fired up, we'll be waiting. You don't want any more bruises. Things like that don't heal overnight."

Things like that wouldn't heal at all.

"Battery is a felony," I said. "You'll need a restraining order."

"Are you mental?"

"No, I'm not mental. Think about it. There's hundreds of classes of felony. Battery's got to be at the top of the list."

She frowned. "You are mental."

Absolutely. No cops. No inquiry. I was *insane*.

"This isn't Nevada, Clo. This house—him, me—who cares what class of felony it is?"

"I guess you could say having sex with Ryan for information was a felony?" I blurted.

"I hated every minute of it," she said, super quick. "Lying to him, pretending we'd get married. Do you know how awful it is when someone loves you and you don't love them back? How sad?"

I did. Sadness was like a fever that spread throughout the body, manifesting itself overtly in the face. The eyes. The mouth.

Her face.

She scraped her hair behind her ears with shaky hands. "If there's anything I've learned, it's this: If you don't have that crazy love for someone, the type that knocks the breath out of you, then you don't have a shot to go the distance."

She was milking me for all the sympathy she could get, but I didn't care. "Is that how you feel for Kimball?"

"I think so. I thought so."

She closed her eyes, dark lashes fanning out over sallow cheeks. For a moment, she looked vulnerable. I didn't know if she was in love with the possibility of Kimball more than the reality of him.

"You know what he told me?" She looked pale, and her voice was unsteady. "Marriage among the middle classes is a bargain. Among the free it would be compromise."

I had no idea where Kimball dreamed up the platitude or whether he had taken it from a car bumper sticker. But I said amen to that.

"He loves me in his own way. He gave me a ring. He's already told his wife."

"How did she take it?"

"Better than he expected. He told me she wouldn't contest it. Unless he screwed her out of her fifty percent."

"Will he?"

"I doubt it."

"What's his net worth?"

She shrugged. It had to have been cathartic for her to talk about it, to keep the fantasy alive. I could have run all the way home by now but I had to finish what I had started.

"There's nothing for you here," she said, almost reading my mind. "You can leave if you like?"

Leave? Hell no. I wasn't leaving without knowing what that sick son of a bitch had done to my husband. My *ex*-husband.

"I need a drink," I said.

I could almost see Ryan standing here in this very kitchen, stirring his own drink with a fork handle. But for all my musings, he wasn't here. I was.

Finding the videos—proof of his infidelity—was irrelevant. It was the money he had taken out of the bank I wanted back. Every single dime.

I discovered a few bottles of Evian in the fridge and handed her one. She nodded, mind emptier than the bottle in my hand.

"What he did to you," I said, "is extremely violent. What if he lost control?"

"He didn't."

"But he could."

"He wouldn't let it go that far." She sounded sad. For a woman patched in welts and scars I couldn't for the life of me imagine why.

"Come on, Marion. He hits you and tomorrow's another day? It's abuse."

She drew a breath, took another sip. "Not if it's consensual."

That shook me for a moment. It proved to me he had done it before. "Have you considered deleting it? The video I mean."

She leaned forward, elbow on the countertop, thumb and finger massaging the glass. "No. He likes to study it. Like a director. He makes me do it again and again until it's perfect. Then he edits it, shows it to agents. They reject it and he takes it out on me. That's the cycle, Clo."

What kind of agents reveled in violence? I kept looking into those black, depthless eyes fastened to mine. I lifted the glass to my lips, water glowing against the rim. It tasted bitter, like fermented lemons.

"It's also a memento," she said, "of our times together. I like to think of him watching it. Watching me."

Somehow I thought that was unlikely. If Kimball was a narcissist, he was watching himself.

"I wonder if he worries about you all alone in this mansion."

"Don't be ridiculous," she snapped back. "He can see me anytime."

I took the word *see* to mean watch. "Do you go out to dinner with him sometimes?"

"Not often. He thinks it's inappropriate."

"But you're living in his wife's house. Isn't that inappropriate?"

"It's his house. Not hers."

"Minor discrepancy."

"It was *his* before the marriage. In any case, she'll get three houses once the divorce goes through."

A fair division of spoils and no disputes. Marion was being unrealistic. Lucy Kimball would be the first to sniff out her husband's lair if he failed to come home.

"Do yourself a favor," I said, glancing at a pan of vegetables steaming on the stove and a serving of oysters covered with a glass lid. "You don't want him to see this."

Marion ran the hot tap until her forehead glowed. She kept shaking her head and asking me to repeat what Kimball had said.

I repeated; I consoled; I offered to get her another drink. Pinot this time.

"No, I don't want one."

"You're sure?" I tensed because I knew what was coming next.

"I don't feel good. My stomach… I feel like throwing up."

"It will calm your nerves. You can leave it if you don't want it."

"I don't want it."

"Don't be snarky, Marion. I'm only trying to help."

She winced again. "I know you are. Of course you are."

"Then shut up and let me get you something."

I ran to the hall, shoes skidding across tile as I swerved around the door to the dining room. A sedative would take the edge off.

I poured two glasses of Lafite, one with a liberal sprinkling of Xanax. Things were galloping ahead now. *Total number of deaths = 1.*

I wanted to congratulate myself on the lack of evidence, at least anything that could be traced back to me. But I was minus a gun.

It was no use leaving the glass on the kitchen island and hoping Marion would drink it. Those little white granules were hard to come by and I hadn't been stingy.

Marion was gripping the elephant's trunk of a faucet and chasing foam down a bronze-rimmed drain when I returned. There was a tube of hand cream on the countertop, which she upended and squeezed three drops into her palm. Rubbing, massaging. She was tense.

"Hey," I said, nudging her elbow. "Let's make a toast."

She backed up a little as if I was putting the moves on her. "To what?"

"To you. What's the betting he'll propose later this evening?"

She shrugged.

"I know he thinks the world of you. I can tell," I said. "And I don't mean that in a creepy scumbag kind of way. He thought it was you he was kissing, not me."

"We don't know that. Doesn't mean he *definitely* thought you were me."

I could have launched into another of my stories but her movements were jerky as if she was in shock.

"I'm sorry," she said. "For everything. It's some scary shit when someone takes your husband. I wouldn't have done it if I had known."

Bullshit, Marion, you do it every time you sign on to that sordid little webpage and talk to desperate, sleazy men.

I put on my most good-natured smile and raised my glass. "To us."

She grinned. Took the glass I held out and repeated the toast. I can't say she glugged it back like a good kid taking cough syrup, but it was damn close.

She drank.

I watched.

"Why don't you finish cleaning the kitchen," I said, "while I make sure the rest of the house is tidy. When he comes downstairs, I'll disappear."

She grinned. "Thanks."

"Don't mention it." Besides, I had an urge to look in Kimball's car.

I made a few scraping sounds with the chairs in the dining room and listened, while knives scraped crockery, dishwasher door slamming. I had to be quick.

Taking a hand towel from the downstairs cloakroom, I ran a corner under the cold tap. I had to use something to chase away the fingerprints.

Outside, the air was crisp and moist, rain pattering against the eaves. Then a rhythmic ticking followed by a long hiss. I nearly jumped as the lawn sprinklers sputtered into life. Redundant in light of the rain.

I stared at the Porsche in the driveway, its broad haunches glistening like the shell of a tortoise. To car enthusiasts it was a beautiful beast. To me, that beast could activate a range of doors and gates. I wanted to know if my car was in the garage.

The fob buttons were dedicated to the car alone and I opened the driver's door with the face towel, shoehorned myself into the seat and opened the armrest. A wallet and money totaling $760 in cash. There was a driver's license in the name of David M. Kimball. Height: 6'1". Eyes: BLU. DOB: 08/21/1955. Organ donor.

Perhaps it had been safer in the car rather than inserted in his jacket pocket. Kimball wouldn't have trusted Marion to know the address of his house. The house he shared with his wife.

Looking in the glove compartment, I rifled through car insurance papers and an owner's manual, and tossed in the right-hand corner was an additional set of car keys. Mine. I folded my hands around them and let out a breath.

Think, Clo, think. Find your car. Open the garage.

In all my experience of driving assorted clunkers nothing could prepare me for such an exotic car. The smell of leather, a cockpit of lights and an acceleration where a driver's contact lens could literally vibrate off the side of his eye. The temptation to burn a trail out of Southampton triggered a gnawing fear. Stealing cars was not a crime I wanted to add to my résumé.

I glanced down at the gear lever, saw an assembly of haptic buttons and what appeared to be a smart tablet mounted into the dash. Studying the constellation of lights, I had no idea which one would open the garage.

The overhead keypad looked promising. Before pressing the first button in a bank of three, I had to be sure it didn't activate some inner door and alert Marion, who should have been feeling a little groggy by now.

Knock on wood for a little superstitious luck. I knuckled the dash.

I pressed the first button. A distant hinge, a rallying yelp. A flicker of light and the garage door scrolled upward. My fingers twitched. I squinted. Tires, tail lights, four cars, two wrapped in tarps, two glossy under the lights. A white Mazda and a black Buick. Hers and mine.

I could feel cold air coming in through the open car door, wind hesitating as if taking another breath. The only other sound was a *sssh-chk-chk-chk*. The wet ratchet from the sprinklers as they shut off.

I wiped my fingerprints from the steering wheel, the fob, everything I had touched and swung the hand towel over one shoulder. Fatigue threatened a landslide and my legs twitched forward as I ran on adrenaline fumes toward my car. I wrenched the door open and found my handbag still on the passenger seat and my cell phone tucked down the gap between the console and the driver's seat.

One call. Lieutenant Joe. I almost sobbed.

I pocketed my phone, stowing the keys and my handbag behind the driver's seat. Instead of using the door from the garage and the kitchen, I streaked back through the front door. My nerves were buzzing and my stomach was in knots as I retrieved my suitcase from the cloakroom and locked it in my car.

What was I missing?

Kimball's phone. I hadn't checked his trouser pockets and I hated the idea of going back upstairs. And then…

"Have you finished in the dining room, Clo?"

The dining room? "Oh, yes. Nearly."

Kimball's phone or the bottle of Lafite. I juggled the options.

Then her voice. "I'll be right there."

Bottle of Lafite.

I checked the drawers in the cloakroom vanity and found a flashlight and a stack of drawstring trash bags. I dropped the bottle of wine and glasses into one and maneuvered myself through the doorway.

I jerked back.

Marion met me in the hall, teeth chattering and hand dragging across her snotty nose. "He's not waking up."

"You went upstairs?"

"I don't think he's breathing."

"Of course he's breathing, Marion. He has to be breathing."

"I'm not taking the blame for this," she said, hand waving in the air. The same hand that held a cell phone. Kimball's phone. "Because if anything happens—"

"Nothing's going to happen!" I let the neck of the trash bag slip through my hands, where it came to rest on the floor with a muffled clunk. "You can't have checked his pulse properly. He was breathing when I left him."

Her forehead creased into a frown and she took a deep breath. "How much was he drinking?"

"Well, when you do the math—alcohol consumed, his weight and the hours he spent drinking—what he actually consumed wasn't that much. But a seizure's a seizure, isn't it?"

She merely stared.

"Did he eat anything?" I asked, my eyes locked on that cell phone.

"No, I don't think so."

The pathologist would do a thorough investigation of Kimball's stomach contents and I wanted to make sure it appeared he had died from a blend of alcohol and sedatives.

"Marion, do you have an attorney?" I saw the shake of her head. "Know any?"

"No. Only—"

"Clients? That won't do."

I needed information about invasion of privacy laws. Bugs, taps, hidden cameras, anything of which a resident was unaware. I understood it was still a gray area, but exactly how gray? Wasn't an unauthorized phone tap a federal offense?

"What have you got in *there*?" she asked.

I followed her gaze down to the trash bag and up again at two narrowed eyes. "Trash."

"You know where the dumpsters are?"

"Of course."

"I can't go back up there, Clo. I can't… I'm afraid. But you can. You can see if he's okay."

I could and I would. I nodded. Couldn't think of anything to say.

"I'll pour you another drink," she said. "Wine?"

"Oh, yes, fine."

"Are you hungry?"

I wasn't.

"We don't want the oysters to go to waste."

"Alright. Sounds good."

"I called a friend," she said. "He'll be here in an hour."

48

Shit!

Who was this friend? It was unlikely he was law enforcement given the nature of Marion's profession. He had to be someone with whom she felt safe.

I had one hour, possibly less.

A mist of rain greeted me in the darkness and I nearly tumbled over an egg carton. A piece of paper poked out from under the lid, limp and slowly turning to pulp.

I closed the front door and walked down the driveway to the dumpsters. I was screwed. How had I ever worked up the courage to come here? It was not only the future that frightened me now but the past. A past I had no desire to revisit.

The stench of rotting food caught my stomach as I hurled the Lafite over the side of the dumpster, hearing the clunk of glass as it hit the bottom. My fingers were sweating inside the rubber gloves and I stood there wondering what to do with them. The cops were a canny lot and K-9s were worse.

A clatter of rain against plastic.

A clatter of rain against plastic. I turned my ear to it, calculating it was somewhere behind the guesthouse.

About fifty feet in front of me was the hedge that lined the dead-end lane to the beach. Everything sheened; puddles forming against the neatly trimmed lawn and the house, which stood like a mausoleum against a slate sky, was reflected in the rear quarter panel of the Porsche.

The sound could have come from a bag of fertilizer, but in such immaculate surroundings, where the gardener maintained the property three times a week, it was doubtful the bag would have been left there. The flapping was louder now and, running the beam of the flashlight across the lawn, I could see a flowerbed tucked close to the patio between the guesthouses.

A mixture of scents played under my nose and refused to let go; a troop of glistening roses, plump buds and open petals spilling across the lawn like a wedding toss. Beneath them, an amorphous mound, a drainage bank as if the dirt had been pushed up against the rose stalks.

I took a deep breath and let it out slowly. Whether by instinct or some inner voice, I inched closer and angled the flashlight, almost jumping at the sound of the bag buffeted by the wind and glossy and black like a slick of tar.

I gazed into a yawning tear. A flash of gray. A face. Then each tiny detail fell in order like dominoes toppling in a line. My fingers tugged and ripped, hands paddling the soil. A torso turtled on its back and I covered my mouth with one hand, elbows slamming into the ground. For a breathless second, the image seemed to flutter like ripples on water.

The flashlight spilled a ribbon of light, framing the area between the gap of the man's pants and a button-down shirt. A knife protruded from a thin fuzz of hair that formed a seam down his belly and I knew I couldn't touch it. I scooted back a little, disgusted by the thing that lay there rotting in the mud. The thing they had destroyed and buried.

I choked out a name. "Ryan."

He seemed to stare at a ceiling of stars, mouth ajar as if collecting spikes of rain. I stuttered his name again and again but I couldn't train the flashlight on his face because I knew his eyes were dull. There was not even the tiniest essence of him, or who he had been.

A groan scoured through my throat and jerked its way into my mouth. A giving birth groan, one that drags and burns. Deep and primal. I tried to stand, tried pushing against the ground but my legs were like two feeble twigs, bending and flopping.

Time seemed hazy and I let my mind drift. For a long moment I just stared at the ripped plastic, wrenched back and forth by the wind. White noise that sent images of Ryan through my brain, skipping in and out until my head buzzed with it all.

It was then I noticed a pair of glasses lying a foot from the right side of his head. Crimson drips skated down the lenses and pooled in the grass. I wiped my hands on the grass as if wiping away imaginary stains and I tried hard not to vomit.

I couldn't decide if it was sweat trickling between my shoulder blades or rain and my feet braced against grass as I shifted back a few feet on my butt. A grumble of thunder made me jump and I crabbed my way across the lawn to the driveway, palms slamming into wet concrete. The wind squalled closer, branches groaning, leaves rattling. I could hear the pulse of rain against the tarp behind me, a distant drumming now as if forcing Ryan further into the ground.

Did I touch anything?

My brain clicked through a range of emotions and settled on rage. It was rage that urged me to stand. Rage that lifted me up and rage that propelled me toward the house.

Think, it said. Breathe, it said. *Kill*, it said.

The front door was closed and I loped through the open garage, elbows driving like pistons. My mind switched gears. Was the door between the garage and kitchen still locked?

It was a deadbolt, key protruding from the slot, which, in most garages could be unlatched from the inside. The lock turned in my hand, the knob followed as I maneuvered myself into the kitchen.

Darkness. The house was quieter than a meditation grotto. She had to be upstairs. Holding Kimball's hand, rubbing his knee, talking to him as if with a comatose patient her voice would bring him back to life.

There was no sign of her in her room or mine and I was hesitant to climb the attic stairs in case he wasn't up there. Or he *was* up there, flesh rapidly decaying and eyes bugging from a taut face.

Buffeted by a fresh wave of fear, I mounted the stairs and stood inside the mirrored room. Inching closer and closer. I couldn't touch him. It would drive me insane.

He had to be dead. He would have moved otherwise.

I stood alone in that room, soaking up the silence. Studied his face. Not a twitch. The air conditioner played with a strand of hair that had fallen over one eye and there was a mottled pallor to his skin.

Then a sudden whiff of bile mixed with alcohol and I nearly gagged.

Keep it together, Clo. Almost home free.

A door slammed downstairs and I froze. Knees almost bending inward as if forced together by a magnet. I backed up toward the door.

There it was again. A *thunk*. Not a slam.

I felt my jaw drop, as though someone had attached a ten-pound dumbbell to my lower teeth.

Marion. The bitch.

I launched myself downstairs, air making a fast passage through my nostrils as I stumbled, slid and powered to the kitchen. The lights were out.

I was met with a gasp of cold air. An open window?

I took out my phone and used the flashlight, brandishing the beam like a wand. I called out her name. No answer.

The beam hovered over two glasses of wine. My heart raced. One was empty. I caught a dim reflection of myself in the oven door, hair in weeds and skin bluer than blue. I could hear rain slapping against the deck. A door beating against a latch.

Splattering into the hall, I heard the wind howl and the French doors squeal. My vision began to bend and I blinked a few times as I stepped out onto the deck.

"Marion!"

49

If Marion was to run away, where would she go?

Not far, I thought, running to the edge of the deck and squinting through the haze. An image caught in the beam of the revolving buoy as well as a light pole outside the neighbor's house. She was on the beach, slouched over a coil of cigarette smoke, hair beating around her head.

I tried to understand why she hadn't hightailed it to the tennis club for help. Then I realized why. She didn't want the police poking their noses in Kimball's sordid little world. Or hers. Nor did she want them to find a dead man in the rose bed.

What she didn't know was worse. She was drugged up to the eyeballs, only that drug was taking a long time to take effect.

"Marion!"

She flinched, drew the hair out of her eyes and turned at the sound of my voice. I waved my outstretched arm back and forth like a metronome and from the look in her eyes, I realized she had become untethered from the present.

I rushed down the steps, shoes cutting through a thick swath of sand. The wind pounded like a heartbeat, rain slapping against my thighs.

"Kimball... He's inside, isn't he?" she said, throwing the cigarette in a wet runnel of sand. "I heard the garage door."

"No, Marion. He's dead."

"No... no." Her hand fluttered against her chest and her eyes streaked down the beach to the dinghy. "He never said goodbye."

"For goodness sake, Marion, he was too stoned to remember his name."

I heard the resignation in her voice, the slurring of words. It started to hit me. Marion wouldn't know how to live without Kimball. Wouldn't have the house anymore. Better yet, she wouldn't have to find a way to forgive him every time he hit her. It was all coming together very nicely.

"I found Ryan."

Her head snapped up. "Ryan... he's here?"

"Dead. Stabbed." I patted my stomach. "Why? How could you do it?"

"I didn't... No, you don't understand."

I watched in fascination as she ran a finger along her bottom lip, reached into her pocket and brought out a tube of lipstick. As if it mattered what she looked like? The type of woman who could stand in front of a podium surrounded by a bunch of detectives and give a speech to reporters about her dead lover. And still, her hair and makeup would be perfect.

"Where's the phone, Marion. Give it to me, dammit!"

I crouched and clamped a hand around a lock of her hair. I wanted to hit her, scratch her face, even out here on this musty pit of a beach where a lone walker could see me.

Then she yowled like a cat, arms thrashing. Lipstick slipped through her fingers and thudded onto the sand. I couldn't tell if she was laughing or crying. She might have been the only person I knew who could do both at once.

My nerves crackled. Strands of her hair locked between my fingers like a trophy.

She managed to crawl away like a dog hit by a truck, still awake and determined to stay that way. For a brief moment she just stared out to sea. The wind picked up and Kimball's fishing boat rocked a little on the sand, halyards snapping against the mast. I was standing over her now.

She gripped my leg, eyes pleading. "What did he say to you before… before he died?"

"Who?"

"Kimball."

I had no idea what she was talking about. There was so many things he said and only one that stuck out in my mind. "I believe his exact words would have been 'You're not Marion.'"

"Did he kiss you?" she asked.

Was she asking me because she hadn't been watching through a monitor? Or was she asking me because she was jealous? "Yes."

"Did he… did he… ask you to get undressed." She speared me with a glare.

"Undressed… well, yes. He didn't exactly ask. He unclipped."

She twined her fingers in the hem of my jeans and her gaze sunk to ground.

"What does it matter?" I asked. "He's dead."

"No…" She was rocking back and forth, one arm clasping her waist. "No, he's up there. I can see him."

I crouched, my face inches from hers. "You're a lying, thieving bitch. All you care about is yourself. The house. The money. You didn't think it through properly.

Marion… Marion, look at me. It's your fingerprints the cops will find. Not mine."

The words bubbled from my mouth before I could swallow them down. It was hard to believe how she had seduced a man, all because Kimball wanted to keep his ass clean. In the same way it was hard to believe how she had bought into it all, how she still loved him after all the abuse he had put her through.

I wrenched the keys from her neck and rammed them in my pocket. She had access to the entire house.

"There was a reason you wanted me to take your place tonight."

She tried to shake her head, bat a hand, but nothing was cooperating. She couldn't even speak.

"You know how the story ends," I said. "We know Evelyn was drugged by her benefactor and sexually assaulted. But I was thinking—wondering—why Evelyn's name is the last one on Kimball's list."

Marion's pupils were large and her breath deep and ragged. Be subtle, I thought, just in case she was faking. Only I was past that point. "You've played all of the girls except her."

"You're crazy," she slurred.

Marion rolled sideways, cheek slapping against sand. She reminded me of a yeast ball, cocooned in a shrink-wrapped bowl waiting to rise. I lay down beside her. I needed eye contact.

"Not crazy enough, it seems. You knew Evelyn marked the end of the game. And you knew in Kimball's version, she dies. Were you going to kill me too, Marion?"

Her eyes were suddenly on mine. A rheumy stare that tore right through me, tongue churning in her mouth. I guessed her gums felt thicker than a wad of cotton and it was an attempt to whip up a little spit.

Holding my breath, I stiffened, curiosity mutating to impatience. I saw tiny constellations of sand whirl above her head and dissolve in the moonlight. The wind was strengthening.

Her eyes skittered to somewhere over the top of my head. Again I saw it: the resignation, the loss for words, and the defeat. Then she mouthed something I couldn't hear.

"What?" I leaned forward and heard her whisper.

"He can see us."

"Who?"

Her eyes closed and I watched her for a moment, heart going a mile a minute. In her delirium she must have thought Kimball's sordid little security system reached as far as the beach.

I could have left her where she was because if anyone found her they would assume she was coked out of her mind. I studied her lying there like a beached squid and almost lost my nerve. I shouldn't have done it. I shouldn't have followed her. She would never have a grave or a headstone. Was that fair?

But my prints and hair were all over her and I was afraid.

Reaching inside her pocket, I pulled out Kimball's cell phone. Not one outgoing call had been made to an emergency number or to law enforcement. Two had been made to a private number over twenty minutes ago indicating she may have been greeted by voicemail and tried again.

I checked incoming calls. Nothing. The person Marion had called had not received the message yet, although there was no knowing how long it would be before I heard sirens approaching the house.

Doing what I had come to do seemed redundant now. Ryan was dead. What did he care?

Fingerprints. Fibers. All detectable to the law enforcement eye.

It wasn't until I thought of Ryan, the pallor of his cheeks and the coolness of his flesh, that a fresh surge of hatred overtook any feelings of loss.

I hooked my hands under her armpits and hauled her toward the fishing boat. The voice in my head urged me to be quick and I pulled and strained, shoes slapping against wet sand. Then ankle-deep in tangled seaweed. I couldn't drag her up against the gunwale unless I flipped her over on her front. The boat listed to one side, rowlocks rattling as she flopped face-down, forehead striking the bench. Bending her knees, I pushed her closer to the stern, where she lay huddled on the bottom boards, face in shadow.

I streaked toward the dunes, to the sandy hollow where I had left the scuba belt. I couldn't take the phones into the water and, skimming off my hair band, I wrapped Kimball's and mine in a neat bundle and left them there. I strained my eyes through the yellow haze beneath the light pole, and the beach yawned before me like a pale tongue, littered on one side with broken teeth.

This time, I caught movement near the neighbor's house, something bobbing on the sweep of dune near a sagging fence. It could have been a dog or a bird. It could have been nothing.

Hooking the scuba belt over one shoulder, I took a deep breath, gathered courage and struck out toward the boat.

50

The moon was a big eye watching as I searched the boat for oars. They had been here. I hadn't imagined it.

I could see grooves visible in the sand. Drag marks starting from the stern and reaching as far as the dunes. Blood fizzed in my veins. Lips opening and closing like a thick-lipped flounder.

Someone had removed them. Recently.

I tried to analyze. Tried to keep my mind clear. Perhaps Kimball had an agreement with someone in the neighborhood. Someone who regularly borrowed the oars or had picked them up for re-varnishing. The fact was if I couldn't row, I had to sail.

Marion was clear of the center and bows, room enough to slot the boom into the mast. I shackled the halyard to its head, feeding the mainsail into the mast track. Hoisting was heavy going and I was almost out of steam before the luff was tight enough to cleat off the halyard.

The sail began to fret and beat, boat tossed back and forth by the incoming waves. Only one thing for it. I jumped into the water and pushed off from the beach, waist deep before hoisting myself back over the stern.

I sheeted in the main, pushed the tiller away and she came slowly up into the wind. The sail filled as the bows crunched and surged over the water. Tiny white caps winked in the swell and I counted three stars to the left of the buoy. It was further than I had imagined, light beam swinging out to sea and leaving the dingy in a track of shadow.

The boat had no lamps and the thought of sailing blind filled me with terror. Having studied the beach two days ago—the dinghy and the distance from the shore to the buoy—I hadn't determined any obstacles then. There shouldn't have been any now.

My hands gripped the tiller and I glanced behind me to the beach. I could hear the waves breaking and beyond the dunes, the sparkle of village lights were slowly receding. The dinghy must have been pushing a few knots and I had a feeling she could outsail almost anything in her class with nothing but a jib and somebody's shirt.

The first tendrils of panic prickled my spine as I turned back to the buoy. In the dark water, the beam speared down in undulant points almost to the bows of the dinghy. Nausea ballooned inside me and then I reminded myself that if anyone was watching, they would see a woman at the stern, a brunette with a ponytail. A woman just like Marion.

Drunk girls drown. Sad girls drown. It happened all the time.

I couldn't determine the distance of the buoy to the beach but the tides were strong here. The incoming tide was almost turning and the thought of swimming against it didn't fill me with much enthusiasm.

I braced myself. Thrusting the tiller away from me, the mainsheet played through my fingers. The dinghy slipped forward a few feet and then came to rest in the trough, mainsail beating a sprightly rhythm and boom swinging dangerously.

Keeping landmarks and reference points in position to orient myself, I pulled and heaved, and slumped Marion part way over the gunwale. Her forehead tapped against the hull and her hair and hands streamed in the current. She was almost overboard. Leaning over, I fastening the scuba belt around her waist, making sure the buckle was facing front. Checked her clothes were free of the cleats and let her droop there for a while like a stepladder.

I tried to make some sense of it all, but kept running into the impenetrable fact that Ryan was the reason for all of this, and Ryan was dead. Where do you go from a starting point like that?

Marion had destroyed my marriage; maybe she'd destroyed hundreds. Here I was intent on making it stop because I recognized it for what it was. Sick.

Did I feel anything? A little guilt, a little terror. But she was going to pay for what she did. She was going to the bottom of the ocean where she couldn't hurt anyone else. I wasn't mad, was I?

Using her legs as leverage, I counted to three and wheelbarrowed her into the water. She dropped beneath the surface with barely a splash. If anyone was going to live eternally in the darkness it would be her. I leaned over the side and saw a once beautiful woman sinking lower and lower, tiny bubbles eking from her lips like a stream of jewels.

Pulling off my T-shirt, I rinsed it over the side of the boat and scrubbed away at any surfaces that might have carried prints.

Scrubbing, wiping. Wiping, scrubbing.

My body was slick with salt water and sweat and I was shaking as I pulled the T-shirt back over my head. Waves lapped against the hull and the continual flapping of the sail reminded me of the tide.

I moved to the other side of the boat and lowered myself into the water. It was ice cold.

I kicked off against the side, arms wheeling, eyes stinging. Lips tasting salt as I swam for the buoy to catch a second wind.

When I reached it, I grabbed onto a rusty rail and the metal belly listed toward me. Gauging the distance to the shore, I sucked in breath and pushed off again.

You can do this. You've done it before. With her.

I don't know if thinking kept me warm but I thought about a lot of things. Retracing every detail of the past few days, scrutinizing which theories held water and which didn't.

I had a list of things to do, words and sentences memorized. Marion's suicide note to write. I was already typing it up in my head. It would need to express depression over Kimball's death and apologize to his wife and friends. Compounded, of course, by Captain Montefiore's accusation of prostitution, the police would see the sense in what she'd done. The townsfolk would dine out on the story for a day or two, forgetting it after a couple of beers.

I couldn't forget that Marion had screwed up my life. Making me into the killer I am. There had to be restitution. A large check perhaps?

There were two things that bound us. Ryan and two hit-and-runs. Hers was premeditated murder. Mine was a lucky escape for which Ryan had been held posthumously responsible. It was very chivalrous of him.

I couldn't hope to escape the premeditation in my own dealings. Marion's death was not exactly the untimely accident the police would think it was. I had stalked and recorded, dieted and impersonated. I should have been in jail. I felt as if I was being sucked out of a plane window, as if I could no longer exist without a blend of Marion's exotically curated life in mine.

There had been no extra layer of soil in the rose bed when I last visited the guesthouse. I would have noticed. Marion couldn't have buried him, nor could she have killed him. She had been locked in the house with me.

It had to have been Kimball. Maybe he had been on the property the whole time rather than driving from one house to another as Marion suggested.

Wouldn't I have seen mud on his shoes and on the hem of his pants? Smears. Footprints. Tell-tale signs of walking through sodden grass. It had been raining on and off for the last few days.

I was treading sand and swallowing water now. Fingers grappling with seaweed. The beach was dark and asleep and I slogged toward the sand dunes, sinking in a clump of grass.

My eyes were heavy.

Glasses. In the grass. Ryan didn't wear glasses.

51

Saturday, 30th July, 2016

I awoke to blue skies and screaming gulls and a trolling motorboat in the distance.

Rolling onto my elbow, I tried to squint through a screen of hair. Flicking the bulk of it over my head, I could feel sand-specked curls heavy against the small of my back.

The coastguard boat ran a few laps along the coastline and there were swimmers further down the beach, barely visible in a haze of sea and sand.

Had Marion's friend responded to her phone call? Would he or she already be in the house?

It was a gamble I had to take.

I walked back toward the sandy hollow, ears trained to a familiar ring tone. Unraveling the head band, it was my phone ringing not Kimball's.

Lieutenant Joe.

"Good morning," I said, trying to sound groggy.

"Did I catch you at a bad moment?"

"No, just woke up."

"I rang the doorbell. Talk about waking the dead."

Talk about bad choice of words.

"I thought we had a date," he said. "I was worried."

"I'm sorry. I ran into a snag but everything's okay now."

"Did you still want to go out?"

I gulped. "Yes."

"You're nervous, aren't you?"

"You could say."

"Don't be. Just because I'm cop doesn't mean I'm going to keep asking questions."

I wasn't laughing.

"So, how about lunch?" he asked. "Oh, wait, it's already past lunch."

What? That was some oversleeping I had done under the stars. I was glad I hadn't been pecked at by a flock of birds.

"Dinner?" he asked.

"I'd like to Joe. But tonight's a little hectic. Going out with some friends from the sailing club."

"That'll be fun." Silence, and then, "Is that a seagull I can hear in the background?"

My mouth went dry. "Might be. They were nosing through the trash in the back yard yesterday."

"I didn't know they came so far inland."

Joe, get off the freaking phone. You've got sodding birds on the brain.

"You know," he said, "Henry found one of those big ones. Albatross, I think it was. He nearly pinned it to the back fence. Must be learning a few tricks from his dad."

Why do owners always refer to their dogs as kids?

"Can I call you, Joe? In a day or so?"

"Sure. Anytime."

I hung up. The seagulls were starting to screech further down the beach.

I needed a shower. Rather badly.

Grasping two phones, I climbed the stairs to the deck and saw the French doors still open, drapes snapping back and forth in the wind.

I peered in. Maybe I was thinking too damned hard. Planning. Understanding. This was not an intelligent move without knowing who was in the house—law enforcement, emergency personnel—and getting to my car and making a dash for it was senseless.

I listened. A breath of air-conditioning. A fan guttering as it shut off. I could have done with a glass of iced water from the fridge…

The first blow stung the back of my head. The second axed my stomach. The phones tumbled from my hand and I teetered forward on one knee.

* * * * * *

I opened my eyes in the darkness, arms instinctively curling around my burning stomach. I had no idea where I was. A cramped stall, no bigger than a bathroom. Small, stifling, windowless.

A shrill ringing in my ears and a throbbing at the base of my skull. I tried to stand, legs almost shooting out from under me as I staggered back against a wall.

I circled the room with one hand, fingers feeling for a door knob. Up and down. Both hands now, patting the cool surface. Shelves. Books. The same on the other side. I was in a closet.

I heard the swish of a runner beyond the wall. A sliding door. Then a rattle—a doorknob. I hurled my shoulder against it. Pounding, scratching, even though I knew I couldn't get out.

I screamed. I yelled. I told myself I was stupid for coming back because now the police were here and my prints were everywhere.

Kimball wasn't dead after all.

I jiggled the handle, slamming my hip against the door. Don't let me die like this. *Please* don't let me die. He had abandoned me. Gone off in the car and left me here to face my worst fears. Trapped with no phone. Trapped in a tomb.

Think! If someone rattled on the doorknob they must be right outside.

The first panic attack I had ever had was when I was fifteen. I was sitting in the classroom listening to a silky male voice explaining linear equations. His name was Walter Cherry. Long hair, a beard and a stutter. When it came my turn to answer, I heard a hissing inside my head. Felt my skin prickle, temperature shifting from a Saharan sweat to ice cold in barely a second. I couldn't stand in a room that warped and curled like a scene from Harry Potter. It was the same thing now. I tried not to give way to panic with each breath I held, forcing myself to exhale.

In and out. Slowly. Refusing to think that the closet, as small as it was, could deplete itself of oxygen in less than a few hours.

I tried again, this time straining every muscle as I pummeled against the door. Feeling the low, agonizing pulse to the back of my head. Sensing a tiny give in the frame.

This wasn't happening. Worse, I had nothing with which to lever the door open.

"Stop!" came the voice on the other side.

I stopped.

"You don't get to choose anymore!"

Not Kimball. Another voice so familiar it wasn't logical. But then none of this was.

"You don't get to *choose*, Marion. Do you hear?"

Marion? No. Wait. "It's me. Clo. Let me out!"

The sound of rapid-fire laughter. Then a kick against the lower panel. Streaks of light leached between the hinge and the frame. But the door held.

"You're not going to push me away, Marion. You love me. You told me you loved me."

If I could hazard a guess, he was pounding his chest with a fist because if she had dumped him, he was going to make darn sure it hurt her.

"You can't just screw a guy and walk away." Sobbing. Gasping for breath. "You faked it, didn't you? You faked it all."

So far, his language was very restrained. It was admirable. But it also creeped me out. He was still in love. Still in control. That meant Marion had given him hope.

"He can't hurt you anymore."

Sobbing. Gut-wrenching howls that made me stroke the door as if I was consoling him.

"I knew you would call... I knew you had changed your mind. Babe, *please*... Don't let me have to do this."

More sobs.

"I'll do anything for you, Marion."

Oh God, it was *him* Marion had called from Kimball's phone. *Him* she had called for help. Manipulated. Lied to. With some sick love-talk to get him to clear up her mess. The man who had seen us on the beach because he had been watching all the time.

"You do love me, don't you, Marion?"

It dawned on me that this was my only escape route. There was nothing else except stand here in the impenetrable blackness for what could be hours. Days. I couldn't risk it.

"Yes," I shouted, ear pressed against the door panel.

"I want you to show me... the way I like it."

I tried to cover my ears to the things he wanted Marion to do. With her hands, her body... The things she had done to make him love her.

I slid down the wall to a crouch, vision exploding into stars. I couldn't shut out the sick longing of a man for a woman. Every tiny memory made me want to hurl.

"I want to show you what I did. To prove it to you."

"What did you do?" I asked.

Breathing. Panting. I could hear it through the door.

"I got the videos, Marion, the laptop. There're all here, babe."

More sobbing.

"Thank you," I said, hoping I sounded grateful.

"He didn't… he didn't go home that night."

I wanted to ask who, but I settled on why. "Why? Why didn't he go home?"

"I had to do it. I couldn't let him use you anymore. I-I stabbed him…"

I clutched my belly even tighter. The letters. They hadn't been from Ryan. All this time, Marion had been egging on another lover. I winced. What a terrible pun. The egg boxes. So many of them. So many Marion had never ordered.

His words burned in my ears. Sad words. Feelings all of us have. Feelings we are told to repress because it's the first time. And first times are purely experimental. They are not meant to last.

You leave a part of yourself behind and it's hard… because that person has that part. Always.

His voice again. It made me jump.

"I buried him. He didn't feel it, Marion. He didn't feel anything. Don't you see? He can't hurt you. Like he hurt *her*. Because he would have."

He was talking about me. Clo. Ryan's abandoned wife.

"Kimball was there. He saw everything. We drove his car to the end of the road," he said. "Pushed it into the pond. They won't find it."

If he was taking about the police, they would find Ryan's rental like they find everything.

"Marion, are you there?"

Where would I go? "Yes, I'm here."

"He's dead. They're both *dead*."

In all my hatred and my darkest thoughts, I couldn't have killed Ryan. But I knew I had to kill her.

"Marion, I love you," he said.

I stood and eased back into the closet.

Inhaled.

Fists by my sides. Blood pounding in my ears.

"I love you too," I said.

A clunk. The door swept open and I barreled out into the light.

52

Jax was sprawled in front of Kimball's desk.

I should say behind it. That's where the closet was. A small 6 x 8 room, a hole-and-corner door set into the bookshelves.

He was breathing. Just knocked out. I remembered the sound when his head hit the corner of the desk. Now it was angled slightly to one side, blood trickling down his temple. He would be out for a while.

I had never seen Jax wear glasses. Sunglasses, yes. Maybe he wore contacts.

I scooped up the laptop and raced down the stairs to Marion's room. There was so little time. Paper. Pen. I fumbled in the drawers of her vanity. Found a scrap of gift wrapping and using my left hand, wrote on the white side.

Remember how you told me to spread my wings and set myself free. Well I have. I have died for you. Marion.

I left it under a paperweight and pelted down the stairs to the living room. Phones. Where are the phones?

One was wedged against a baseboard and a table leg, the other had scooted under the skirt of an easy chair. I scooped them up and hurried through to the garage, punched the door opener on the wall and locked myself in the Buick.

Dropping the laptop into the passenger foot well, I reached behind the driver's seat, hands fumbling for my handbag. I turned it upside down, saw a hurl of keys, wallet, tissues, and lipsticks as they bounced onto the passenger seat.

Panic built inside me, surging up through my chest and pushing to get out. I grabbed the car key, turned the ignition, hit reverse and pumped the gas.

The car sprung backward, just as Jax burst into the garage. I couldn't hear what he was shouting. A blur of words muffled behind glass.

I mashed the lock button, swung out into the driveway not caring what I hit. Backing far enough from the garage, I pulled on the wheel, slotted the gear into drive and accelerated in a tight circle. That's when I noticed the front gate. It was closed.

Jax was running, almost level with the driver's window, hand fisted against the glass.

While keeping my eyes ahead, I reached over onto the passenger seat for the fob, fingers rooting among a detritus of maquillage I swore I would never again need. I looked down briefly and grabbed it, noticing Jax in my rearview mirror, veering over to the passenger side of my car. I had no idea what he hoped to achieve. Whether he could somehow disarm the gate from opening before I got there.

I pointed the fob down the driveway, pressing the unlock button, *every* button. There was no response. I cursed the battery for an ill-timed malfunction. It was possible the fob only opened the garage and if so, I had to hope the gate was equipped with a proximity reader.

I was halfway there when the idea struck. Jax was sprinting parallel to my right front fender. Tugging slightly on the wheel, I heard a thud as the car swerved into his left thigh, forcing him off the drive.

I yanked the wheel back again, breath whimpering in my throat. Running a car toward a closed gate was a bitch to do in a hurry. I slammed on the brake and slowed to a cruise. The gate panels shuddered, opening several feet per second. I almost pumped the air with a fist.

I checked my mirrors. No sign of Jax. Not on the lawn or behind me. My hands trembled on the steering wheel, counting the seconds off in my head. What had I done?

Had I killed him? Had he been tossed over the hedge? I couldn't stomach a death, especially not another one caused by me.

No, he couldn't have been tossed. I hardly nudged him.

The blast was so sudden, I must have screamed. Glass spilling over my shoulders and into the foot well. I tasted blood, felt a sting on my lip.

My gun. He had *my* gun.

My foot slammed on the gas and the car surged forward, engine roaring as I swung right onto Gin Lane. I wasn't going to stop now and I don't know if I was still screaming all the way to the gas station on Hampton Road.

All I do remember is dusting myself off, fingernails tweezing glass out of my bottom lip and checking there was none in my mouth.

My head slammed back against the headrest and I gasped and shook with the horror of it.

What had I done?

My hands were trembling again, and I couldn't get Marion's face out of my mind. Dark eyes. Parted lips. White teeth. What was she saying? What was she thinking? Where was she?

My throat was raw and I needed a bottle of water. My legs wouldn't accommodate a trembling body.

It was the lady by the pump who startled me. Head

down and peering at the shattered window. A baby on her hip. A panhandler. She only wanted a few bucks.

I ushered her over and gave her a twenty for herself and a five for me. Asked her to get me a bottle of water from the store. She nodded and went in.

It was quiet outside, except for the rumble of traffic and the ticking of a nearby engine. A man leaned under the hood of his car, children and mother sleeping in the back seat, oblivious.

The woman came out of the store and brought me my water. I unscrewed the cap and glugged it down. Couldn't stop. Couldn't help pouring some on my hand and patting it on my face and neck.

I thanked her and asked her to do me a favor. I pressed a few quarters in her hand and pointed at the payphone outside the store. Asked her to call the cops and gave her the address of the house on Gin Lane.

"There's been an accident," I said. "Will you do that for me?"

She nodded. Said something about not needing the quarters to call 911. I told her to take them anyway.

Shuffling back toward the store again, she swiveled the baby to her other hip and lifted the handset.

53

I left the Buick in Mrs. Nita's garage and made sure there was nothing of mine inside. I was sorry for the shattered window. But there was nothing I could do about that now.

I took the battery out of Kimball's phone and ditched all of it in Mrs. Nita's dumpster. No one would think to look there. No one, that is, but me.

When I arrived home, my house smelled different. Mustier, I guess. Closed windows will do that to a house. The most significant difference was that it was mine. Not his. He would never come here again. Never sleep in our bed. Or eat at the table next to me. I began to look around with fresh eyes.

I left the laptop on the kitchen counter, peeled off my clothes and rammed a good few capfuls of soap in the washer. A shower never felt so good. It was twenty minutes before I got out, wiped the condensation off the mirror and had a damn good look at myself.

A brunette. Different. Wiser.

I padded around naked for a while, feeling the cool of the air conditioner against my back. Then I dried my hair and ironed it straight.

If they came, and they would, I wanted to look my best. I wanted Lieutenant Joe to be proud of me.

I patted my face with a little foundation and dressed in jeans and a white button-down shirt, no socks. It reminded me of Chef Robert.

My kitchen was strange in its familiarity: microscopic and old. Nothing compared to Kimball's canyon of cupboards and million-dollar views. Here, I could reach both walls in less than two steps. Empty and lackluster, except for a laptop lounging on the kitchen island. I had a feeling I would find the password in these words. *The Golden Child, EdeB, 2001.*

I typed in several versions of the title. Some with initials. Some without. The last try broke through the lock screen and brought me face to face with a list of files. Buried within the picture library were two folders. One labeled *CCTV*, the other labeled Video. Both locked.

'TGCEdeB2001' wouldn't work on these. In fact, I could have been there all night trying to work out the initials of anyone he once knew. An old dog. A hamster.

In a way, I was glad. I would never have to relive that terrible night. A man hoisted over my car and nearly killed. Could the FBI restore the files even if I threw the laptop under a bus? Probably. What if it was incinerated? Maybe.

The only option was to slide it under the cabinet where no one would find it. Without the gun, the laptop fitted snugly between the floor and the lower shelf, until I could find a friendly hacker to unlock the files.

Left adrift, I returned to the living room and lay on the couch. Leaning my head against the armrest, I closed my eyes and dreamed of pale skin drawn over cheekbones and moonlit limbs. Hair shuddered in the current and eyes, her beautiful brown eyes, were open...

A stuttering bell. It was dark and I knew who it was

before I opened the door.

"Clo," he said.

Just one word. My name.

He hovered. Faltered. Started forward a few steps, hand reaching for mine. I couldn't look away. Then his gaze dropped down to our linked hands and he mumbled, "I want to tell you… We need to talk."

He led me to the living room. Made me sit next to him on the couch, arm trailing my shoulders and eyes finding me again. They were pleading, with creases playing in the corners of his eyebrows as if there was something he needed from me.

"We found Ryan."

My lips mouthed the word *where* but the sound never made it out of my mouth.

"He'd been stabbed."

I heard myself say 'Who? Why?' in a disjointed voice that could have belonged to a stranger.

"We don't know, babe. He didn't make it."

I lowered my face into my hands. Sobs. No tears. All I could feel was Joe's hand rubbing my back.

The explanations made no difference to me. The relationship between Ryan and Marion. Marion and Kimball. Marion and Jax.

"Looks like Mr. Kimball took an overdose. Drugs and alcohol. We'll have the results in a day or two. Would you like a drink?"

I stuttered a yes, hearing the vocal fry in my voice.

Joe walked into the kitchen, started opening cupboards. He must have found a bottle of wine in the fridge because he came back with two glasses filled to the brim.

I slugged mine. He told me to slow down. Then the tears came. Thank God.

"Marion Kurchel," he began, "the lady that lived in the house. She's disappeared. No one's seen her. Not even the neighbor boy."

"Neighbor boy?"

"Jax De Becker. They found him on the beach with a gun. He was dazed and bleeding. They think he might have shot her, what with all the things he was saying."

"Oh God…"

The thought of him, the young man whose name I couldn't say, forced a sudden weight of darkness so black it terrified me. Couldn't hold back the tears now.

That lovely gilded boy, his mother's golden one, who occupied her soul and ran through her veins. The boy that once collected shells. The boy in the painting above the spare bed. The loss of him would kill her.

"I'll stay if you want," he whispered.

I couldn't say no to Joe and in some way my involvement with him would make the neighbors less wary. They couldn't home in on the old adage that the next of kin is the one to watch. Why would someone suspected of a nerveless murder date a cop?

Joe gazed at me for a while, the longest and most infinite of seconds. I hoped he hadn't seen the thing between us. Transparent to me and with the ugliest hint of black.

I fixed my gaze on his face, lips moving, voice dribbling with compassion. While I thought of a young man who would soon stand up in court and receive a verdict of guilty on a charge of murder in the first degree. The victim in this case was Ryan Shepherd. *Was*.

Final statements would be made, the defense would outline a rebuttal to the prosecution and a jury would sit in the deliberation room, blistering with reasonable doubt. While newspapers outside reported the miserable faces of the accused and his mother. You could smell it in the air.

My pulse accelerated and my fingers tightened around his. I couldn't shut out the sense of loss, the building grief. I couldn't shut out Joe. The muscles of my abdomen unclenched and I looked at him and wondered if I could ever tell him what I was.

There was no smell I treasured more than the scent of his skin and a trace of tobacco in his hair. I didn't want to lose all this, because then there would be nothing left of me.

He carried me down the hall. Drew me down on the bed, watching my face as if he knew the grave state of my nerves. Fingers easing between the buttons of my shirt, his breath humid in the air. I could hear his gasp and mine and I realized—for the very first time—that my life was entirely in his control.

I was hazy drunk, studying his eyelashes, thick and dark against the curve of his cheeks. My hand floated to his chest and I could feel the heart beat beneath it. A fast pulse against my fingertips.

Thump-thump. Thump-thump.

I wondered if that heart could ever break, because I had been carried along by dangerous forbidden things and he would uncover it all and hate me. Burn me like a witch.

A flash. An intuition.

Then I looked up at him. His big-hearted smile had all flattened out, traded for a half-open groan. I weaved my fingers into his and felt my body arch.

There was a slow flutter in my belly in the silence that followed. I watched the flex of his fingers, each dark hair and crescent nail more tanned than they were before.

I felt as if I had been turned to stone, unable to move even if I wanted to and I wondered how long I could make these final few hours last.

54

It was three more days before the news was abuzz with a development. That's what they called it anyway.

Joe cooked a pizza and came over to my house, bomber book tucked under his arm. He brought Henry with him this time. The dog snorted around the living room and finally settled in a tight curl in front of the TV.

We sat on the couch, Joe's hand flat against my thigh. He took the remote and muted the sound.

"They found Marion Kurchel weighted down with a scuba belt. Her body was washed up on Rogers Beach."

I couldn't believe it. I'd thrown her overboard less than half a mile from the house. How the hell did she get down there?

"You wonder who the last person was to see her alive," he said. "If she was depressed, they should have done something."

I was the last person to see her alive. I did do

something. Rid the world of another marriage breaker. Someone would thank me one day.

"There were teeth marks on her legs," he said. He saw the frown on my face. "Sharks."

Wait, there were shark nets out there to stop that type of dining. Something wasn't right.

I heard him say how sorry he was that Marion hadn't called the police sooner. That they had found a camera in her room—close-ups of bruises and cuts—and a suicide note.

I felt a gnawing of remorse. I didn't know if it was the pizza or the wine but I needed someone to talk to.

"Janice De Becker's a mess." Joe kissed me on the cheek. "In her son's statement, he claimed he was having an affair with Marion. *Way* too young for her."

"Nothing wrong with age," I said, tugging at a gold locket around my neck.

He kissed me again. Murmured something about finding Jax's glasses in the grass near the body.

I liked Joe. Steady, you know? The type of guy I could listen to for hours because there was something about his voice. Can't describe it. Deep and kind, I guess.

"You can understand how that went down. Ryan…" He tailed off and looked all sorry. "I probably shouldn't say."

"Yes. Say."

"Ryan was at the house that night. Came out the front door and collided with the knife the kid was holding. According to Jax, he thought it was Kimball."

I could only assume that while Kimball was walking along the beach, he heard the roar of a car and returned to the house. Jax was waiting outside the front door and knifed Ryan on the way out. What the police didn't know was how both men dragged my husband's body into a makeshift grave and then disposed of the car he had been driving. A rusted-out shell in the bottom of the pond.

The police had sprayed Luminol in the guesthouse, where blood spatter lit up the walls and revealed a glow of drag marks on the Persian carpet. According to Mr. De Becker's statement, Ryan had staggered to the guesthouse after being stabbed. Jax refused to say who had beaten him but the coroner confirmed the gash in Ryan's skull matched the corner of the coffee table.

"Mrs. De Becker said Jax hated Kimball for what he'd done," Joe said, lines cutting a swath in his forehead. "Broke his mom's heart when he refused to marry her. Apparently Kimball was his dad."

"His dad?"

"Yeah. Anyway, Jax won't talk to anyone. Not even an attorney. But here's the kicker. Someone beat the crap out of him. He wouldn't say who. But they gave him a right shiner and a bruised spine."

I had seen it on TV. The reporters had already beat Joe with that bit of news.

"More pizza?" he asked.

I nodded. Couldn't stop thinking what a shitty thing it was. Marion. Kimball. Ryan. A waste. Who would live in the house now? A house that would permanently echo with the shrieks of the dead. Perhaps I could. After all, they were my dead.

I wish I knew what had happened to the missing girl Kimball had entertained. Katherine Ainsley. Trouble was, I couldn't ask. I wasn't supposed to know. She was probably a Jane Doe, lying in a morgue somewhere with a tag around her big toe. I thought that was sad.

The other question I couldn't ask was did Jax have a dog? I had never seen one. What had been written on that soggy note in the egg box left by the front door? A last message to Marion? I would never know. But I kept the Christmas tree of shells he had given me.

"My friend concluded, and this is confidential," Joe said, tapping his nose, "that Marion Kurchel committed suicide."

It may have looked as if Marion Kurchel had committed suicide because her prints were on the champagne bottle and no doubt the police had found the iPad that controlled the CCTV in her bathroom. Joe wouldn't tell me any of that. But I knew how it looked.

"Had she lived," he said. "She would have been charged with Kimball's death. Probably couldn't live with that. I know I couldn't. Seen the inside of a jail? Awful beds. Wouldn't get a wink of sleep."

The look on Joe's face almost strangled the words in my throat and yet he rambled on.

"She had depression. It was all over her website. I don't know if she knew Kimball's rap included sex games and kidnap. But there was evidence of another missing girl."

"Evidence?"

"A driver's license. That's all they found. Ongoing, so I can't really talk about it. As for prints, tons of them. Partials mainly. We'll get the full report tomorrow."

I nodded as if I understood. But I understood more than Joe realized.

I couldn't keep my mind on the news. Or Lucy Kimball's statement that her husband had exhibited early signs of Hodgkinson's disease. If it were true, I was glad I hadn't emailed her. For some reason the news footage kept highlighting the house and the beach, and I asked Joe what would come of it.

"I heard the wife didn't want it. So I guess it will pass to his next of kin. A brother. Ah…," Joe snapped his fingers. "Some funny name. Began with a Z or something."

I nodded slowly as if I was trying to pull up the information from way down in my subconscious. But I knew the name. Marion had told me.

Xander. With an X.

"You know what you need," Joe said, arm shifting on my shoulder, fingers massaging the base of my neck. "A vacation. Somewhere far away. Well not too far away otherwise I'd lose you."

I smiled. I had plenty of money. Ten thousand dollars in an envelope. Quite a generous donation.

"Somewhere soon," he said. "It'll be good for you."

I didn't want him to ask me if he could go too. We both knew he couldn't. Work. Dog. Helping people. Too many things for Joe to consider.

But I could. And I would.

55

Thursday, 4th August, 2016

It takes fingerprints to make up my mind. So many all over the house and the guesthouse. Unique to every person. Including me.

They don't know yet. But they will. No matter what a clean freak Marion was, mine will surface with all the others.

Joe finds me walking down Berkeley Road. I don't have a car now. At least not one I can drive.

So he pulls over in his cruiser and asks me where I'm going. I say nowhere. Just walking.

Really, I need counseling.

It's funny how he knew I would be walking at that time of day. It's not like he usually comes home for lunch or anything. He knows something's up. But he doesn't ask.

He glances at my weekend bag and asks me if I want a ride. I say no, I need a cab.

Police officers can't take family members in the front of their cruisers and I wouldn't want to ride in the back either. In the cage where the villains sit. Although one day I expect I'll have to.

He nods and makes a call. I stand by the open window and he strokes my hand over the sill and we talk about food. It's Joe's favorite subject.

We talk about Henry and how Joe thinks it's time to make him a new dog house. A Christmas present. I like that idea. I like Henry. He's the child I never had.

Joe asks if he can call me sometime for dinner. So we can celebrate.

Celebrate what, I ask?

"You and me," he says.

I don't feel much like celebrating. My face is heavy as he opens the taxi door and settles me inside. I lift my eyes to him and thank him. The change in my expression must have traveled all the way to the soles of his feet. I know this because he gives me a look.

One hand is braced on the door, the other is braced on the seat behind my head. "What's the matter, babe?"

"I had a nightmare last night."

Luminescent spots of light that roam among the algae.

"Be patient," he said. "Pain fades, you know?"

Pain never fades. It dulls.

I like the way he doesn't ask me where I'm going. Doesn't get all jealous like Ryan did. It's not his business and he respects that. So I tell him anyway.

"I'm going to get counselling. You're right. I think I'd feel better."

"I'm proud of you, Clo."

"I'll come back all new. You wait."

"And I'll give up smoking. Promise."

He plays with a ruffle of curls at my neck with a finger. Twisting, tugging. Not hard. Just enough to make me smile.

"Did you mean what you said back there?" he asked.

That I love him. I'm not sure. "Of course."

He slants his head to my ear and says, "I love you too, Clo."

Weights that have anchored you into the bottom of the world.

"You have fun." He kisses the side of my face. "Call me."

I can smell the cologne through the opening of his shirt. I give a tentative wave.

The stench of seaweed and rotting things.

Joe nods and slides a finger down my cheek and blows me a kiss. I catch it with a hand. I smile

He shuts the cab door and stands briefly on the curb. Then he strides along the pavement toward his cruiser. He puts on his sunglasses and slides into his car.

He will probably get a call from dispatch. A triple homicide perhaps. I don't know where. He's one more suit among the many, touring down the sunny blue streets. Maybe he will be late home tonight. Maybe he won't come home at all.

Loneliness. It's a gutting feeling.

The driver of the taxi says, "Where to, ma'am?"

We inch forward past Joe's cruiser and I mirror the wave. If our hands could have touched through glass, it would have been a high-five.

Bubbles dart through an open mouth and then a final sigh goodbye.

I lean back against the seat and then I say, "To the airport."

ABOUT THE AUTHOR

Claire Stibbe grew up in Norfolk, England and now lives in the USA. She is the author of the Detective Temeke Crime series - *The 9th Hour, Night Eyes, Past Rites, Dead Cold, Easy Prey* and *Silent Admirer*. Winner of the New Mexico/Arizona Book Awards for crime mystery, her books have also been Amazon bestsellers, reaching the #1 spot in the top 100.

She is also a reporter for Stand True 4 Blue, which features a Nationwide Newsletter dedicated to law enforcement, supporter of the Victim Impact Program and a member and graduate of the Citizen Police & BSCO Sheriff's Academy. A former journalist and magazine editor, she now writes full time.

Find out more about Claire at www.clairestibbe.com Twitter and Instagram @CMTStibbe.

Sign up to Claire Stibbe's New Release Mailing List at: http://eepurl.com/bqCQhv

For more information on Claire Stibbe.
www.cmtstibbe.com

ACKNOWLEDGMENTS

My thanks to my mother for giving me a safe and loving home, and to my father who gave me his love of language and books.

Special thanks to the invaluable services of Bookpreneur, Twisted Ink Publishing, The 13th Sign and Famelton Publishing. A huge thank you to editors Jeff Gardiner and Sandra Mangan, and the wonderful proofreaders at Booklab for molding the clay into something worth reading.

As always, I owe the greatest of thanks possible to my husband Jeff for his love and support, and to my son Jamie for his encouragement and humor.

Claire Stibbe
Albuquerque, New Mexico
2018